THE SOUND OF YOU

A J LOVE

Edited by: Ewelina Rutyna
Cover & Formatting by: The Graphics Shed

"I think the hardest part about being a teenager is dealing with other teenagers - the criticism and the ridicule, the gossip and rumors."

-Beverley Mitchell

CONTENTS

Chapter One

Hallie

WELCOME TO THE UNIVERSITY OF MICHIGAN

The sign glows like a golden chalice. It's like a message from God, free tickets to see your favorite band, and all other forms of awesome things rolled into one substantially epic thing.

I love that word - *Epic*. I even love the way it's overused, which is surprisingly not something I'd normally like about a thing, or a word. No, what I like the most about the word 'epic' is the way *everyone* uses it. Whether they are young or old, rich or poor, weird or wonderful, the word is everywhere and I kind of like that.

Anyway, all that rambling aside, after a long ass day of driving I am finally here. I am over five hundred miles away from my home back in Des Moines, and it couldn't be far enough. Four years of working my ass off at high school, surrounded by small-time losers, and it's finally paying off. And pay it is with a full ride, accommodation included, scholarship at UM. Seeing how I wasn't aware accommodation was included until last week, I've even got some cash saved up from a part time job I got a year ago, plus the money sperm donor has sent me every month since freshman year at high school. Not that I told my mother that, I mean I only told her I was coming away to college yesterday. Her response - "Have a good trip Hon."

My mom doesn't exactly have an *active* role in my life. I know she loves me and she does her best, but I also know that her varying boyfriends are always, and will always be, priority number one. We haven't been close since I was able to dress myself. She'll barely notice I'm gone. I learnt to get things for myself, which is why when I started high school, I set my sights on the University of Michigan and never let anything get in my way. Not the string of men Mom had parading around me, not the girls at school that called me names, and definitely not the sperm donor that helped to give me life and nothing more. I wasn't interested in boyfriends or dating. I've only ever been on one actual date, which had ended in me losing my virginity, and then never speaking to the guy again. His choice, not mine.

Yes, Ladies and Gentlemen. Jason Evans is an asshole.

He was also the most popular guy in school, and when he asked me out sophomore year, I tentatively accepted, unable to resist his cute dimpled smile. *God that smile.* I was stupid and naive. He picked me up early one Saturday morning and spent the whole day being the perfect gentleman. I decided then and there that maybe not all guys were like the shit heads my mom attracted, and so I let my guard down. By nightfall he was back at my place and in my bedroom. He was sweet and gentle with me as I gave away my innocence, and then when it was done, a smug little smile crept over his face. I stared at him, confusion clouding my features, as he dressed, and then he laughed and told me that I just made him fifty bucks richer, which was when the realization and shame had settled in. In that moment I lost control and I vowed it would never happen again. I would never again lose sight of my end game.

The rest of high school was hell. When the news of what Jason did filtered through the masses, the name calling and the taunts began. I became a version of myself I never knew existed, more guarded, and cold to everything and everyone around me. I got what I needed from guys then moved on. Branded a slut from the day I lost my virginity, and with no advice on how to handle it, I gave them what they wanted – a rumor girl with no shame.

Can't beat them join them right?

I fooled around with guys for the intimacy I craved, but nothing more, dropping them as soon as it was over. It was easier that way. I left them before they could leave me. I discovered alcohol and its ability to numb logic, and so with the two combined, I became Des Moines' very own party girl. Guys wanted to sleep with me and girls wanted to hurt me. I had zero friends and I didn't give a shit. But high school is over now – finally – and not a single person from my class is headed here, which means I can be anyone I want to be. My plan is to be a much more sensible and respectable Hallie, a Hallie that doesn't drink twice her weight in tequila, or make out with random guys.

Plus less sex, yeah definitely less sex.

I park my grey Ford Focus (about the only decent thing sperm donor ever did for me) in a space at the back of the lot, and walk over to where I can see people gathering to sign in. I ignore the eyes I can feel coming from of a small group of guys who are watching me walk across the car park. I'm used to this. I have my mother's long brown hair, my father's deep brandy eyes, and I work out twice a day. Not to mention the more than healthy chest I have thanks to a long line of big breasted women in my family. Guys always look at me, never do anything about it though. My tough exterior means I'm intimidating to the opposite sex. I know that, I planned for it. I want boys to be intimidated by me. It keeps the assholes away, which is always priority number one.

I stroll right by without offering them a glance, and ignore the obnoxious wolf whistles. I find the line for FLINT CAMPUS and join it. Sorry guys, but the new sensible Hallie doesn't fool around with guys she hardly knows. Or fool around full stop. *Yes, that is better.*

Two hours later I'm hauling the only bag I brought with me, and my old, poorly tuned guitar across the campus to the Trisler Building, dorm 182, where I get to meet my roommate. Apparently I'm rooming with another full ride scholar and we have a private dorm with two separate bedrooms, a communal lounge/kitchen, and a separate bathroom. Using the little keycard I got from student sign in, I let myself into the building, and then walk over to the front desk where a guy, who looks as though he'd rather be facing a firing squad, is sat. His eyes are cast downwards, over-gelled blonde hair drooping over them, as he focuses solely on the laptop screen in front of him.

"Can I help you?" He asks, without bothering to look up.

"Yeah, my dorm room is 182. I'm supposed check in or something?"

"Name?" He responds, as he brings his grey eyes slowly up to meet mine.

I fight back a smirk when I watch his entire demeanor change before me. The boredom that was once on his face is now covered with sickly charm and cocky confidence. Confidence he doesn't deserve to have - at all. His hand runs through the sticky mess on top of his head as he leans back in his chair.

"Hallie Clarke," I reply.

He leans forward and taps a few keys on the laptop before bringing his gaze back to me and smiling wide, revealing crooked, not quite white teeth.

"I've got you. I'm Westley your RA and you can come to me for anything." He licks slowly across his bottom lip. "Literally anything."

Is that supposed to be sexy? It's really, *really* not. Without any permission from my brain, I feel my mouth scrunch up like I've been licking lemons.

"Awesome," I answer, sarcasm choking my words.

He must not notice, as he smiles even wider and informs me he'll show me up to my suite. I'm not sure I like that he knows where I'm going to be living. I'm getting major creep vibes. He walks away through a door to the left. Against my better judgement, I follow him through. Westley is waiting at the foot of some stairs when I reach him. He smiles again with that sinister, crooked grin and motions me to go up ahead of him. I'm confused about the gesture for all of two seconds until I feel his eyes on my ass. *Pervert.*

We walk in silence when we reach the right floor, and soon arrive at an open door with '**Codie Barnes and Hallie Clarke**' written on to the white board fixed to it. I follow Westley in, and find myself standing in a medium sized lounge with two comfy looking chocolate brown couches facing a large television, that's set onto a pine unit. Music is playing out from it, and I silently cringe at the cheesy pop beats as I walk in further and look around. Sat cozily behind the longer of the two couches is a circular dining table, four wooden chairs surrounding it. Set back from the cream walls of the lounge is a long breakfast bar that holds a full kitchen behind it. A door leads off to a hallway from there which I assume are where the bedrooms are.

"Codie?" Westley calls, and a tiny, blonde haired girl comes bounding down the hallway.

Her hair is pulled back into a preppy ponytail at the top of her head, wide blue eyes twinkling as she comes to a halt in front of us. I survey her discreetly: black Mary Janes, white sundress and a soft blue cardigan. I almost laugh. We couldn't be more different. I drop my bag and shove my hands into the back pockets of my jean shorts.

"Hey, Westley," she says, and even her voice is preppy.

"Hi gorgeous. This is your new roommate, Hallie Clarke. I'll let you give her the rules and regs. I'll be downstairs if you need me for anything," he turns to face me. "Hallie, welcome to University of Michigan."

He winks at me, and I try not to barf as he walks out the door, leaving me with a very smiley roommate. She turns to me as I stand there idly, her eyes dancing from my worn out combat boots to my black leather jacket.

"Hey."

She smiles wide again before replying.

"Hi! I'm Codie Barnes! And holy shit you are stunning! I *love* your boots! Also, ignore Westley. He's a total sleazebag. My brother warned me about him when I got here earlier," she beams, then hugs me whilst I stand there like a statue. *Wow, she's friendly.* "Oh let me show you your room so you can put your stuff down, and then I can help you get the rest of your things if you like?"

"This is all my things," I reply, and I follow her down the small hallway to a bedroom on the right.

"That's it?" She asks me, causing me to chuckle under my breath from the shock in her voice.

I'm not surprised by her reaction. I witnessed girls all over campus carrying suitcase after suitcase into their rooms, with cars piled with stuff. I decided to pack light after I'd seen in the dorm room welcome pack, that all the essentials would already be provided. After going through the list of what will be waiting for me in the suite, I realized I only needed to bring my clothes. Everything else is already here. I also watched as people were being waved off by their parents, and ignored the tiny pang of sadness that had threatened. My mother would never have made this trip, and my father would have paid someone else to do it. George Clarke would never be seen on a college campus that isn't Ivy League. He doesn't even know I'm in college. *Yet.*

"Yeah this is it," I say, as I dump the bag on the bed.

She continues to talk as I unpack my clothes into the wardrobe and drawers in the room. She tells me all the rules about visitors and noise levels and how my key card is also how I pay for food in the lunch/dinner hall. She also tells me about herself, that she's from Ohio and her brother, Jace, is a sophomore here. He's in a fraternity and so she gets automatic invites to the big parties, meaning me too apparently. I'd rather die - painfully and slowly. I ask her if she's going to join a sorority which causes her to literally laugh in my face.

"Definitely not. Sorority bitches are the worst!"

Maybe this girl isn't all bad.

"What about you? Where are you from? Brothers? Sisters? Tell me more about Hallie Clarke. I can already see that you play guitar," she asks, sitting down on the chair in front of the small desk in the room.

"Not much to know. No brothers or sisters, and from Des Moines, Iowa. Yeah I play a little but don't worry it won't be loud," I tell her as I put the light purple duvet cover on the comforter and make my bed.

"Oh don't worry about that. What classes are you taking?"

"English major, Anthropology and History, you?" I reply, feigning interest.

"Physics major with a minor in Bio, and then History too as a filler class, Wednesday and Friday right?"

I nod in agreement, remembering my schedule. I guess I have a study partner for History then, a chatty one at that. Great. She leaves me a little while later so she can go finish unpacking herself. When she's gone I kick my boots off, sit on the bed, and lean my back against the wall, bringing my crappy old acoustic to my stomach and letting my fingers pluck lightly at the strings. I strum a soft tune, wincing at the poor quality of the sounds. I really need a new guitar. Unable to take it anymore, I look around at the bare, pale green walls, making a mental note to go buy some pictures or something to cover them up. *So depressing*. My cell phone rings, distracting me, and when I look at the caller ID I see my dad's name flashing. *George Clarke*. I groan as I bring the phone to my face.

"Hi."

My father is a difficult man. He's judgmental and often downright mean.

"Hello Hallie, how are you?"

"Fine. What's up?"

I hear him release a frustrated breath. "I'm in Des Moines later this week and I thought we should meet for lunch. When would be suitable?" He asks me, and I smile to myself. At least I finally have an excuse now to get out of the bullshit lunches and dinners I'm often forced to go on.

"I'm not in Des Moines, so sorry but I can't."

There's a quick clatter of something being dropped before he rushes out a response. "What do you mean? Where are you?"

"College."

Again, his response is rushed.

"Since when do you go to college?" He asks and I can hear the disbelief in his voice. Does he really think I'm lying? Really?

"Since I applied, received full scholarship, and drove here today." I let my thumb brush softly across the strings of my guitar as I answer his questions in quick succession about where I am and how I got here. *What classes are you taking, Hallie? Is your car okay, Hallie? Where are you living, Hallie?* Blah Blah Blah. I respond to everything, never once letting go of the flat tone in my voice.

"Why didn't you say anything?" He asks after a deafening lull of silence.

"You never asked. Look I'm really busy with moving in and stuff so I gotta go."

Not entirely true but I've had enough of this conversation already. I don't know why he's suddenly interested, he never has been before.

"Fine. I will send some money to your account to help you whilst you're there. If you need anything else then please just call. Goodbye Hallie."

I put my phone down on the bedside cabinet then climb

off the bed and grab my toiletries. I need a shower and to wash away the disappointment I feel in myself every time I speak to him.

Thanks Dad.

CHAPTER TWO

Hallie

"Hallie, you ready to go?"

I groan silently. That would be my new roommate shouting to me to go for dinner with her. I tried to back out, but she pleaded with me to go with her so she wouldn't be alone. I take one last look at myself in the mirror, just to make sure I don't look too horrific. It's not that I cared all that much, I'd just rather not start the semester off with a major image malfunction. The plan is to blend in as much as humanly possible. Complete invisibility would be the best outcome. I smooth down my hair, letting it fall in long waves down my back, then pull on my leather hooded jacket over the vintage band tee I have on. I guess it's time to go and be sociable. I can hear voices as I approach but I ignore them, having no interest in who they are or what they're saying.

Wow, no wonder people think I'm a bitch. They're probably right.

"Yeah I'm ready," I say to my blonde roommate, whose eyes are trained on the door.

"So have any of you got names?" I hear from the direction of Codie's stare, and turn to come face to face with a guy leaning on our door frame. I take him in, looking him up and down, as I size up what kind of guy he is. My gaze falls from his black spiky hair and sky blue eyes, down to the rich boy sneakers on his feet. That, and the cocky smirk tugging at the corners of his mouth, tell me he's a player through and through. A rich player, the worst kind. I whip my gaze away, having satisfied my curiosity.

"If you're busy I can meet you there?" I ask Codie, ignoring the original question from the guy.

"No, no I'm coming now," she answers, then looks back to the guy. "I'm Codie Barnes and my *super friendly* roommate is Hallie Clarke." My eyes roll involuntary at the sarcasm laced in her voice.

"Nice to meet you girls, I'm Ryan Turner and this sexy bastard is Nate Harris. We're your new neighbors," the guy tells us, and I turn in time to see him inclining his head at his friend on the left.

Who is that?

My eyes scan him as he looks at his friend. Messy brown hair, strong square jaw, broad shoulders covered by a tight black shirt. The starts of a tattoo creep out the neckline of his shirt, and my body begins to react to the vibe coming from him. He lifts his arms to lean against the door frame, his shirt rising and revealing that perfect V that every girl goes crazy for. The man is hot, like holy shit hot.

"Hey," new guy says, his voice coming out as more of a grunt.

I can appreciate that, this get to know your neighbors crap is horseshit.

He turns to face me and our gaze locks on each other. His deep emerald eyes search mine, and I search his back.

His stare is penetrating, piercing even, and I fight to keep my face passive. I don't know what it is but there was something about this guy. With more difficulty that I'm willing to admit, I place one of my many mental ice blocks in front of him and break the contact, blinking a couple of times before turning to pick my bag up off the couch. Holy crap. This no sex thing is going to be harder than I thought. One look and I want this guy's pants off.

"Heading somewhere nice?" Ryan asks, talking mainly to Codie now.

"Just the dining hall for early dinner," Codie replies brightly, as she leaves through the dorm door.

I follow her hesitantly, my mind contemplating whether I could get away with just staying in the suite. I trail behind, not wanting to be involved with the nauseating flirting going on between my roommate and Mr. All American up ahead. His friend, Nate I think it is, walks beside me. I can literally hear him thinking, and can feel it every time his gaze flicks over me.

"So... do you ever stop talking?" He suddenly asks me, and I have to stifle a smirk at the obvious joke.

Of course he's funny too. Good grief.

"No, I'm real chatty and friendly," I reply dryly and he chuckles quietly.

"Yeah I can tell."

I don't answer him and instead walk ahead, arms folded, until I reach where Codie has stopped and is giving Ryan her number.

"So I'll call you later, yeah?" Ryan says.

"Definitely," she calls back to him as we walk away, offering him a wink for good measure. I roll my eyes as we head off in the direction of the hall.

My first thought of the dining hall? *Too many people.*

My second? *What the hell did I do to deserve this?*

I'm sat with Codie at a long table, where we've subsequently been joined by her brother and one of his greasy frat friends, Toby, who thinks that it is appropriate behavior to call me *Baby* and feel my leg whilst I try to eat a chicken sandwich. Moron. They're both talking about a 'slammin party' tonight that Codie is going to and she's trying to convince me to go with her. Uh, no.

"Are you sure you won't come with me tonight? It's the first party of the semester," she whines, as I stand and re-shoulder my bag.

"Yeah, sorry I'm beat. Next time definitely," I lie. There will absolutely be no next time.

"These parties are a good way to make friends you know," Jace offers, and my only reply is to raise my eyebrow slightly.

I thought I made it obvious that I wasn't really into friends. I'd only agreed to come here with Codie because she gave me a look I couldn't say no to. If I'd have known she was going to be asking her brother and this creep to join us, I probably would have found it easier to decline.

"Come on Baby, I could show you a good time," Toby winks.

Oh that's gross.

I turn to stare at him. From what Codie was telling me about him on the way over here, he's been Jace's best friend since they started college. He's on the football team, and apparently has girls hanging all over him. I can see why, the guy's attractive but he's far too leery for me. *Leery*. Is that even a word? Jeez, I'm supposed to be smart.

"Doubtful," I reply, tossing my half eaten sandwich in the trash, and then leave hastily before anyone can respond.

I'm walking back across the campus towards my building, when my mind drifts to Nate. He is insanely hot, all muscles and tattoos with an 'I'm cool as fuck' vibe. It had almost killed me to ignore the prickly heat I felt all over my body as he watched me, and then when my eyes had locked with his jewel green ones, I was lost for a few seconds. But right now I need to stay away from boys. Especially dangerously sexy next door neighbors, which would be a lot easier if Codie hadn't set her sights on his all American roommate. That guy has player written all over him, so it should be interesting to see how it plays out. Codie is definitely not a one night stand girl and we live right next to them.

I reach Trisler then walk up the stairs and towards my dorm, my mind still amused with thoughts of Ryan trying to avoid Codie mission impossible style. He's good looking, but he's no Tom Cruise. Plus he looks about as subtle as a marching band in a library. I round the corner on my corridor then bang straight into a solid wall of abs.

"Damn it!"

I look up and see a topless Nate smirking down at me. Topless? Why the hell did he have to be topless? What kind of creep walks around the halls of a dorm block naked from the waist up? An extremely sexy one would be the answer, one that looks like he's been carved from god apparently. Still, he's a creep none the less. I mumble a quick apology then move around him to get to my door, ignoring the feeling of his eyes on the back of my head.

"Hey Hallie, wait up!" He calls after me so I begrudgingly turn around and force down the highly inappropriate thoughts I'm getting at the sight of his perfectly crafted body.

He couldn't just be a fat, lazy slob could he? No of

course not, because that would be too easy. This must be a test. He's been put right next door to me as a test to my will power. I think I may fail.

It's such a cruel world.

"You wanna get coffee with me?"

Jesus, wasn't almost knocking me on my ass enough? Now he wants me to get coffee? Why? I've hardly even spoke to the guy, although his line earlier about be not stopping talking was amusing. And he was able to capture my attention for longer than I'm willing to admit. Now he's standing there all cocky and confident because he knows he's hot, and you can bet your ass he's expecting me to fall over myself at a chance on a date with him. I arch my eyebrow at him.

"As friends, you know, to apologize for almost knocking you over then," he adds quickly as he shifts his stance.

I've seen the move before. Hands in pockets, head cast down a little, and looking up with fake innocent eyes so he comes across all cute and embarrassed. Nice try. I almost laugh.

"Just friends?" I reply, not believing him for a second. I can tell this guy wants me by the way his eyes linger on my chest.

"Yeah. We can be friends, right?"

I smirk at the cute boy next door look he's trying to pull off.

"Sure."

I move my hands to my back pocket pushing my chest out ever so slightly, and his face lights a little. He's not the only one who can put the moves on. Cocky confidence radiates from him as his eyes roam me from top to bottom. I keep my face impassive, mad at my body as it begins to react to his gaze.

"So, you wanna grab some coffee now?" He asks.

"No thanks."

I force myself to turn and walk through my door shutting it behind me. I almost feel bad for him, but guys like that need a little rejection sometimes. I've met his type before. He knows how hot he is and every girl in sight probably knows it too. I bet no one has ever said no to him before. Well, I'm not about to be a notch on anyone's bedpost here, no matter how much my body seems to want it. I've worked too damn hard.

Nate Harris is a big NO.

Knocking at the door is causes me to reluctantly stand from my comfy position on the couch. Codie came back an hour ago and has been begging and pleading with me to go to this stupid party with her, whilst consecutively getting herself ready. She's invited Ryan next door so I figured he'd be showing up here at some point soon, of course accompanied by his friend. Nate has invaded my thoughts over the last couple of hours. I've been unable to get his well-defined abs out of my mind, and (oh my) those eyes that haunt and pierce right through me. It was safe to say that my thoughts haven't exactly been clean. I stroll over to the door and fling it open, annoyed at myself for letting a guy I don't even know consume me this way.

"Oh hey, I'll get Codie now," I mutter, barely sparing either of them a glance. I wander back into the suite leaving the door open, not caring one single iota that they're both witnessing me in sweats and a hooded jumper. It's probably a good thing. Maybe this way he'll stop looking at me.

"Hallie I'm going to beg you one last time to come with me," Codie whines at me as she enters the lounge area.

"Nope. Have a good night," I say back to her, dropping

back down onto the couch and curling my legs underneath me.

I can feel eyes on me but I ignore them and un-pause my movie. It's just me and Mr Tatum tonight, absolute perfection.

Chapter Three

Hallie

The light beaming through the thin material covering the lonely window in my room wakes me. I stretch out lazily then roll myself out of bed. I need a run, but first... coffee. Slowly, I make my way into the kitchen only to walk into a very sleazy looking Ryan as he tries to sneak out the door. His eyes go wide as he notices me and I smirk.

"Is this where you tell me that you're just heading out for breakfast?"

His face pinks as he tries and fails to stutter out some sort of apology, and I have to fight back a laugh. Talk about awkward.

"Don't mind me," I tell him, then turn towards the coffee maker we have in the kitchen, no longer interested in what he's doing.

I hear him sigh and then the door opens and closes. *Things are about to get very interesting around here.* The love struck expression on Codie's face last night when Ryan and Nate came for her did not go unnoticed. And I'd bet my last dime that sleazebag Ryan noticed it too, which makes him the ultimate asshole for playing her. Never mind, what's college without a little drama?

Grabbing my mug of coffee, I make my way back to my room to change into my running clothes, and idly wonder if I'm supposed to tell Codie that her one night stand has left. No, if it was me I'd want to find out for myself. Then again, if it was me I would be the one leaving. I finish my coffee as I dress, then take the mug back through to the kitchen, and grab a bottle of water out the refrigerator to take with me. Still no movement from Codie, although it is only 8am. She looks the type to sleep in. I, myself, very rarely sleep past 7. I hope she's not upset later when I return. I'm not sure how I feel about living with a girl that cries. She was so excited when she got off the phone to him yesterday after him telling her that he'll go to the party with her. She ran around like a crazy person getting ready for it, changing her outfit at least four times. I open the dorm suite door and then stop still as I watch another awkward exchange happen.

"Okay so you will call me later baby won't you?" A tall half-dressed girl asks Nate, the desperate tones in her voice almost making me cringe.

I step back so I can watch him without being seen, the exasperation on his face clear as day. The girl is twisting her fingers in her raven black hair as she waits for him to answer her.

"Um... yeah sure," he replies, his hand clasping the back of his neck.

Asshole. It is one thing to just hook up with a girl but to do it and then lie about calling her after is just low. Not even I'd do that. Whenever I hooked up with someone, they always knew I wasn't in for long term. I step further out the door and close it behind me, probably louder than I should.

"Oh, hey Hallie," Nate calls to me and I turn flicking

my glance between him and his girl for the night, my eyebrow rising slightly.

"Hi, I'm Tami," the girl says as her whole demeanor changes from desperate one night stand victim to confident sorority bitch. *Insert eye roll.*

"Hey," I reply because I feel like I should, and then begin to turn back towards the direction of the stairs.

"I don't think I saw you at the party last night," Tami comments.

I groan inside as I turn back to them, again. Jeez! I just want a run, not a conversation.

"I didn't go."

"How come? Everyone was there."

My eyebrows rise fully. Nosy much?

"I guess that makes me no one then, huh?" I answer then turn and walks away before either of them can say anything else.

I leave through the main doors of the building, plug my earphone into my ears and switch my iPod on shuffle. Pink Floyd's See Emily Play fills my senses and I smile to myself, impressed at my own taste in music. I hit the ground at a quick pace, desperate for the solitude. I've always liked being on my own. I block out all surrounding noise, and thoughts of a particular hot as hell neighbor and his mega bitch new girlfriend, as I run through the gates of campus and then down the long road leading to the park I'd looked up before arriving here. I'd heard about the river trails and park trails near the college before and so I made sure I knew how to get there.

I've always loved running, just me and the path in front of me. I love feeling the wind pass through me and the sound of my feet slapping against the ground below. I surrender myself to the steady beat of my shoes against the pavement. This is the way I always release my energy, and that's exactly what is happening now. I'm elated; my soul is at its summit. I am running, and I am free. Free from all the bullshit that surrounds my life; the rumors, my parents, the juvenile college drama already unfolding in my dorm block. None of it matters here. Sweat trickles down my back and my muscles stretch as I push them harder, maintaining the punishing rhythm beat for beat. The cold wind moves through me and my throat dries but I keep running until I can feel the back of my legs burn hot and my chest tightening. When I'm mere seconds from passing out, I find a bench to take a short break. I pull my earphones out and bring my water bottle to my mouth, sighing as the cool liquid soothes my throat.

"You okay there?"

I look up and find a young guy standing in front of me, his blond hair slick with sweat as he peers down at me. The expression on his face is equal parts amused and concerned. Not that I can blame him, I probably look insane.

"Yes."

"What's your name? Do you go to school at UM?" Like I'm going to answer that; he could be crazy or a psychopath. It doesn't matter either way as he continues, dropping himself on the bench beside me. "I go to school there, I'm a sophomore. My name's Adam."

Yeah, just because he says he goes to my school doesn't mean he isn't a psychopath. In fact, I'm pretty sure that's exactly what a psychopath would say. If I was a psychopath, it would be my response. I give him a small smile that I hope tells him I'm not interested before standing and taking off down the trail without a word. What kind of moron just asks a girl her name after a three second meeting, and then asks where she goes to school? I halt my feet. Oh God, what if he does go to UM and then I'll see him and it will be mega awkward. I think about this for a minute, all the while knowing I look insane to anyone passing by, and then decide I don't care. I stand by my decision to bolt. Plus, awkward situations have never bothered me, if anything they amuse me.

When I reach the Trisler building, I swipe myself in and thank my lucky stars that I make it to my room without another surprise collision with Mr Solid Abs next door. Why did he have to be hot? I'm trying to be more sensible and avoid sex yet all I can think about when I see him is how much I'd like to rip his clothes off, with my teeth. Well I was until I saw him letting out Miss All American Sorority Bitch. Why do I care? *Come on, Clarke.* I can do this. I've worked too damn hard to get here. Maybe I should've give Adam the friendly psychopath (if that's his real name) a chance, burn off some steam and push a certain neighbor out of my brain. No, no boys. I will not end up like my mother, whose life revolves around whatever man shows some interest. I shake off the thoughts as I walk into my bedroom to get my things for a shower then head into the bathroom to take said shower. I switch the temp on full then let the water cascade around me, taking my time in there.

My first couple of days at college have been a strange. Meeting my over enthusiastic roommate, then Nathan and his lady killer friend, Codie's brother and his too-handsy friend, then literally bumping (or banging) into the brick wall that is Nathan's chest, catching sleazebag Ryan sneaking out of the dorm, then catching sleazebag's equally sleazebag friend saying an awkward goodbye to his very own one night stand, and finally a possible chat with a psychopath/fellow college student. Hopefully tomorrow will be less interesting. Classes are starting then so I only have today to get through before I can lose myself completely into school work. I climb out of the shower then quickly towel dry my hair before walking out the bathroom wrapped in a larger towel.

"Hallie?" I hear Codie call from the other side of her bedroom door.

I sigh heavily. This roommate thing is going to get annoying, real quick. I should have requested a single room. I take a deep breath then stroll into her bedroom where I heard her shout from.

"Hey, what's up?" I ask, and then notice that she's curled up in her covers crying.

"He fucking played me, Hal," she sobs, and I sit down on her bed carefully avoiding the discarded tissues all over the place.

Hal? My name is Hallie not Hal. That is going to stop. I guess she woke up and found Ryan gone, huh? And holy shit! How many tissues did she go through? I was only gone a couple of hours. She must have woken up right after I left. Maybe it was when I banged the door to make my presence known to Nathan. My bad. I watch her, unsure of what I'm supposed to do or say. I've never been in this kind of situation before, I've never really had friends. Are we friends? Do I want to be friends?

"What can I do? You want me to go kick his ass?"

She smiles small. "No. It's probably my fault. I knew he was the type of guy to do this, they always are. I don't know what attracts me to them so much?"

In all the cheesy bullshit movies I've seen, this is the point where the 'friend' tells the crying one that she's better off without and then offers ice cream.

"He's an asshole and you should never cry over an

asshole," I say quietly and she smiles wide. I've used the same line on my mother a few times.

"You're right. You're absolutely fucking right! He is an asshole!" She exclaims.

Well that was surprisingly easy, and no ice cream necessary.

"Exactly," I tell her then make to stand up assuming my job is done.

It isn't.

"And oh my God, Hal. He was useless in bed," she giggles and I gape at her.

There's that Hal again, and I'm also sure I could have gone on in life without that information.

"It was so disappointing considering how hot he is and how nice he was to me all night. I was going to let it slide, thinking maybe he was just drunk or whatever, but seeing as though he disappeared before I even woke up this morning..."

She trails off and I pick up her meaning straight away. She's planning on telling everyone about his apparent non-existent bedroom skills. Bad idea. Very bad idea. A girl I went to high school with did it once and the whole thing got turned around on her, and she was the one made to look ridiculous. That just isn't how you deal with guys like that. I look over at Codie and can see the hurt behind the mischief in her eyes. That's all this is, she's upset and she wants him to be as upset as her.

"I know what you're thinking, but you shouldn't. It won't end pretty."

Why am I getting involved in this? I should just let her make her own mistakes but she looks so damn unhappy and she's been nothing but nice to me since I met her yesterday. Not to mention, if (when) shit hits the fan, I live with her and so I'll be dragged into it anyway. Isn't that something to look forward to? *Not.*

"You're probably right but I can't just let him get away with it," she sighs, and then falls back on her bed.

"You've got to play him at his own game."

She casts a curious glance in my direction so I reluctantly continue and give her the small amount of wisdom I have from watching my mom.

"He'll be expecting you to be falling over yourself for his attention and to be desperate to have him as your own. Guys like that get off on it. If you wanna get him back then you've got to ignore him. Like, barely acknowledge him at all. Play him at his own game. If you see him in the hallway just offer him a casual wave then walk on by. If he calls you or texts you, don't reply. It will drive him crazy that you're not interested. Of course if you want to play this kind of game then you've got to be sure that you'll be able to resist him when he turns it back on you. Because that's what he'll do, he'll switch on the charm and pull out all his moves in an effort to get you under him again."

Her eyes are wide as she stares at me.

"What?"

"How to you even know all of this? Have you had to deal with a lot of these guys?" She asks me in awe. *If only she knew.*

"I've known guys like him, yes," I say vaguely and stand up as thoughts of the many men my mother has been with filter through my mind.

I'm done playing the best friend role now, it's exhausting. I tell Codie that I'm going to get changed then groan out loud when the door knocks and she begs me to answer it. I'm still wrapped in a damn towel. What now? I walk over and fling the door open letting my frustration show as I see Nate standing either side.

"Twice in one day, aren't I lucky?" I say dryly as he gapes at me.

"Yeah uh... I'm sorry... I... uh..." He clears his throat. "Ryan left his uh phone here and I um... I was wondering if I could get it back. Probably best that I came instead of... uh... him you know because well..."

I can't help but smirk at his stuttering. He's acting as though he's never seen a half-naked woman before. His eyes are darting everywhere in an attempt to avoid looking at me dressed in just a towel, my damp hair dripping on the floor below me. I open the door wider then lean back against the frame and watch him as he takes hurried steps inside. Where's all your swagger and confidence now, Asshole? He walks over to the kitchen and picks up the black iPhone that's sitting beside the microwave then turns back to face me.

"So how was your run?"

He strolls back over, apparently finding his easy charm in the kitchen with the phone.

"Interesting," I reply simply then stand straight as he passes by me to go back out to the hallway.

My thoughts briefly drift to Adam the Friendly Psychopath. Okay maybe psychopath is a bit harsh but still, anyone who asks a girl her name and where she goes to school in the middle of a park when they've never seen them before is a big old creeper in my book.

"Why interesting?" He presses as he leans back against the wall opposite the door.

"You kind of had to be there. So if that's everything, I'm going to shut the door now."

"What's up, Clarke? Scared to talk to me?"

A smug smile tugs at his lips. Idiot. Scared? Is he fucking kidding?

"No I'm not scared, *Harris*. I'd just rather have some clothes on. You're welcome to come in and wait." I turn and walk straight back into my dorm leaving the door open.

I hear it close behind me and silently pray that it was him being a gentleman and shutting it for me before going back to his own dorm. Not that I'd mind him waiting around for me. If he wants to play games then I can too. Hallie Clarke is not scared of anything. I walk straight into my bedroom without looking back. Guys like him really piss me off. They're all the damn same. I rifle through my wardrobe for clothes, eventually pulling out a pair of light blue skinny jeans and a white tank. These will do. I slip them on then add a cream colored cardigan over the top, fastening the brown wooden buttons halfway up. I dig out my favorite combat boots from the bottom of the wardrobe. My mind is still reeling with thoughts of Nate. *What the hell is wrong with me?* I pick up my hairbrush from the top of the drawers and sit on my bed, crossing my legs like a child as I do. Why can't I get the guy out of my brain? I mean, he's just a guy nothing special yet something about him calls to me. I can't explain it and it pisses me off. I brush out my long curls of my hair then bring it all up into a messy bun, securing it with a simple black hair tie. When I'm finished I walk back into the lounge area and can see he's still there. He's also placed two cups of coffee on the small table between the TV and couches.

Oh sure, make yourself at home.

I sit down at the edge of one of the couches and wait for him to speak, his eyes boring into me. Something is different about him. Normally when a guy takes interest in me I feel nothing, but now, with Nate it's as though a little trail of heat is left wherever his eyes roam. I can physically feel where he's been looking and it doesn't freak me out or give me the creeps. It makes me hot. What the hell? When he still doesn't say a word I debate asking him if he plans on watching me go grocery shopping when I hear my cell ring. I pull it out of my front pocket and check the caller ID. Sperm Donor. Again? Ugh. Ignoring Nate's curious face, I lean back on the seat and answer it. He'll only keep calling if I don't.

"Yeah?"

"Hello, Hallie. I just wanted to let you know that I transferred some money to your account."

I don't know why he bothers. He knows I hate it when he sends me cash and by his tone of voice, it's obvious that he isn't exactly thrilled about it either.

I sigh as I answer. "That was unnecessary but thank you."

"Of course it was necessary. Now, I'd like to visit you soon and then maybe you can tell me why you felt it *necessary* to keep quiet about college until yesterday."

Ah, this is why he's pissed. The man isn't happy that I did something for myself, out of his control. I turn my body so my back is away from Nathan.

"Sure, then you can tell me why you all of a sudden care."

"Do you have to have that attitude with me?" Shit. I didn't mean to mumble that out loud. I groan inside as he continues, "That's not true and you know it. I do nothing but defend you. Do you know what it's been like to have to listen to my colleagues tell me all about the normal things that their children do with their friends, and to hear the endless stories of how you parade yourself around half naked, offering yourself to anyone that's willing?"

My breath catches in my throat as I push back the tears that are trying to spring from my eyes. Of course he'd believe the bullshit that gets said about me instead of just asking me about it. He always does. I force my tone to be level and uncaring before responding.

"Yeah must be horrible to realize what a slut for a daughter you have."

I stand and begin to pace around the room as his clipped voice lectures me.

"I never used those words, but you have to see where I'm coming from. You haven't been the same since the whole Jason Evans fiasco. Maybe college will be good for you, maybe you'll make some friends and..."

I cut his words off with my own, unable to reign the anger.

"And what? Move on from it? Forget about that asshole? Is that what you're trying to say?"

He sighs. "Never mind, I just wish you wouldn't be so closed off with me."

There are reasons I don't open up and he is part of it. My voice is ice cold when I reply.

"Don't take it personally, it's not just you."

"Hallie..." Again I cut him off, not wanting to hear whatever comes out of his mouth next.

"Sorry George I have to go and, you know, parade around half naked. Goodbye."

I hang up the phone and hurl it across the room letting some warped sort of growl rip from me. Closed off? Is he kidding me? And what the fuck? *The Jason Evans fiasco?* Is that what we're calling it now?

"Hey, are you okay?"

I turn abruptly, Nate's eyes imploring into me. Damn it! I forgot he was here. I can't be dealing with this. I fix my usual emotionless expression on my face, somewhat difficultly.

"I'm fine," I say as I again fight away the tears that are threatening.

I will not be weak for an asshole, even if he is my damn father. This is not the first time George Clarke has made me want to cry. My cell rings again from where it's lying on the floor beneath the window. It can stay there. I can feel Nate's gaze on me as I stand in the middle of the room shaking. I don't need him to see this. I grab my bag and my keys and walk over to the kitchen where I pick up the shopping list I made yesterday with Codie then head out of the dorm room door and down the hallway to the stairs. Nate is walking after me but I don't stop. I'm close to losing it and he's already seen too much. My relationship with my Dad is messy at the best of times.

"Hallie!" He calls as his hand wraps gently around my arm.

"What?" I ask him impatiently, ignoring the warmth from his contact.

"Do you want to talk? I mean, it's obvious you're not okay."

"No, I'm going grocery shopping."

I rush away from him and disappear down the stairs. Do I want to talk about it? Is he insane? I don't even know the guy, nor do I wish to discuss my feelings about my father. I'm the product of a one night stand between him and my mom, and his stiff upbringing and immaculate manners are the only reason he's in my life at all. He does what he's responsible for and nothing more. When I turned 18 I told him that he needn't bother anymore seeing as how I'm an adult now, but he maintains the empty contact and constant cash flow to keep up the appearance that he's an outstanding family man and stand up member of society.

As the CEO of a large insurance company, his image is very important to him. It also means that he isn't exactly strapped for cash, which pisses me off seeing as though my mom usually was when I was growing up. We were never poor but we didn't have overly nice things either. Our house is full of donated mismatched furniture, and a lot of my clothes are from Walmart and thrift stores. Not that I care about that stuff, I'm more than happy with what I got. My mom has always done her best by me. Not George though. His image is also the reason he hates that I'm not as sociable as his colleagues' kids. He's attempted to force me into hanging out with the children of the people he works with and his clients on several occasions in order to make him look like the easy going family guy that he definitely is not. He wasn't happy about the whole Jason thing. How he found out I have no idea but I remember him calling round after it asking how I could be as stupid as to let a boy use me like that. He'd lectured me like the whole thing was my fault. Our relationship wasn't great to begin with, but that moment right there pretty much buried it. It's now beyond salvable. We are just too different. I'm not the daughter he wants, and he sure as hell isn't the father I need. I reach my car, climb in and turn my stereo on full, again pushing the tears back. Maybe I should call my mom; all of a sudden I miss her.

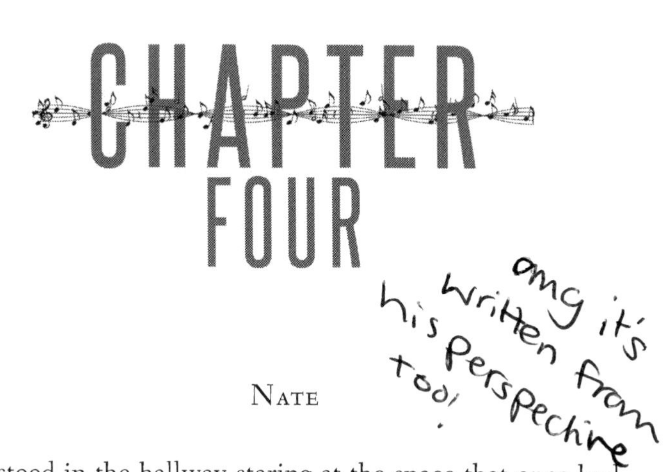

NATE

I'm stood in the hallway staring at the space that once had Hallie in it.

What the fuck just happened? I don't know what was being said on that phone call but she looked like she was about to cry. I think it was her dad. Yeah I'm sure she called him Dad at some point. I guess they aren't close though seeing how she tensed up the second she looked at the caller ID. My pathetic efforts at comforting her were pushed aside so she could go grocery shopping. Fucking grocery shopping. I know she was trying to push her feelings down, I could see it. Damn girl never gives anything away. Her face is a blank canvas but this time I saw it. I saw the hurt in those big brown eyes as her phone flew across the room. And fuck she has quite the arm too. She blanked them again though when I spoke. It was as if she'd forgotten I was even there. I'd been staring at her, the way she walked in all casual with her fuck the world attitude. I was about to ask her to get that coffee with me when her cell started ringing. The way her face dropped slightly was an instant mood killer. I should have left, I should have let her have that call in privacy, but I couldn't. I just couldn't bring myself to leave that room, to leave her.

What the fuck has happened to me?

I shake my head and turn to go back to my dorm. I have to get this girl out of my head. I thought banging that Tami chick would have done the job. She was all over me within minutes of walking into the frat house where the party was last night. I found her cute at first but then she became just as annoying as the rest of them. She spent the entire night clinging on to my arm as she talked constantly about her sorority sisters and how she thought I should pledge a fraternity because it was the 'absolute it' thing to do.

Yeah, not going to happen.

Frat guys are fucking morons. My dad was one and he's the biggest moron I know. I hadn't really planned on bringing her back to the dorm but then I overheard Codie talking about Hallie with her brother. He was asking about her and I got pissed, pissed at myself that I was again letting Hallie into my thoughts and pissed that this guy wanted to know her. It doesn't make sense, I don't even know the girl and she's nowhere near my usual type. Sure she's hot, but she's also hard work and practically fucking mute. I could probably count the amount of words I've heard her say over the last two days on one hand. But I'm so damn curious about her. I want to know what gives her that haunted look in her eyes. I want to know why she's so closed off. I want to know what made her that way. And most of all, I want to know how to fix it.

I'd been tempted this morning to run after her when she darted from the corridor after witnessing me bullshit Tami outside my door. I was going to grab her and make her talk to me so I could tell her that I'm not that big of an asshole even though it must of looked like I was, asking her out for coffee then letting some other girl out of my apartment a day later. I wanted to explain myself to her and then that's when it hit me. Why the fuck should I? I don't owe her anything. I was done with that, with her, which was why I'd agreed to go and get Ryan's phone back for him because he sure fucked up this time. Fucking your next door neighbor is never a good idea. My mind was elsewhere as I walked over there. I'd been secretly hoping it would be Codie herself who opened the door but no. Of course it was Hallie, and of course she was in just a towel. It had taken me walking inside and away from her to stop me babbling at her like a little fucking girl. This chick is killing me.

I pull a soda out of the fridge and swallow half the contents. What to do today. My best friend is still snoring in bed so I put his phone on the kitchen side. Maybe I should wake Ryan up and force him into hunting down a gym with me. Nah, the guy will just slow me down. Besides, from the sound of him I doubt he'll be opening his eyes for a while yet. Then again he does deserve some form of punishment, seeing as he's put us in a very shitty situation with our neighbors now by doing the unspeakable with one of them. Yeah, I'm thinking waking him up is a fine idea.

"You better be dead or dying bro," he groans as I bang on his closed bedroom door.

"Nope. Now get out of bed shit head," I chirp, opening the door and flicking on the light.

"What the fuck did I do to deserve this?"

I laugh loud. "Well my mentally challenged friend, I'm glad you asked. What you did, was our happy go lucky neighbor who we have to live next door to for a year."

He groans and I smile, satisfied. Good. I'm glad he's feeling shitty about it.

"How pissed is she?" He asks, sitting up and rubbing the sleep from his eyes.

"Dunno, I didn't see her. Got Hallie instead."

"Michigan's number one ice queen. She caught me sneaking out this morning, dude, if looks could kill I'd be dead."

Shit, no wonder she looked so pissed this morning. She'd witnessed him and then me doing the same thing just after. I bet she thinks she's living next door to a couple of jackasses. That's not so far from the truth I suppose. Why do I even care?

"Bro, we need to do something. I can't stay in this room all day," I tell him and he groans again.

"Can't you play out on your own? Or go find that Tara or whatever."

"It's Tami you dick, and no. Now get your lazy ass outta bed. We need to go get groceries or something", I say then leave his room before he can complain anymore.

Idly, I wonder through the kitchen opening drawers and cupboards. They are literally bare apart from the usual kitchen accessory bullshit. Neither of us can cook so we'll probably just buy chips and sodas but least it's something.

"Alright Asshole, let's go," I hear my best friend say from behind me a few minutes later.

This should be interesting.

I park my truck in the lot outside the grocery store and my eyes immediately spot the smokin' brunette that's been on my mind since yesterday. She's stood by her car, at least I assume it's her car, talking with a couple of guys. *So she has got a voice.* Wait she's not talking, she's arguing.

"Hey isn't that our resident ice queen over there?" Ryan says from beside me.

"Yeah," I mumble, my eyes still watching her.

Both guys are trying to make a move on her but she's pushing them back. Well trying to anyway. She's tiny compared to them. Well to one of them anyway. The other could quite possibly be smaller than her.

"Shit. I wouldn't like to get on the wrong side of her," Ryan states and a small part of me is amused.

I saw the way she launched her phone across a room. She really has got quite the arm, I'd hate to be on the receiving end of it.

"It's obvious she isn't interested, why are they still trying?" I mutter, more to myself than anyone else.

The taller of the two has now got his arm wrapped around her waist whilst the other is teasing her, playing with her hair. I look at her face, and the expression clouding it makes my stomach drop. Fear, pure fear. I'm out of the car without a word to Ryan and heading over to where she is. Within seconds I'm close enough to hear their voices.

"Come on, baby, I can tell you want me," the smaller guy sneers at her.

"I really don't," she answers then makes a perfect O with her mouth as her eyes meet mine. Totally the wrong time to be thinking about this, but the things I'd like to do to that pretty mouth of hers.

"Don't worry, babe, we're willing to share you," tall guy purrs and she tries to push them both off again, her eyes not leaving mine as I come to a halt directly beside them.

"Get your fucking hands off her," I say firmly, keeping my voice as level as I can. I'd learned very young that shouting never gets you anywhere, only escalates a situation. The perks of having a lawyer for a dad I suppose.

"Is this your boyfriend?" The small guy laughs, not even sparing me a glance.

"Nah it can't be, she's got slut written all over her," the

other guy smirks, pushing himself closer to her. "You don't seem like the one man type."

Fuck this. My hand reaches for him and I clasp my fist around the back collar of his shirt, before pulling him hard. He stumbles a little before falling.

"What the fuck do you think you're doing?" Small guy shouts, stepping away from Hallie and right in front of me. I almost laugh. He pushes his chest out and squares his shoulders. It's a typical asshole move, trying to make himself look bigger.

"You really don't wanna do that bro," I hear Ryan say from behind me and I fight back a smirk. We'd been here before. I don't need to turn around to know that he has picked up the lanky half of this clown duo.

"Hallie, you good?" I ask, looking over this dicks shoulder and locking my eyes with my neighbor. She nods quickly and then crosses her arms over her chest. I can see she's struggling to keep her shit together so I pull my eyes away, switching to glare at the guy in front of me.

"Time to go buddy," Ryan says, pushing tall guy over to the side then adds, "take your miniature boyfriend with you too." He shakes his head in disbelief. "Seriously dude, how tall are you?"

Small guy glares up at me for one last second before turning swiftly and following his friend into the opposite direction of the store. Pussies.

"Fucking douche bags. Do you know those guys?" My best friends asks Hallie and she just shakes her head no before muttering a quick thanks and rushing away towards the doors of the grocery store.

Well then. You're welcome?

CHAPTER FIVE

Hallie

How fucking embarrassing! Of course, it would be Nate that shows up to play white knight when I'm being harassed by a couple of assholes. Couldn't just be a nice simple stranger. And let's just ignore the way my heart kicked up a couple of notches when I saw him approaching.

Let's definitely ignore that.

What the hell are they doing here anyway? I pull a cart out from the line of them just inside the store door and quickly move up the aisle, clutching the list of things I need. Thanks to that little spectacle I'm in the store a lot later than I want to be. My mind flashes back to what just happened and I shiver. Fucking guys.

She's got slut written all over her.

Maybe that jackass was right, I wonder idly, as I pick off the items on the list, adding them to the cart. Maybe I am a slut. I've always attracted idiots like that so maybe I do give off some kind of 'my legs are always open' vibe.

"Hallie!"

I groan inside at the sound of my name being called. What the hell does he want now?

"Look, are you okay? Those guys were assholes," Nate says when I turn around.

Assholes. Yeah, that pretty much sums them up.

"Yeah I'm fine. Nothing I haven't dealt with before. Thanks though," I say, and then turn back to face my shopping, concentrating harder than any person needs to on the contents.

The truth is I was scared. Not as much as a normal person should be, I've been waiting for something like this to happen to me for a while. You can't live the way I do (or used to) and not expect to find yourself in a few tough situations. Still, I was concerned. The way that tall guy snaked his arm around my waist, pulling me into him, and the little dude digging his fingers into my hips, his sweaty breath suffocating me. No. I don't even want to think about it.

"Hallie," Nate says softly, his hand touching my own shaking one.

I jerk away. What happened in the parking lot has left me feeling jittery and I hate it. He tries to say something else but is cut off when his friend approaches us.

"Hey, Hal! Can you cook?" Ryan asks with a wide smile on his face.

Seriously? What kind of question is that? And what the fuck is this Hal business? First Codie and now him, it's catching quicker than herpes.

"Can I cook?"

"That's right," he nods and I look over to Nate for some kind of explanation. I don't get one. He just shrugs, clearly used to this kind of thing from his friend.

"Um, yeah I can cook. Why?" I ask and regret it immediately as his eyes fill with mischief.

Oh sweet Jesus.

"Well, if I pay you a handsome amount, would you be

willing to come to our dorm and cook for us every night? Naked," he smiles, his face showing no sign of a joke.

He's gotta be kidding right? Guy just has no boundaries. He slept with my roommate last night and now he's asking me to get naked.

"You have no shame."

"None whatsoever. So what do you think? None of us can cook and there's only so much pizza a guy can eat," he continues and this time I don't even bother to reply. I just laugh quietly and turn back around shaking my head.

"Is that a no?" He calls to my back and I continue with my shopping, not looking behind me. "Come on Hal, I thought we could be best buds! I'm willing to ditch this loser to make friendships bracelets with you," he adds and I chew my lip to stop the smile threatening to take over my face.

Fucking idiot. It's a shame he had to go and sleep with Codie, he's actually quite amusing.

I finish my shopping, vaguely aware of my two neighbors fucking around behind me but I don't turn to speak to them. I also don't comment on the shit they have piled into their cart when I see them at the checkout, nothing but Gatorade and Cheetos.

Has neither of them ever heard of an apple? Or an actual balanced meal?

People with poor eating habits seriously annoy me. There's no excuse for it. Surely between the two of them they could at least make a sandwich. The thought of them next door eating nothing but chips follows me the whole drive home, then plagues me as I change, and is still present when I'm putting away the groceries in the dorm room. I force myself to try and let it go but it crawls at me, driving me insane.

"Who the fuck goes to a grocery store and just buy Cheetos and Gatorade?" I blurt out as I make coffee for Codie and I.

"Who bought Gatorade and Cheetos?" She asks confused and I look up to see her right next to me.

Jesus. How embarrassing. I'm apparently thinking out loud now.

"Whilst I was at the store, I saw Dick 1 and Dick 2 there, and that's literally all they bought. What the fuck is wrong with that? How is that keeping them healthy? Good God it's not difficult to make simple meals. They're 18 years old for fuck sake. Have they never cooked anything? I mean seriously?"

She laughs hard. "Dick 1 and Dick 2, nice. I like that." When I don't respond she continues. "This has really pissed you off hasn't it? Why do you care?"

She picks both of our cups and moves over to the couches. I follow her and then flop down on one of the seats. Why do I care?

"Thanks," I say, taking my coffee from her. "I hate stuff like that. I feel like I need to feed the pair of them now," I state and she raises her eyebrow at me.

What the hell is wrong with me? I did exactly the same thing back home and it always confused people. Why can't I just leave it alone? No wonder people think I'm weird. Even Codie is looking at me now like I've grown a second head.

"Hey don't look at me like that. If it weren't for you being mad at one of them, that's exactly what I'd be doing right now," I tell her and she nods thoughtfully for a second before speaking.

"Go invite them over."

I study her face, looking for any indication to her mood.

Is she mad? I can't just go over there and invite them for dinner.

"I'm serious. It will give me a chance to ignore Ryan and practice my cold shoulder technique. Nothing says 'I'm over you' like inviting the guy for dinner and ignoring him," she continues and now I nod thoughtfully.

This is so out of character for me but the idea of them not eating something healthy just next door to me is making me crazy.

"There is that." I take a deep breath before standing with my cup still in hand. "Okay I'm doing it. I'm actually going to fucking do it."

I can hear Codie laughing as I open the door to our dorm but I ignore it and continue down the hall to their dorm suit, knocking loudly when I reach the door. I sip at my coffee as I wait for an answer. Why the hell am I doing this? Purposely inviting over a guy that makes me feel things I've never felt just so I can feed him, or them. Not to mention, his friend had casual (on his side anyway) sex with my roommate. Talk about awkward.

"Hey, what's up?"

Shit. I hadn't even noticed the door opening in front of me. I have got to stop spacing out like that. I bring my eyes up to Nate's and empty my face of expression. He has seen far too much of me today.

"Come over at six, and bring the other one," I say, and then walk off back to my dorm.

"Hallie! What's at 6?" He calls and somewhere inside I smile. I'm going to sound crazy. I really shouldn't get off on that.

"Dinner."

"So are they coming?" Codie asks as soon as I walk through the door.

"No idea," I reply then head over to the kitchen, my head trying to decide what I should make for dinner.

Codie is flapping around beside me, questioning me on what I said and I explain to her what happened as I begin to pull ingredients out of the cupboards and refrigerator.

Lasagna. Everyone like lasagna right?

"I need to look hot, like I should change and look smokin' hot right? I need to make him sorry he ever left here this morning," she asks me and I turn to face her. She's obviously not going to leave me alone unless I answer her.

"Just wear something casual that shows off your," I consider what word to use, "assets." That will do. "Low cut shirt or something."

I need to get moving. It's already four and I told them to be over at six. That's if they even come, it's not like I waited around for an answer. It's not like I even care. If they don't show I know I'll just make them a plate each and take it over. It's a compulsion that I have no idea how to ignore, even if it will be awkward. Never mind, time to get to work.

I spend the next two hours cooking and setting the table, declining all offers of help from Codie. Instead, she sits on the breakfast bar watching me and talking to me about the party last night and how much I missed. I don't have to talk back as she says enough for both us. I'm just putting the side salad on the table when I hear the knocking at the door. I send her to answer it as I'm finishing up. *Here we go.*

The Italian aroma fills the dorm as I pull the lasagna out of the oven and place it on the kitchen counter. I breathe it in softly, secretly impressed at my own culinary skills. I've always liked cooking. The second I got old enough to be left in the house by myself, my mom took full advantage by dating more. Sometimes I'd get home from school and she'd be so preoccupied with getting ready to go out, or she'd already be out, that I'd go without dinner. I learnt then that I'd have to do it myself and after a few failed attempts, I actually started to enjoy it.

I turn and watch from the kitchen as the guys enter, stifling a laugh as Ryan's eyes stare at my roommate's ass. She's gone for tight jeans and a low cut shirt, barely containing her breasts. It's doing the trick, he can't take his eyes off her. I feel a strange sense of satisfaction for her. I turn back to the kitchen, opting to finish preparing the salad as Codie makes small talk with them. Why have I done this to myself? I've always been the same. It's not something I can really explain. I just have this need, or compulsion, to make sure the people around me eat properly. Back home, I used to make casseroles and then take them to the homeless shelters and orphanages in the area. I'd do that at least twice a week, often stick around to help them serve or clean up. Not many people know about it. In fact, thinking about it I need to check out the shelters here. I make a mental note to look into it then turn to the cupboards to grab some glasses.

"Hal, I'm pretty sure you were supposed to be naked," I hear Ryan say from behind me so I turn.

He's leaning against the breakfast bar, smiling wide at me. I fight back the smile. There's just something about this guy. I've never seen him be serious, even with the whole drama at the store earlier he made a complete joke about it. It's light and he's funny. Not that I'm going to tell him that. It's very obvious the guy's ego is big enough.

"My name is Hallie, asshole. Go sit down."

I watch him as he saunters over, taking a seat next to Codie at dining room table.

"Hi, baby," he purrs at my blonde roommate and I shake my head in disbelief. He really doesn't have any shame.

I walk around from the kitchen, carrying the glasses and

a jug of water, then go back for the lasagna and place it in the middle of the table. I feel Nate watching me as I take me seat beside him.

"Holy shit, Hal! You weren't lying when you said you could cook. This is fucking awesome!" Ryan shouts as he shovels some of his food into his mouth. I smile slightly in response.

"It really is good, Hallie. I've completely lucked out in the roommate market," Codie adds, throwing a wink at me. This whole situation seems insane. My roommate banged one of these guys just last night and here they are chatting away like nothing happened.

"So how come we got invited?" Nate asks me.

I turn to him, my head tilting slightly to the side and study him. I keep my face impassive and lock my eyes with his. His gaze bores into me, giving me the sense that he's seeing behind the bullshit and right through me. The feeling gives me a surprising calm that I can't even begin to explain in words.

"Because you both lack nutrition," I state simply before pulling my eyes away. That's all I'm giving him. There is absolutely no chance that I'm going to be telling them that I can't help it. To be fair, it's the truth. They really should be eating better.

"I knew you cared. You totally want to be my best bud and make friendship bracelets all night with me," Ryan winks and I roll my eyes at him, again hiding my amusement.

"I really don't."

"Sure you do. I can see it in your eyes," he says smiling wide.

I smirk. "I'm not really the friendly kind."

We spend the next thirty minutes or so eating, the

Fuck off Ryan

others talking idly about what classes they're taking and all that kind of shit. I don't speak, just listen and watch. Conversation isn't something I do easily. The last group of friends I had turned on me viciously after everything went down with Jason Evans. They believed his lies and chose their popularity over their friendship with me. It didn't matter that I needed them. I knew then that having friends wasn't something I ever wanted again. I never want to have to go through all that bullshit again. It's behind me now and I have no interest in looking back. The past brings nothing but trouble and heartache.

"So Hallie... Jace was asking about you last night," Codie says as we all finish up eating.

"Jace? That's your brother right?" I answer as I sip at my water.

"That's right and he was all uptight that you didn't show at the party. I think he has a thing for you."

The guy doesn't have a thing for me, he has a thing for my ass. I couldn't be less interested if I tried.

"He's told me to make sure you're at his frat party in two weeks," Codie continues and I tense. Getting out of this isn't going to be easy. I can see the determination on her face.

"I don't go to parties," is all I say before standing with my dish, collecting the others and walking over to the kitchen. I really don't want to go.

"Oh come on, Clarke, everyone likes parties! Booze, beats, and babes. What's not to like?" Ryan shouts to me and I can't help but let out a sarcastic laugh. The guy has no idea.

"Sorry *Turner*. Booze, beats, and babes aren't really my thing."

"You know, these parties aren't so bad. Everyone has a

good time. Plus after a fortnight of classes, it could be fun to let loose a little. Come on Hallie... please please please. I'll do all your laundry for a full week if you agree," Codie whines at me.

I turn then, eyeing her suspiciously. I've known the girl a couple of days and she can already tell I hate laundry. Plus, it will be a good test of my strength, to see if I can still say no in the face of temptation. I just have to steer clear of the alcohol and I'll be fine.

"All week?" I ask carefully and her face stretches wide, nodding in agreement.

Oh Jesus. What am I doing?

"Fine I'll go," I answer then slip down the hallway to my bedroom.

I need to run.

duh nuh nuh nuh nuh

Hallie

Oh thank holy Jesus this week of classes is finally over. I am so ready to get back to my dorm, find some pajamas, and not leave for the whole weekend. I've been working on my excuse all day to get out of going to the stupid party tomorrow night that I promised Codie I'd go to. Why, oh why do I do this to myself? The old Hallie would have been totally up for getting smashed at some college party but not the new sensible Hallie. This Hallie stays home and does her college work, runs and cooks. Because this Hallie knows that if she goes out and gets drunk, she will come home with company. Or not come home at all. Either way, that isn't how I want to live anymore. My cell chimes, distracting my thoughts and I pull it from my pocket. A text from Codie.

Codie: *You. Me. Candy. Channing Tatum. Tonight. Not accepting no as an answer. MWAH!*

I can't help but smile a little. Over the last couple of weeks, we've come to be sort of friends. She's actually a lot more relaxed than I'd originally given her credit for and we have more in common than I thought too. She's smart and her school work comes before anything. I've heard her turn down several dates over the past week as she only goes out on weekends. She even turned down one from Ryan next door who's been following her around like a lost puppy. It's hilarious. Poor guy isn't used to being turned down. He's not so bad though. I surprisingly found him in my anthropology class and now he saves me a seat. We seem to have an ongoing joke where he asks me for sex and I generally just flip him off. I send Codie a quick reply back to say I'm on my way to the dorm now then pocket my cell. The browning leaves crunch beneath my shoes as I hurry back through campus. The air is moist so I know it's only a matter of time before the rain hits. I'm desperate to be back after the encounter I've just had with Adam the Friendly Psychopath. Yeah that's right. Turns out he's not actually a psychopath. He's actually in my English class. He also doesn't have hard feelings about me running away from him and wants to know if I'd be interested in being his running partner. I think not. I'm still not convinced. The jury is most definitely still out on that one. My dorm block is only a few minutes away in the distance when I hear my name called causing me to groan inside as I stop and turn.

"Hallie, wait up!"

I stand impatiently as Jace, Codie's brother, runs over to me, the first drop of rain falling onto my bare arm. I knew it. I knew I'd get caught in this damn rain.

"So my sister said you're coming tomorrow night," he says as he stops right before me.

My eyes roam him discreetly. He's got the same blonde hair as Codie, styled in the just got out of bed look that guys everywhere seem to have. *Hurray for conformity*. His hands are pushed into the pockets of his black jeans as he rocks back and forth. He's staring right at me. What am I supposed to say to that? He didn't ask anything just made

101

an observation. I literally have no reply to it. The rain is now falling heavy and I'm getting wet waiting for him to elaborate. Fuck this.

"Was there something else?" I ask him and he lets out an embarrassed chuckle before responding.

"Uh yeah, I was hoping, I mean wondering if you want me to pick you up before it."

Oh dear. If I agree to this then I'll have to actually go to the damn party.

"I'm going with Codie," I tell him and he nods quickly.

"I know, I can pick you both up," he replies, pushing a hand through his hair nervously.

Seriously? Why couldn't he have just called his own damn sister to arrange this?

"Sure, whatever. Call Codie and arrange it. I really need to go," I say, pulling at my now soaked through t-shirt.

"Yeah shit, sorry. Kay, later Hallie," he mutters before walking off shaking his head.

He might be my roommate's brother, but my God he's an odd one. I turn back towards the direction of my dorm and begin to jog, cursing myself the whole way back for not having a jacket with me.

"Looking good, Miss Clarke," Westley shouts from his usual perch as I walk through the main door of the block. I can't stand this guy. He's an absolute creep. He just leers at the girls here as they walk by. "You need a hand drying off?" He calls after me as I stroll past him towards the stairs.

I don't respond, instead choosing to ignore him and running up the stairs. A night in with Codie watching the God that is Mr Tatum on the TV is sounding better and better. Shower first though I decide as my shoes squelch along the corridor. Or maybe a bath. Yes a nice long steamy hot bubble bath. I like that. A rare smile spreads across my face as I reach the dorm suite door.

Finally.

What is wrong with this picture?

Everything, that's what.

All my hopes and dreams of a nice hot bubble bath have been shattered. Destroyed by what is sitting on one of the couches talking with my roommate. Or I should say who is sitting on one of the couches.

"Hallie."

I look up to the sound of his voice as water from the rain drips all over the floor. Ugh, what fresh hell is this?

"I need to change," I respond quickly before walking down the hall to my bedroom.

What is he doing here? I pull off my wet clothes when I reach my room, quickly changing into sweatpants and a tank. There is literally no reason for him to be sat in my dorm right now. Has something happened? Is it Mom? I add thick socks, my UGG boots and rush back out to the lounge. I don't want to leave Codie stuck with him for too long.

"Hallie, how are you?" My dad asks me when I enter the room.

He's perched perfectly at the edge of the seat, as though he's scared the damn thing will suck him in. I watch him as his eyes scan the area, disapproval etched all over his face.

"Fine. What are you doing here?" I answer, not wanting to prolong this any further.

"I'll just run to the store for that stuff, Hal," Codie mutters before flashing me a reassuring smile and dashing at the speed of light out the door.

Not that I can blame her, the tension in here is thick, heavy and extremely noticeable. I'm almost choking on it myself. I haven't spoken to him since I hung up our call a fortnight earlier. Codie knew something was wrong without me telling her anything as she'd seen me ignoring my cell over the last few days. I'm still pissed at him.

"Well you weren't answering my calls, I had no choice. You could have been dead for all I knew. I tried to ask your mother but she says she hasn't heard from you either," he replies to me once Codie has left.

I doubt my Mom even remembers that I'm gone. She probably thinks I'm just out at the store of something.

"Sorry, I've been busy. You know, offering myself to anyone willing," I deadpan and he sighs heavily.

"Hallie, I want to know why you felt it necessary to hide coming here from me. Are you ashamed because you know I went to Ivy League? Is that it?"

My eyes widen is disbelief. He's really not going to apologize for practically calling me a slut last time we spoke. Plus he's throwing in my face that I'm not anywhere near as smart as he is, nice Dad. Maybe I should tell him how I got offered a place at fucking Yale and only turned it down because I didn't want to use *his* money to go. They wouldn't accept my scholarship request because *he* earns too much money.

"I never hid it, it just isn't any of your damn business. Now I have plans so could you leave please?" I say firmly as I walk over to the door and open it wide.

I'm eighteen now and this is my fucking home. If I don't want him in it then he has to respect that. Whether he likes it or not.

"Hallie you're acting like a child and I've done nothing to deserve this. You will have to talk to me at some point. What you do is my business, I am your father," he states as he walks reluctantly through the door.

Where the hell does this guy get off?

"You may biologically have helped to give me life, but you sure as shit are not my father."

I will not raise my voice. I will not let him get a hysterical reaction from me. I know that's exactly what he wants.

"That's not fair. I'm a good father to you. I get you anything you need despite all of the things I have to hear about you," he responds and I groan inside.

"I never realized I was so popular."

I'll never admit to him how much it hurts knowing he believes all the bullshit rumors and not me.

"Hallie you used to be so full of life when you were younger and now it's like you're dead inside. If you keep shutting people out then soon there will be no one left," he counters and I harden.

Of course, because he gives me money everything is okay in his book. Where the fuck was he when I needed him? Maybe if he wasn't such an image obsessed ass I would let him in once in a while.

"One can only dream," I answer him dryly and stifle a laugh at the way his jaw begins to twitch.

"That flippant attitude right there is why you had no friends back in Iowa," he tells me stiffly and I roll my eyes. I had no friends in Iowa because I didn't fucking want any. I fix a cold expression on my face as he continues. "And I'm guessing you only have your roommate as a friend here which doesn't count for anything because she has to speak to you. I can only imagine the stories I'd hear if I stayed around campus long enough."

Of course. Hallie Clarke, daughter of George Clarke, and number one slut. That's all he sees. He doesn't see past the rumors. He doesn't know me, or anything about me.

"That's right, I'm obviously fucking all of them," I state coldly.

"I don't know where you get that language from but that's no way to speak to your father young lady," he scolds and I sigh inside. He lost the right to tell me what to do a long time ago.

"Well we have established that I'm not America's fucking sweetheart. Now I'm sure you have lots of meetings and phone calls to make, all of which will be more important and of more interest to you than your moody, dead inside slut for a daughter so goodbye, George," I say then close the door on his face.

Fucking jerk.

CHAPTER SEVEN

NATE

Ouch. I'd hate to be that guy.

"Did you fucking hear that?" Ryan half whispers beside me.

"Yeah," I mutter. We'd just opened the door to head out for dinner when I stopped abruptly, the voices from the corridor freezing me in place. It was Hallie and, who I can only assume, her dad. Arguing. Well it was more like her dad giving her sly digs and Hallie brushing them off in a completely awe worthy manner. I didn't want her to know we could hear her so I'd pushed Ryan back into the suite, wincing at the words that were said.

"Shit. I knew she could be blunt but fuck she was ice cold then," my best friend comments and I nod agreeing.

The way she spoke to him, I can only imagine the blank expression on her face. The same blank expression I get from her and have done since I met her. We haven't spoken at all since the night I went over for dinner, not that I've tried to. I've been working my ass off on keeping her out of my mind, concentrating on working out and school. Whenever my mind had started to wonder, I've called Tami. It makes me an asshole using her like that, I know, but I have told her I don't want anything serious and she seemed to accept it. Although she does text me 5000 times a day. That's just a chick thing though, right?

"So we gonna go eat now, bro?" Ryan says beside me, nudging me out the door.

I nod and we both walk down to my truck. We see Codie there talking to an older guy, and from the sound of his voice I know its Hallie's dad.

"I don't really know what I can do to help, Mr Clarke," I hear Codie tell him as we approach. "I mean, I don't really know her that well yet."

"Hey baby," Rye purrs, sliding his arm around her waist.

I can't help but admire how little he cares that he's just interrupted them.

"Oh hey. This is um, Hallie's dad," she introduces us, pulling away from Ryan.

"Sup bro, we live next door to the girls." I watch as the older man's face sours, grimacing as he forces a professional smile onto his face. His eyes roam the both of us and I smirk as they hit me.

"Don't worry, none of us are banging her," Ryan continues and I have to stifle a laugh at the face the old guy pulls - sheer distaste.

"Well, that's very good to hear. Codie if you could tell my daughter that I will be in touch soon, I'd be grateful," he responds before walking away quickly.

"I guess that's where Clarke gets it from then," Ryan muses after we all watch him drive off.

"What do you mean?" Codie says defensively.

"The whole walking away abruptly thing, whether you're finished talking or not."

He has a point. She does do it a lot. I watched a guy

trying to ask her out two days ago and she literally walked off before he's even managed to spit the words out. Poor fucker.

"Yeah well I'm gonna go check she's okay. Later guys," Codie chirps as she heads back to the building.

Part of me wants to go up there and check she's fine myself, but I can't. That would be counterproductive to my no Hallie plan.

"You gonna be at that party tomorrow night?" Ryan calls and I chuckle under my breath.

I've never heard him sound so desperate. He's been moaning about her lack of interest none stop, pulling every move he has to get her back in bed. Nothing has worked. It seems she's taken a lesson from her roommate in that department, freezing him out. At least she's friendlier about it.

"It's Jace's party, so obviously I'll be there. Hallie too if I can get her out the room," she shouts over and I can't help but smirk. Good luck with that one. She doesn't seem the let go and have some fun type.

"Come on man, let's go eat." I say to my best friend, patting his back in brotherly support.

"I just don't get it bro, she was all over me that first night."

I chuckle as we walk back to my truck. This whole situation is going to be real amusing to watch.

So the last thing I want to be doing right now is partying with a bunch of frat boy assholes who think they own the damn college. But here I am, surrounded by them as I watch my best friend grinding with some red haired chick. We got here four hours ago and he's completely fucking wasted where as I'm ready to go home and have been for the past 3 hours and 59 minutes. Parties like this just aren't my thing.

"Baby, come and dance with me," Tami slurs from beside me.

Uh, no.

"I don't dance. Why don't you go with your friends or whatever," I reply, bringing my beer to my mouth and draining the cup.

I'm going to need more of this if I'm to get through the night.

"Fine," she huffs before stomping off to a pack of girls in the corner.

They may as well be a pack of wolves the way they're all staring at me. God this is uncomfortable.

"Nate!"

I turn and see a guy from my class is calling me over from where he's stood by the keg. Thank fuck, an excuse to move.

"Sup, Carter," I say as I reach him, handing him my cup so he can fill it.

Brody Carter - The only frat boy I've met here that doesn't instantly piss me off.

"S'all good here. Saw you trying to get away from QB so figured I'd offer a helping hand," he laughs and I snort.

QB is what all the guys call Tami. It stands for Queen Bee. Apparently she rules the girls here. The very idea of that makes me piss. She wouldn't last two seconds in New York.

"Looks like your girl has got some competition for the title," he mutters as his eyes look over my shoulder.

Confused, I turn slowly to see what he's staring at and come face to face with the hottest thing I've ever seen. And

I'm not the only one who thinks it. She has the attention of every guy in here, all of them gaping at her, jaws to the floor. *Hallie.*

I watch as she shifts uncomfortably whilst Codie whispers something in her ear. She nods firmly then follows her dancing blonde friend into the kitchen.

"Holy shit man! Who the hell is she?" Carter hisses when they've left the room.

"That's Hallie Clarke, the blonde is Codie Barnes."

Everyone knows Codie, because of her brother Jace. He's some big shot around campus; everybody wants to be his best friend, or boyfriend. I want neither. Guy has douche bag written all over him.

"You know her? Because I wouldn't mind being introduced," he comments and I laugh small as his eyebrows wiggle. Can't blame him, she is a babe. I didn't even know she was here, how long have they been here?

"Hers and Codie's dorm room is next door to mine."

He lets out a whistled breath. "You're a lucky bastard you know that," he laughs and I smile small.

I'm not that fucking lucky.

"I'll catch you later man," I say to him before heading out to the back patio.

It's far too hot in there, I need some air. I push my way through the crowds of horny teenagers and out into the cold night air, sitting down at a bench to the far side of the garden. My cell beeps and I reluctantly pull it out of my pocket. This will be Tami wanting to know where I am.

Ryan: *Bro? Where the fuck you gone?*
Not Tami. At least that's something.
Me: *Out back.*

He doesn't text back. Instead I'm greeted with his shit eating grin as he strolls across the grass towards me, his arm wrapped around a stumbling Codie.

"Look who I found," he laughs, coming to a stop in front of me.

"Hi Nate!" Codie shouts then giggles. "Ryan is going to take me home because apparently I've had too much to drink," she continues and my eyebrow rises.

"Assholes in there pawing all over her man, I can't leave her with them. You coming? Or staying?" Ryan asks me and my eyes search over his shoulder for any sign of Hallie.

Where is she? She's always with Codie and she doesn't seem like the party girl so I don't think she should be left on her own. I'd feel bad if I didn't make sure she was okay. That's all this concern is. *Sure, keep telling yourself that dude.* Who the fuck am I kidding?

"Where's your roommate?" I ask Codie, trying not to sound like I care.

Codie's smile widens. "Hallie is still in there, fending off frat boys. She's a damn pro at it." She giggles again. "Jace said he'll get her home or she can crash here if she's drunk so don't worry about her," she laughs and my pulse quickens.

Something just doesn't seem right about that. I know Jace is her brother but I've met guys like him before. He'll get an inexperienced girl smashed and take advantage then because of all his little followers, she'll be the one who looks bad. Maybe I should just check on her? Or would that be weird? Why the fuck am I second guessing this shit? Why the fuck am I even thinking about her again?

"Okay, let's go then," I tell them both then head back through the house, not waiting for them to catch up.

About three feet from the front door I groan inside at the small manicured hand that wraps around my arm.

"Baby where are you going?" Tami moans and I force a smile at her.

I need to get rid of this chick, for good.

"Back to my dorm," I answer her sending a pleading look to Ryan who's approaching at snail speed.

Thanks bro. I know he hates her, but he could at least help a guy out.

"But I thought you could maybe come and sleepover at my place," she offers and again, I groan inside.

I look down at her. Her eyes are filled with hope and a drunken glaze. This isn't going to be easy. She has to be the clingiest girl I've ever met.

"Sorry Tami, Nate needs to help me get Codie home," Ryan chirps, saving my ass.

"Oh Nate, I'm sure they'll be fine without you," she whines and it's like knives to my ears.

Shit. I need to deal with this now.

"Look, Tam, I just don't think we should see each other anymore."

Her eyes widen as shock takes over her features.

"You're drunk," she states and I let out an exasperated breath.

"Not even a little bit. Look the sex was good but we just won't work together. I told you, I don't want a relationship," I say then turn to leave not waiting for her response.

"That was harsh bro. Not that I'm complaining, she's all kinds of crazy, but she's gonna throw a fit," Ryan laughs as we walk towards the sidewalk in front of the house.

"Fuck her. She's just a pain in my ass."

He laughs a little more agreeing, and then the three of us hit the sidewalk to head back to the building talking idly, only stopping when a familiar voice distracts us.

"Come on Hal, just stay over."

I turn and see Hallie walking towards us, masking my surprise at how quick she is walking in the high shoes she's wearing. Jace is rushing after her.

"Look I'm sorry okay? Just come back inside," he pleads with her.

She doesn't even turn back to look at him. My eyes drift up to study her face but she's giving nothing away. It's as blank as usual.

"Hallie what's wrong?" Codie asks when her friend stops beside us.

"Nothing," she mutters as Jace also joins us.

"Hal, where are you going? It was just a joke," he says to her and she glances at him.

"My name is Hallie, not Hal," she responds before marching away.

"Jace what the fuck happened?" Codie demands, her voice slurring slightly as she looks frantically between her brother and Hallie's now disappearing figure.

"Nothing, she just got the wrong end of the stick about something. Make sure my sister gets home alright guys," he tells us before dashing off suspiciously to the house.

What the fuck was all that about?

CHAPTER EIGHT

HALLIE

My body shakes as the cold wind whips around my bare thighs. Two fucking weeks. I'd only managed to avoid parties and drinking and guys for a pathetic two weeks. Why didn't I just say no? I can hear Codie and our two neighbors rushing behind me so I walk a little faster, not wanting the company right now. I know she's going to be asking me why I just practically ran away from her brother the second we get into our dorm. Although, I can hear her giggling and stumbling so maybe she'll just collapse in bed when she gets inside or maybe Ryan will be staying over. They look pretty comfortable right now, holding each other up. She'll regret that in the morning. Either way, I won't be telling her that her brother just propositioned me.

"You know Hallie, I know a couple of guys, including myself, that would pay a lot for you..."

Absolute ass.

Is that really all people see when they look at me? My feet ache as I speed along the road towards my dorm. Damn heels. Whoever decided that these would be the social norm for girls to wear should be made to go up against a fucking firing squad. Naked. *I bet it was a fucking man.* I don't stop moving or look back until I reach the main doors of our building. It's there that I realize Nate has caught up to me and is standing right behind me. The suddenness of his presence causes me to stumble slightly as I reach for the door.

"Careful," he murmurs, his arm coming around my waist to steady me.

God why does he have to smell so good? He reaches across me with his other arm and uses his key card to swipe us in, pushing the door open ahead of me.

"Thanks," I mumble, and then pull myself reluctantly away from his hold to step inside.

"Good night, Hallie?"

I turn and see Westley smirking at me from behind the desk in the reception area of the block. His eyes are dancing all over my body causing the acid in my stomach to boil. Fucking creep. I am so sick of this shit tonight. I stand taller, squaring my shoulders discreetly and stare at him. I keep my face passive as I tilt my head slightly to the left, watching him carefully. Sweat begins to bead on his forehead and he shifts uncomfortably from one foot to the other as I continue to stare at him in silence. I can smell the anxiety on him and my inner bitch roars. I've done this before. Guys like Westley are leeches. They prey on girls they think are shy and vulnerable, something I'm automatically assumed to be just because I don't talk much. They shit in their pants when someone shows a bit of confidence with them. I usually just ignore his advances. Over the past couple of weeks he's called obscene things to me as I've walked past and I'm pretty sure he told a couple of people that we had sex. Gross. Tonight though, I've had enough. I'm done pretending.

Tonight he'll see the old Hallie and he'll see just how cold I can be.

"What do you want from me, Westley?" I ask him in the most pleasant tone I can summon as I walk further to him, leaning over the desk and putting my face inches away from his.

"Um... what?" He stammers and I force back a smile.

I knew he was a pussy. I'm aware of Codie and Ryan stumbling through the door but I don't avert my gaze from Westley. His eyes are flicking around the space, never once locking with mine.

"You make all these comments about my sweet ass and I know you notice me in class. I've caught you staring at my tits several times then readjusting yourself," I explain, glancing down deliberately at his crotch then back up to his face. "So what I'm asking, Westley, is what do you want from me? Do you want to keep telling your little friends stories about our apparent wild nights together whilst you check me out from afar?"

His eyes widen as his face takes a rosy color. Yeah, he's definitely been telling people we've had sex. Fucking pervert. Why would somebody do that? Did he honestly think I wouldn't find out? God, guys are stupid.

"Do you want me to take you up to my room right now and show you just how wild I can be? You wouldn't mind wearing earplugs for the night would you Codie?" I continue, glancing at my roommate.

"Not at all, Hal," she smirks, knowing exactly what I'm doing. We'd talked a few times about Westley and I've told her a little about how to deal with morons like him.

"Or do you want to run off into the sunset, get married, and have babies?" I finish, bringing my eyes back to him. He doesn't respond. Instead he glances around the area, looking at each person nervously, and then leaves abruptly through a door behind him muttering under his breath.

"Oh my God! Hallie, that was awesome!" Codie gushes at me.

"He's a dick and I'm done with feeling his eyes on my ass everywhere I go," I shrug then turn to leave. I'm done here. I leave the three of them and walk through the door to the stairs. I'm so ready to get into bed. And to take these damn shoes off.

I'm looking through my purse for my key when I feel him behind me, watching me.

"You wouldn't be checking out my ass right now would you, Harris? Especially after you just heard me down there?" I say, turning to face him with a smirk on my face.

He smirks back and then leans casually against the wall opposite my door.

"That depends. Do I get the same options that you gave Westley? Because I'd definitely pick the wild sex please," he answers me and I don't even attempt to fight back the small laugh I let out.

I must be drunk, because the only thoughts I have right now are to push myself against him and have him right here. I don't get to reply, Codie and Ryan stumbling along causing my head to whip round to where they're coming from.

"Hallie! Ryan is going to sleepover but don't worry, I told him that we're not going to have sex," my roommate grins at me and I can't help but smile.

"That's great," I comment back to her and her grin gets wider.

Jeez. She really is smashed.

"Come on babe, let's get you to bed," Ryan laughs as he

leads her over, taking the key from her then strolls through the door as Codie leans on him.

I turn to watch them and then chuckle softly when Codie causes Ryan to walk into the couch. She isn't the most graceful when she was drunk. I've witnessed her a couple of times falling into the furniture at all hours of the night. Ryan, for sure, has his work cut out for him tonight.

"So where were we?" Nate asks from behind me.

I turn back to him slowly.

"I believe you were asking me for wild sex," I reply and he chuckles darkly.

He pushes his body off the wall and takes two steps closer to me. The atmosphere around us stills as his earthy scent fills the air, his glowing green eyes burning into me.

"And I believe you were about to give in and beg me to have my way with you," he says, his voice low and seductive.

My skin tingles. I want him, I want him bad. I tell myself in my head over and over how bad of an idea this is but my body has other ideas. I take a step closer, closing the space between us. I feel him inhale as I lean in close to his ear.

"Do you think you could handle me?" I whisper and his hands go to my hips, twisting me so my back is to his chest.

I feel his breath on my neck, my heart beating so hard I'm almost certain the entire block can hear it.

"I could do more than handle you sweetheart," he whispers back and my lower stomach heats.

His confidence and arrogance are turning me on. I don't think I can fight this.

"Just say yes," he says softly into my ear and my resolve slips away.

I'm not sure how, but I find myself nodding tentatively.

"Say it Hallie," he growls and I clench my thighs together.

The reaction I'm having from only his voice and proximity is baffling. I don't want to analyze it right now though, I just want him. I don't want to think. I've avoided being near him because of this, because of how he makes me feel. I'm done avoiding it. I need to get this out of my system then I can move on from it.

"Yes."

His hand takes mine and without a word he leads me to his dorm, unlocking the door in record time and pulling me inside. I don't get a chance to look around. As soon as I hear the door click behind me he's pushing me up against it, pinning my arm above my head as his mouth crashes onto mine. I can't stop myself from kissing him back with an equal urgency as he presses his hard body roughly into mine. He traces his tongue across my bottom lip and I open it allowing it into my mouth. A heat, stronger than I've ever experienced, burns hot in my stomach as the kiss deepens. I embrace it as he moves his free hand down my back, squeezing at my butt before pulling away from me. His eyes lock with mine and I know it's because he wants me to tell him again that I want this. I don't tell him. Instead I pull my arm free from him and start to slowly undo the buttons on my white satin shirt, keeping my eyes locked with his the whole time. His eyes fill with want and lust as I let my shirt fall to the floor. He wastes no time as he pulls me through the suite and to his bedroom, shutting the door behind him then turning back to me. He brings his hands to my hips pulling me close to him and kisses me deep. I wrap my arms around his neck and he lifts me onto the drawers behind before moving closer and standing between my legs, setting my stomach alight. My shoes fall from my feet as I trail my hand down his chest and stomach feeling the hard ridges of his abdominal muscles, stopping at the hem of his t-shirt. I pull away and look up at him as I gently lift his shirt up. He moves slightly so I can take it off and I bite my lip as I look at his super toned lean body. Fuck I forgot how hot he was! The heat burns bright in my lower stomach as I feel my need for him rise. I trace the small star tattoos he has that are littered across his hip and along the V of his groin as he places soft kisses across my neck, moving down and along my collar bone before bringing his lips back to mine. I can feel his heart beating strong as he presses closer to me causing the blood to run hot through my veins. My mind clouds as he gently traces his fingertips down my neck and between my breast before bringing them back up and repeating over and over again in a torturously slow rhythm causing my nipples to harden in anticipation of him. My breasts feel restrained so I bring my arm back and unclip the clasp of my bra. He pulls back and watches as I slowly remove it, letting it slide to the floor. He licks his lips as his hands move gently up my legs, over my skirt and rest on my stomach.

"Hallie, you're beautiful," he whispers before once again pressing his lips against my neck making the skin feel tender.

I need him.

I watch him under hooded eyes as he trails kisses down my collarbone again and over the swell of my breasts, gasping as he softly pulls my nipple into his mouth. His tongue flicks over it and the feeling I get is exquisite. I throw back my head and moan softly as he starts to tease the other nipple.

"I love that sound," he growls in my ear as he brings his

mouth back up to me, kissing me full of passion and nipping at my bottom lip.

His hands trail up my legs again and I moan again as his thumbs circle the inside of my thighs.

"Baby I'm going to make you feel things you've never felt before," he whispers in my ear and I warm between the legs.

I nod slightly, unable to form words as my body feels as though it's on fire. His fingers trail higher up my leg and he again locks his eyes with mine. I can see the need and lust clouding his normally clear green eyes and it only makes me want him more. I moan and he covers my mouth with his as his finger strokes lightly over my underwear again and again, getting firmer. I feel the heat inside me rising as he pulls my panties to the side. I desperately try to hold myself together as I feel like I'm about to explode any minute. I moan into his mouth as he slowly slips a finger inside me. I don't know how much more I can take. The heat bubbles in my lower stomach and I'm desperate for some sort of release. He groans in the back of his throat and it's sexy as hell! He pushes and withdraws his long skilled finger inside me and presses the base of his thumb against my clit. My hands grip his shoulder desperately as my breathing comes out in harsh pants.

"Hallie, let go," he demands and it's my undoing.

I cry out as I shatter around him and the feeling is indescribable. Oh my God. Wow. I'm so turned on right now. I lift my head and look up into his eyes which are watching me carefully.

"My turn," I tell him before sliding off the drawers and pushing him back to his bed. I make quick work of the button on his jeans then push them down his legs with his underwear. I lick at my lips as he stands to attention before me.

"And what do you want me to do now, Miss Clarke?" Nate asks and I smirk.

"Sit down," I tell him firmly and he obeys then smiles wickedly as I sink to my knees between his legs.

"Hallie," he breathes as I wrap my lips around him.

I slowly suck the length of him, taking it in as far as I can then back out again. I let my tongue flick over his end, tasting his arousal as his hand tangles in my hair. He groans when I swallow him again, letting the tip of his cock touch the back of my throat before withdrawing it, repeating it over and over again. I swirl my tongue around as I do this and his other hand finds my hair, pulling at it roughly. I lift my eyes to his, staring as his breathing becomes labored.

"Baby that's so good," he moans and my pulse quickens.

Heat is rising in me again as I watch him coming undone. It was a beautiful sight, and knowing it was my fault is the biggest turn on I've ever had. I keep going until I can feel him tensing in front of me.

"Hallie... I'm going to... shit," he groans as empties his salty taste inside my mouth, pulling slightly at my hair.

I stand back up and flash him a triumphant smile as he wraps his arms around my waist, pulling me into him. He kisses across my stomach and his hands pull on my skirt until I'm left standing before him in just my panties. Slowly, I remove them and push him back gently so he's lying on his back then climb over to straddle him. His hands immediately begin to move over me softly, grazing at my nipples but I stop him and move his hands to his sides.

"Don't touch, just watch," I whisper.

I place one of my hands on his shaft behind me as I trail the other lightly down my stomach, keeping my eyes on his and I bring it lower touching my core gently. I begin to stroke his balls softly as the fingers of my other hand rub at my clit causing him to groan. That has to be the hottest sound I've ever heard.

"Shit, baby, you look so fucking hot right now," Nate gasps and I bite my lip seductively.

I can feel him hardening again as the heat inside me gets hotter. I need him, all of him. His eyes fill with lust and he gasps as I wrap my hand around his hard length. He moans as I move my hand gently up and down.

"Hallie... fuck," he growls and my back arches as I moan full of pleasure.

Nate sits suddenly and brings his mouth to mine, kissing me full of need. I allow his tongue into my mouth and his hand moves up my back holding me close to him. He pulls away, both of us breathing heavy.

"Tell me what you want Hallie," he says in that low sexy voice that gets me hot.

"You. Now."

His hand reaches into the draw beside the bed and he pulls out a small foil packet as his lips find mine again. I hear him tear it open then feel his hands as he rolls the condom on, never breaking from the kiss. If I wasn't so enthralled by him right now, I'd probably admire his multi-tasking skills. He moves his lips onto my neck causing me to tingle all over and I rise in anticipation of him, the whole world disappearing around us.

"Are you sure?" He asks me and I nod my reply.

I've never been surer of anything else. He positions himself below me and I slowly lower myself onto him, allowing him to enter me. I moan as he fills me and he positions his hands on my hips.

"Baby you feel exceptional," he says as he brings his

tongue to my now erect nipple. He flicks over it whilst using his hands to guide me as I slowly rock on top of him. I moan softly and quicken my pace, bringing my hand into his hair and pulling it softly to bring his face back up to mine.

"I need to see you."

I continue to move as his forehead rests on mine.

"You have the most beautiful eyes," he whispers.

I can feel him deep inside me and the sensation it's giving me is causing my insides to boil like lava. It's bubbling and threatening to blow any second. My breath is coming out in short pants and the pure desire in Nate's eyes makes me hotter for him. My hips move faster as he kisses me hard, biting at my bottom lip. I throw my head back, the heat becoming almost unbearable as my legs begin to tremble.

"Let go with me baby," he urges as he tenses beneath me.

I cry out his name as he brings his lips to mine, the orgasm ripping through me.

"Hallie," he moans against my mouth, stilling below me.

I feel him smiling against my neck and I rest my forehead on his chest to catch my breath.

"Hallie that was..." he trails off.

"Yeah."

He gently lifts me off him before disposing of the condom in the trashcan beside the bed. He lies back on the bed, pulling me close then covers us with the sheets.

"Are you okay?" He asks.

Am I okay? I mean the sex was phenomenal, but have I just made things complicated and awkward? Yes, more than likely. But oh my, that was amazing. It's never been like that for me before. I felt so in tune as he moved inside me. Normally, my mind will wander to inconsequential

I mean, same but that's just my short attention span

nonsense but just then, all I could think about was him and what he was doing to me. God he made me feel so alive!

"I'm fine," I say, and then force myself away from his warm embrace and sit up. "I should go," I add and he sits up, putting his arms around me before I can move.

"No stay, please."

Sleepovers aren't something I do. Even though my body is crying out to lay down with him and let him sleep next to me all night. I let out a long breath and eye him wearily.

"Come on Hallie, Ry is over at your place with Codie anyway," he continues and I force my shoulders to relax a little.

"Okay," I answer simply then let him ease me back down.

I turn on my side and he drapes his arm over my waist, pressing his chest into my back.

"I want to know more about you," he states after a few minutes of silence.

"Like what?"

He chuckles softly, his lips pressed to my head. I ignore the comfort his warm body is giving me. I also ignore the feelings I'm getting from knowing he's naked behind me. If we start that again, I'll never get any sleep. It's going to be hard enough as it is.

"Everything. Let's play a game," he says then continues when I let out a laugh. "Not that. Twenty one questions. I can ask you twenty one questions and you have to answer the truth. Same goes for me. Doesn't have to be all right now, just whenever. Got it?"

I think about the notion. It's ridiculous and juvenile but a part of me likes it. Maybe sex ruined my thought process? I should not be agreeing to this but I find myself nodding. I'm curious about him too.

omg me & Jake used to play that to get to know each other

Same and he's not even real

"Why did you really invite Ryan and me over for dinner that night?" He asks and I can't help but let out a small laugh again. How the hell do I explain this one?

"I told you, you lack nutrition."

He laughs now. "Bullshit. Why would you care? You didn't even know us."

My mind dances over the memory. The call from sperm donor, the grocery store, the assholes that made a play for me, all of it. It was fairly safe to assume I wasn't exactly thinking straight that day.

"I hate it when people don't eat properly, period. Doesn't matter who they are or whether I know them. I've been the same since I was a kid, can't really explain it. I'd never have slept knowing all you had here was fucking Cheetos," I laugh. "Let me ask you something now."

I spin so I'm facing him, letting my finger trail his chest and his hand strokes from my hip and down my thigh.

"Why did you help me that day in the parking lot of the grocery store?" I ask.

The question had plagued me since it had happened. He didn't know me, why would he help me? I was just the icy bitch that lived next door to him. His hand stops by my knee and he lets his eyes close, thick brown lashes fanning on his cheek. How have I never noticed how long they are before? He really is quite spectacular looking. I shouldn't be here, this is dangerous.

"I didn't plan it. We just showed up. I was worried about you when you left that day because of the call you had with your dad but I wasn't about to push you on it. Then when I saw those guys all over you and the look in your eye I couldn't stop myself. Don't ask me to explain it, because I don't know how but it was like I needed to be there, to help you."

I feel like he looks like Nate Archibald but with tattoos

My mind blanks at his words. I was expecting the whole damsel in distress deal, not that he *needed* to be there. What the hell do I do with that? Nothing, which is exactly why I show him a small smile then turn back around, putting my back to him.

"Thank you," I reply softly, and then sigh inside as he presses a gentle kiss on my bare shoulder before wrapping his arms around me tighter.

I lie awake, waiting until I can hear his breathing even out and fall heavy. I'm a bitch for doing this, I know, but I carefully climb out of his bed and collect my clothes and shoes quietly before sneaking out of his room, pausing long enough to look at him as he sleeps. God what am I doing?

I dress in the lounge area, only mildly disgusted with myself when I find my discarded shirt by the front door, and leave the suite. I pad along the hallway barefoot, shoes in hand and into my own dorm. Thankfully, Codie and Ryan are in her room asleep so I'm able to get to my own room unnoticed. I thought I was done with this walk of shame bullshit. In my room, I change into pajamas and climb silently into bed.

Tomorrow should be fun.

Not.

CHAPTER NINE

Hallie

For the fourth time that day I scowl down at my ringing cell. It's not a number I recognize but it seems they won't be giving up until I answer.

"What?" I bark down the phone.

"Who's that?" The voice at the other end asks.

Seriously?

"You called me, asshole. Who are you?" I respond and the voice laughs nervously.

"Sorry, hey Hallie it's Jace."

Are you kidding me? How the hell did he get my number? What does he want? Pretty sure I told him to fuck off clearly enough last night. I ask him what he wants as I slump down on the couch, bringing my knees up to my chest.

"Look I think we should talk. I want to apologize for last night. I feel bad. I was drunk and joking but you obviously didn't see it that way," he explains.

I call bullshit. I'd seen the hunger in his eyes. I'd seen the way he was looking at me like I was some juicy piece of meat and he was the king lion.

With sarcasm prominent in my voice, I answer. “Obviously.”

I hear him take in a deep breath at the other end of the phone. Good. He should feel bad for what he was insinuating.

“I know you’re pissed but do you think maybe we could go for coffee or dinner and start over?” Is he asking me on a date? No, surely not. “I mean, you are my little sister’s roommate and I know she’d be happy about it. She’d love it if we started dating,” he continues and my jaw falls to the floor.

As if he’s trying to use his sister to score. Sorry Codie but your brother is an asshole.

“Wow,” I breathe out loud, unsure of what else to say.

“Does that wow mean you’ll go out with me?” His voice is hopeful, cocky even and I wait before replying. I let the silence get awkward as I stand and make my way to the kitchen, grabbing a soda and swallowing half of it before I speak a word.

“No Jace it doesn’t and I have to go.”

His voice raises two decibels as he lets out a strange kind of groan. “What? No, wait! Why? Shit Hallie, I don’t normally have to try this hard to get a girl.” He laughs nervously again before continuing. ”Most girls are begging for me to take them out.”

Could he be any more of a dick? Does he really think this will get him laid?

“I’m not most girls,” I respond then hang up the call before he can reply.

The last thing I need right now is more male drama. What the hell was I thinking last night? I wasn’t and that’s the damn problem. Now all I can do *is* think about the whole damn thing, the way he pushed me up against that door all dominating and hot. Damn it. I've had to vigorously clean and violently tidy the suite just to stop myself from going over there and demanding round two. This is not good. This is *really* not good. The man just makes me feel so alive. It's not like I can avoid him. He's right next door. Plus from the sound of Codie and his roommate this morning, I'm pretty sure that they're dating now.

Speaking of Codie, she's just walking through the front door. Her eyes regard me warily as the door clicks shut behind her. I can't blame her. When she escaped this morning with Ryan I was psychotically banging things around in frustration.

"Hey, Hal," she says in a small voice and my internal anger cracks a little.

"Hey Codie, I'm sorry about this morning," I tell her and she smiles. I'll never understand how easy this girl switches her moods.

"Don't apologize, everyone has a bad day. Ryan thought you were gonna come busting through my bedroom door and rip his head off," she laughs and I smile small, deciding not to admit that the thought had crossed my mind.

"Must be PMS." She flashes me a knowing and understanding smile. "Look how about I make dinner to apologize huh? You can invite Ryan over if you want. I'll make tacos or something," I suggest, silently hoping she decline the extended invite.

"Oh that would be awesome. I'm going out with Ryan all day today so I'll ask him and let you know. He'll probably want to bring Nate with him though of course," she answers, rolling her eyes and I force a laugh.

She clearly doesn't know what I did last night. After a few more words about where Ryan is planning on taking her, she leaves to go and get ready and I take the chance to throw on my running things. That's what I need, the solitude and burn of a nice long run. I hunt down a bottle of water from the back of the refrigerator, make a mental note to go grocery shopping after and head out the door. Westley is in the reception area when I get downstairs and I can't resist throwing him a sly smirk as I pass. His face flushes and falls immediately and I turn to stifle a laugh. It's probably cruel but he had it coming.

"You know you probably butchered his confidence last night right?"

Oh no.

I look up and see that Nate is smirking at me as he holds the main door open, motioning for me to pass through. I hold my breath as I brush past him, fighting every urge I have in my body that wants me to take his hand and drag him back up the stairs. What the hell is wrong with me? Last night was supposed to get this out of my system.

"He'll get over it," I reply finally when I'm outside.

He follows me out, falling into step beside me.

"So how long after I fell asleep was it before you crept out of my room?"

My stomach tightens as I notice the hurt in his voice. I don't want to hurt him. For the twelfth time that day I curse myself for letting this happen.

"Is that one of the twenty-one?" I ask, curious.

The little game he made up was another thing that had swirled in my head all night. There are things I want to know about him too, including why he's so pissy with me right now. Surely he must be at least happy that he got his dick wet.

"Yeah sure, one of the questions, why not? So answer it please."

"Not long." I answer simply. The point is to not lie.

He exhales loudly. "I see we're back to this," he comments and I turn slowly to face him.

"Back to what?" I ask, although I know exactly what he's getting at.

I'm being a bitch and I'm doing it on purpose.

"I know you enjoyed it last night. You fucking loved it, yet here you arc, back to your usual cold self. What's up, Hallie? Do you have to have a drink before you can say more than four words to me?"

I force all emotion from my face, leaving it a blank canvas I know he'll never figure out. He can't know that I was awake all night last night tossing and turning over my thoughts for him. He can't know that even just being here, with him staring right through me makes me feel things I never thought I could feel. He can't know any of that because I need to be alone. I bring my eyes to his and let them harden before speaking, using the most casual voice I can muster up.

"We had sex, Nate. I'm not sure what the big deal is."

I watch his jaw tighten as his eyes narrow to mine, hitting me with a steely stare that tears right through me. I know he's mad, and I know it's me that has done this. I count backwards in my head as he continues to look into my eyes. I know he's looking for the lie, anything to prove to him that I want him. He won't find it. I mastered the skill to hide my feelings and thoughts a long time ago.

"We've fucked and now you don't think there's anything left to say? Shit, Hallie, I guess I know now why everyone calls you ice," he growls.

Ouch. My arms automatically tighten around myself as a shiver moves up my spine. I'm used to hearing stuff like that, prepared myself for it but it felt like a knife to the gut coming from him. It's not that we connect in any way, it's just I had the feeling that he understood me on some level. Apparently not. He steps to me then, as if suddenly realizing what he just said was said out loud. I step back, not wanting to be near him and his face falls.

"Fuck, Hallie, I didn't mean that," he adds quickly and I snort.

"Sure you did, Harris. Don't worry I get it, you're not the first to call me ice," I tell him then turn away swiftly and start my run, no longer caring if he's following me.

If he wants to think of me as the icy bitch everybody back home did then that's fine. What's fucking new? If I wasn't a slut then I was a bitch. I guess Nate thinks I'm both. My dad would be proud. I seethe the whole way through my run then all the way around the grocery store as I shopped and when I get back to the building and up to my floor my mood is made worse by the first sight I see. Nate is stood in the threshold of his door with that sorority bitch Tami clinging on to him, her hands rubbing all over his chest. She bats her eyelashes at him, making that little girly giggle that guys like to eat up. Jeez. How is he falling for this? I can feel the stab of jealousy clawing at my insides but I shove it down brutally. He can talk with whoever he damn well wants! It's not like I have any claim on him. We had one night of truly fucking sensational sex that's all. He could fuck whoever he wanted, and green is not my color. Still, the fact that he's got some other girl hanging onto him not even 24 hours after being with me is low. Even for a guy. Moodily, I make my way down the rest of the hallway to my suite, making sure I'm loud enough to be heard.

"Oh... uh... Hallie, hey. Do you need a hand with those bags?" He asks me, referring to the two grocery bags I'm carrying.

Seriously? He wants to help me carry my bags now?

"No."

I'll be damned if the guy is going to help me do anything right now. I bend and place the bags on the floor then stand to search for my keys which are at the bottom of my purse somewhere.

"So Ry said that we're coming over for tacos tonight," he comments and my whole body tenses.

I should have known they wouldn't turn down free food, especially with what I revealed to him last night. *Where the hell are my keys?*

"Uh huh. Bring your girlfriend if you want," I reply, throwing a sly sideways glance at him. I don't miss the look on his face - guilt.

Yes! I have my keys. I'd victory dance if I wasn't in the presence of an audience.

"See even *this girl* knows that we should be together," sorority bitch whines and I turn to face her.

This girl? She knows my fucking name. I turn to face her. Her eyes study me and she takes in my outfit - faded and purposely ripped jeans, a vintage Jimi Hendrix tee, and my favorite black hooded leather jacket. I can see the disgust in her eyes and I almost laugh. She's standing before me in a hot pink halter neck shirt, tight black jeans and high heeled boots. Probably thinks she looks hot. I think she looks like a hooker but what would I know?

"Tami," Nate moans, sounding every bit exasperated.

Trouble in paradise I assume. Well that would happen when a man fucks someone that isn't his damn girlfriend. The two of them immediately start talking but I don't listen. Instead, I unlock the door to my suite and walk in with my groceries.

I shut the door behind me a little louder than I probably should and walk over to the kitchen, dumping my groceries on the counter. *This girl.* God what a bitch! I mean I figured we weren't about to run off into the sunset together but to run to her from me is a fucking insult. I know I'm not exactly perfect, far from it, but at least I'm not *that.* I don't dress up like a hooker just to win over some guy. She'd been the same at the damn party. I hadn't missed the way she glared at me when Codie and I walked in with Jace. He'd had his arm wrapped around my waist and her eyes had burned holes through the contact. Codie had told me that she had approached her a few times over the last couple of weeks, wanting to be BFFs or whatever. It's apparently something to do with Codie having the potential to be top of the campus. Have you ever heard anything so fucking stupid? Tami, or Tamara Vincent, is head of a sorority here on campus which apparently gives her the right to be a complete asshat to anyone she encounters. It also helps that the Dean is her father. Spoilt little rich bitch would be the most appropriate title for her. I push thoughts of her and of he who shall not be named today out of my mind and get busy with preparing tonight's dinner. About 15 minutes into it, my cell chimes indicating a text. I look briefly, not recognizing the number then open it up.

Hey it's Nate. R U busy?

Well holy shit. Where did he get my number? Also, yeah I'm busy. I'm busy trying to forget you exist, Asshole. With shaky hands, I force myself to reply then save his number in my contacts for future reference. You know, in case he ever texts me again, or calls me. I know to avoid it then. Yeah, I'll just keep telling myself that and eventually it might ring true.

Me: *How the hell did you get my number?*
Nate: *I have great detection skills. Look seriously, R U you busy? I need 2 show U something. And before U start with your smart ass remarks I don't mean my dick*

Despite myself I laugh at the response. I should have expected it.

Me: *Good to know. What is it Nathan? I'm cooking*
Nate: *Just come over here please*

I don't reply. Instead, a minute later, I'm knocking at his door with my hands on my hips. He opens it wide and I'm momentarily speechless at the sight of him. Why is he never wearing a shirt? Maybe I should ask him? I still have twenty questions left. And this is totally not appropriate right now. I'm supposed to be mad at him. Wait, why am I mad at him again?

"This better be important, Harris," I mutter before brushing past him to walk inside.

He exhales loudly and head over to the dining room table, asking me to take a seat then places a laptop down in front of me. What is this all about? I swear if he puts a porno on there now I'll punch him.

"Look, I just found this after it was mentioned to me. I don't know if you know about it but there's a page on Facebook about you," he tells me reluctantly and I tense. His eyes are clouded with regret and I could swear I see pity. What the hell is going on?

"I don't use Facebook."

What does he mean a page about me? It can't be good whatever it is. I can practically feel the nerves radiating of him. I pull at an invisible loose thread on my shirt as I wait for him.

"I'll open it up for you then go wait in my room. I'm thinking you'll want to be alone for this. Just holler when you're done," he says then opens up the page for me and walk away, rubbing my shoulder softly before he goes.

That was weird. I turn to give the laptop my full attention and gasp when I see what he meant. My stomach curdles but I force myself to keep looking even though it's the last thing I want to see. Well I guess I know why he was pitying me now. I scroll through the page. Images of myself, taken when I've been kissing or dancing with guys litter the profile. I don't remember any of these being taken. I look at the comments then, a knot forming as I read the words of old friends and people I went to school with.

Paid Hallie to take my little bro's V-Card last night. He wasn't disappointed.
Did you know that even her own Dad thinks she's a slut? Can't say I blame him.
Got her to suck my dick last night in the back of my truck, damn that girl can blow

I don't even know who this last guy is. Nearly all of this is bullshit. I scroll down further, my body turning to ice when I read a familiar name and the comment to go with it.

LOL I should get some kind of special award or something for being the first guy in there. The fifty bucks I got doesn't really cover it

Fucking asshole. What kind of scummy douche bag advertises the fact that he took a girl's virginity? I've seen enough. I stand abruptly and storm from the dorm, letting the door bang shut behind me before doing the same with my own front door.

Fuckers! Absolute fucking low life assholes. No wonder the guys at the party were all over me like that last night. They're bound to have seen that shit posted about me. I don't know much about this Facebook bullshit but I know enough to know that almost everyone in the world is on there. Even my dad is there. I bet that's where he's been seeing all these stories about me. Most of the shit there isn't even true. I've never accepted fucking cash for sleeping with someone and I definitely haven't had sex with all the people that are claiming it either. Sure, I made out with a few people but not to that extent. Why were they taking pictures? What kind of jerk does that? How fucking stupid was I to think that moving here would mean it would all go away? Deep down I knew that wasn't how things worked. Once you're in the rumor mill, you never come out. You're stuck, constantly hearing the same half-truth stories about yourself. I stopped bothering to deny and defend myself a long time ago. I stopped caring a long time ago too. What was the point? So instead I set out drinking and hooking up, figuring if they're going to make some shit up I may as well give them some inspiration. If I'd have known it would all follow me here, I might have acted a little differently.

Of course, it had to be Nate who showed it to me. He's supposed to be coming over for dinner in two hours with Codie and Ryan. Things are awkward enough right now with him and I can only imagine the things he must be thinking about me now. This is the proof he needed to show that everything he said to me earlier was truth. I bring my hand to my stomach and breathe deeply, desperately trying to null the sickness. I know the feeling isn't down to the rumors. It was down to the last comment I'd read, from him. How can he be so cold and continue my humiliation like that? Isn't it enough that he let on to the entire school about what we'd done? Telling them all I was lousy in bed and not worth the money he'd won on the bet by doing it. It all only got worse from then. I'll never forget coming home from school one day to my father sat in the lounge with my mom. He'd told me to sit and then lectured me about the whole Jason thing. I was mortified, and angry. My father was supposed to protect me. And now with this Facebook shit. Why hasn't he told me about it? Anger fills me, consuming my thoughts as I remember all the times he should have been there but wasn't. Without thinking, I pick up my phone and dial his number.

"Hallie! I'm glad you finally decided to call."

I barely hear his words as scenes from my life so far flash through my mind. Every time I fell down, or was pushed around. Every bad word, insult or taunt thrown in my direction screams at me. Not once was he there, not one single time did he come to me and help me through it.

"Why didn't you tell me?" I whisper, my voice only just audible.

"Tell you what? What's going on?" I can hear the confusion in his voice but it doesn't condense my anger at all. My body shakes as the rage consumes me.

"About the fucking Facebook page which is branding me a whore, George. Why didn't you tell me?" I growl.

I hear his sharp intake, he definitely knew about it.

"Hallie, I thought you knew," he says softly, an unrecognizable tone from any other experiences I've had with him.

"Does it sound like I fucking knew? Is that where you've been getting your stories about me from? Is that the bullshit you've believed about me?" I ask, already knowing the answer.

I need to hear it though, I need to hear him say it. I need to hear him admit that he believed all of that. I pace frantically across the lounge area, my combat boots clicking loudly.

"Hallie there are pictures on there. And these people know you, went to school with you, why would they lie?"

He's never going to take my side on this. No matter what, he is always going to believe everyone above his own daughter. I don't know why I still expect him to be there for me. I don't know why I still crave his compassion, his love. I wait desperately for him to hold me, to tell me that everything will be alright. That it doesn't matter what other people think of me as he loves me anyway. It will never happen. I'm nothing but a burden to him, a responsibility that he can't give up.

"Why would I?" I ask quietly.

I don't give him time to reply. Instead I hang up the phone and place it calmly on the dining room table.

I refuse to let this get to me. I'm just going to shut it all out, just like high school. I just have to get through these four years of college then I'll have my degree and I can go, leave. Make something of myself and be the type of person I know I am, the person I know I can be. But for now, I have a dinner to make.

So that's what I do for the next hour and thirty minutes. I set it all out on the table, with three place settings. I add a large jug of ice water and three tall glasses. I make sure there is enough for everybody then head into my room to change into my running stuff. I promised I'd make dinner, I didn't promise to sit and fucking eat it with them. I like Codie too much to drag her down with me as the rumors begin to filter through campus. It's the reason I'd been ditched by the only other friends I'd ever had back in high school. All of them quick to back away when shit hit the fan there. I won't do that to her. I won't let her be a part of the downward spiral of bullshit I'm heading towards. I have to be alone. I have to keep myself away from everything. The walls have to go up and I can't let anyone tear them down.

I've just tied the laces on my sneakers when I hear them all coming in, laughing.

"Hallie, why are there only three places? Wait, are you going running?" Codie asks confused when I walk into the kitchen.

"Yes."

I can feel Nate's eyes on me, watching as I move towards the door. I can't return the look though. Just knowing that he read all of that stuff and what he must be thinking right now makes my insides hurt. I don't want to see the look of disgust on his face. I can't.

Turn it off Clarke.

"But aren't you going to eat dinner?" She offers and I push down the guilt.

All she wants is my friendship, and I'm about to ditch her.

"No," I say and leave before anything else can be added.

I need to be on my own right now, I need to punish myself until I feel numb all over.

I push my earphones in to let the hard rock pulse through my ears and ignore the hushed whispers and blatant stares as I pass people on my way to the park. Has this always been happening and I haven't noticed? Or has whoever told Nate, told every fucker else at school? Do I even care? Probably not. I'm not an idiot. This has sorority bitch written all over it. Popular and plastic. They're all the same. The faces may change but the personalities never do. I know she's jealous. I'd seen it all over her face earlier. She's stared me down, looking for any weakness she could find.

Good luck bitch.

I don't have weaknesses. I don't have anything.

I pound my feet to the ground the second I get through the gates of the park, letting the steady beat soothe and relax me. The smooth sounds of Aerosmith – Dream On fill my ears, and I move my legs with the bass. So what if people think I'm a slut. Who gives a crap? I sure don't. I got this far with people thinking I'm worth nothing. In fact I thrived on it, never letting anyone stand in my way. I pick up my pace as I wind down the trail which leads me in and out of a wooded area. There's virtually no one out here this late on a Sunday evening so I revel in the solitude and peace. Being alone is the reason I enjoy running so much.

It takes 3 hours and four circuits of the trail but I finally manage to numb myself from the thoughts in my head. I tentatively sit down on a bench close by the park entrance to calm my breathing. My body aches and burns from the punishing assault I've just put it through but I relish in it. I flip the music on my phone to something softer as the cold air whips around me, cooling my hot skin immediately and I stare idly at the goose bumps forming along my arms. Maybe I should have worn a jacket. Never mind, nothing I can do about it now. With one last gulp of my water I stand and then hobble my way back to towards the dorm.

A nice hot bath and early night is all I need.

CHAPTER TEN

Hallie

I let the music flow through me as I lie back on the couch, my eyes fixed on the ceiling. I bring my legs up and let them hang over the arm rest, my body defeated from the way I've over-worked it lately. I've been punishing myself, pushing my muscles further than they are capable of going, in an attempt to silence the thoughts racing in my head every damn day. And when I do silence them, I have to contend with listening to the people around me. I don't know what's worse. I take a deep breath, letting Kat Dahlia's voice soothe me. I have a couple of hours before my English class and I can't think of a better way to spend it. Music, peace, solitude. Out of the corner of my eye, I spot Codie coming through the dorm door with Ryan. *Damn it.* I offer them a small wave when they turn to talk to me, then point to the earphones on my head, indicating that I can't hear them. It isn't entirely true, I can hear every word they were saying, but I don't want to be drawn into a full conversation with them both the way I have every other time over the past month. It seems there is nothing I can do to get rid of them, and hell I've tried. Codie has dragged more than I'm comfortable with out of me regarding all the crap on the Facebook page, and then completely blown up at half the campus, including her own brother. I have to admit, that was an entertaining day. The poor fucker just stared, wide eyed gaping at her.

I can hear her now, talking with Ryan as though I'm not even here. He's asking how I've been, and she's telling him I'm doing 'okay' as they walk down to her room. I know why he's asking. I know why he's always asking her how I am. I'm not that ignorant to the world. It's about Nate. I haven't spoken to him since he showed me the page. He's texted and called, but I haven't responded. Everyone knows about us now, everyone knows the monumental mistake I'd made by giving into my own damn urges. When would I learn? Now, every time I see him, pain radiates through me. Deep down, I want so bad to be able to just be with him like a normal girl. But I'm not a normal girl. I'm someone I don't want to be, and I'm stuck, lost in a maze of my own ice walls where no one can find me. I can't leave, I can't get out. I'm surrounded by the faces of all the people who make it their life's mission to put me down, and I can't see past them. I've been here before, too many damn times to count. I know how it will end, I've seen it happen too much. It's like the punch line to really crappy joke. The joke being my life, the punch line being me. I'm destined for this, and the stigma will follow me around like a bad smell everywhere I go. I'll never get rid of it, no matter how hard I scrub myself clean. I'm just not pure enough, already tainted with a bad reputation. The song in my ears changes to Chloe Howl – Rumour, causing me to almost laugh out loud at the irony. *Figures.* I turn the music up louder on my cell and close my eyes. I let the lyrics fall from mouth quietly, my fingers tapping out the beat against the soft fabric of the couch.

Just tryin' to work out
How to be like myself
I'm just tryin' to work out
These cards I've been dealt

I sense him immediately, the second he's beside me, and flick open my eyes. He stands there, staring down at me with a peculiar smile on his face. I pull my earphones out quickly and sit up, bringing my hand to my head to somehow ease the dizziness from getting up too quick. I don't know why I bother, or why anyone does for that matter. It doesn't work, I'm still dizzy. All it achieves is me making myself look a complete moron. I silence my inner scolding. My head is messed up enough without the added crazy of my own rambling monologue.

"You sing," Nate says.

I scoff, unable to stop it, and stand.

"No."

He takes a step closer to me, his scent surrounding us, and making my heart beat louder than necessary. Damn it. I need to learn to control this. Why does he make me feel so... alive? Can't he see I'm trying to thwart his advances? He should respect that, surely. In fact, I should be mad at him. I don't really have any reason to, but being mad at him would be a hell of a lot easier than missing him like I'd miss a limb. This is pathetic. I'm giving myself a headache now.

"It sounded like singing to me."

"You're mistaken."

His eyes bore into me, but I don't meet them. I can't. I can't risk getting lost once again in his gaze. He's silently pleading with me to acknowledge him, I can feel his unspoken words as though they're knives to my gut. But I'm too far gone, too far inside myself to let him pull me out.

He's been at our dorm more and more lately, but that's down to Ryan. He and Codie are dating now, which means he's here a lot. I can't even begin to count the amount of times I've caught Ryan naked in the suite. He apparently has no issues with indecent exposure, and is extremely comfortable with his own body. Nate is forever coming over for him, and neither of them ever knock first. It's all just a painful reminder of what I'll never have. I tried to find another dorm room, but administration told me it was too late to transfer. It seems the laws of life are still working their grudge against me.

"Hallie," he starts but I don't let him say anymore.

I hold my hand up and shake my head before grabbing my bag, darting from the room, and out the suite door. I rush down the stairs and out of the building. It's still too early for my English class, but Professor Cooper has been cool over the whole rumor thing, so I know he won't mind me kicking it in his classroom for a while. The man is awesome, and I totally want to pick his brains about the paper I'm currently working on. Happy coincidence.

I ignore the stares of people on campus, and walk over to the English building quickly, stopping briefly at a coffee cart to get us both a drink. I keep my mind focused on the pavement in front of me and nothing else. I find Cooper in the classroom, still wearing his coat, with his feet propped on the desk in front of him as he stuffs the remnants of a cream cheese pastry into his mouth. Fleetwood Mac – Second Hand News plays in the background and I smile inside. Yeah, the guy is definitely awesome. I walk further in and place the coffee cup down on the desk, the noise of it hitting the wood causing Cooper to look up at me.

"Hallie," he smiles and holds up the wrapper of the

pastry. "You've just caught me eating something I really shouldn't."

I return the smile. "Hey, your secret is safe with me. I got you coffee." I let out a breath. "Am I okay to hang here until class?"

He frowns slightly before nodding. I plonk myself down at a desk and pull my books from my bag.

"Do you want me to turn the music down?" He asks. "I know this mustn't be your kind of thing."

I laugh, amused that he'd think that.

"Actually, Fleetwood Mac are a favorite of mine."

His eyes widen a fraction as he laughs and shakes his head in my direction. I shrug, roll my jacket off my shoulders, and straighten out my White Snake shirt. I watch him take it in and then raise his eyes back to me.

"Hallie Clarke, you're a constant surprise."

"I aim to please, shock, and impress," I laugh.

He chuckles softly.

"So, what's the deal today? What have you supposedly done now?"

I smirk. This is why I like coming here. He understands the stuff that goes around about me is bullshit. He doesn't give me inspirational speeches, nor does he judge me on what he has heard. He just makes a joke out of it, and then moves the subject on. It's refreshing, and I can be mostly myself here. He is by far the coolest professor I've ever known. Everyone loves him because of his casual ease and laid back personality. Cooper is in his late twenties, closer to our age than any other teacher. He laughs and jokes with everyone in class, telling us stories of his own high school days. It's a great break from the everyday drone of college.

"You mean besides sex with everything that has a pulse?" I say.

He laughs. "Have they not found new material yet?"

"No, they never do. Same old shit, just a different place."

"You know it's because you're badass right?"

I snort. "Is that a nice way of calling me a bitch?"

"No," he laughs. "I mean, they're just jealous because you can just brush off their insults so easily. Not everyone could do that." He laughs again and stands. "Look at me sounding old and sentimental. How about you make the most of having me all to yourself and talk through your paper." He glances down at my notebook on the desk in front of me. "It's why you've got your book out, right?"

he's your TEACHER

I look up at him and smile at the arch in his brow.

"Well I just have this one little thing I wanted your advice on," I say sweetly.

He laughs and pulls a chair over to the desk. He sits opposite me and we spend the rest of the time before class starts going through my paper on eighteenth century literature.

After class finishes, I hurry from the room. I make the short trip to the on-campus book store then rush back to the Trisler building, taking the steps up to my dorm two at a time. It's thankfully empty when I walk in, but not wanting to risk another run in with Nate, I shut the door and lock it. I see it almost immediately. A neatly folded, white square of paper on the floor, just inside the dorm. For a second I assume that Codie or Ryan, even Nate maybe, must have dropped it until I pick it up, and notice my name written on it in scratchy capitals. I carefully unfold it, more curious than interested. In this generation of technology, who the hell used pen and paper anymore? I let my eyes drift over the words.

Hallie,
Just a note to tell you how amazing you truly are.
Don't let them take that away from you. You deserve to have every happiness you want in life. You can be anything, and soon you'll be my everything.
Thinking of you always,
JC

After laughing hard for longer than necessary, I scrunch the paper up and throw it into the trash. Only in my life, would a girl get motivational words pushed through the crack of a door. Suppose it's better than hate mail. I shake off the note, deciding not to give it too much thought, and head to the safe sanctuary of my bedroom. I change into sweats and lie flat on my bed, pulling my guitar to my stomach. I've had a tune stuck in my head for the past few days, and I'm desperate to imitate it the only way I know how. I clasp my favorite red pick in my fingers and flick it across the wearing strings.

An old friend once told me that every person had their own sound. A theme tune that played according to their personality, their soul. I don't know mine, but I know the strong yet soft rhythm coming from my own guitar belongs to one person. And that person is the reason my nights have been sleepless. Despite the pain, I continue the torturous tune. I let it pollute the room, the feeling it gives me is bittersweet.

Banging on the door disrupts me, and so I begrudgingly sit up, placing the guitar back on the stand, my self-pitying apparently done with for the time being. I open the door and find Codie on the other side, her face hard as she marches past me and into my room.

What the hell?

"Hallie Clarke, I've just about had enough of this shit."

I blank at her words. What have I done now? She continues.

"Get your shit together. We're going out, and I'm not taking no for a damn answer. Get dressed. I'm taking you to see a movie, and then we're gonna go for dinner, and you're going to fucking smile whilst we do it."

"Why?" I ask.

Doesn't she realize I'm avoiding her for a reason? I don't want her dragged down with me.

She lets out a long breath, her eyes softening on mine. "Because I'm your friend, and I'm sick of watching you be like this. I'm sick of you locking yourself away in this dorm, hiding from assholes that don't deserve the damn satisfaction."

I shake my head. She must be crazy if she thinks I'm going anywhere tonight. She ignores it and flings open my drawers. I watch her, slightly amused, as she begins to throw my clothes all over my room. She better clean this up. She turns to me and hands me a white shirt with a faded union jack covering the front.

"Get this on, and your badass bitch boots, then meet me in the lounge. If you aren't there in 5 minutes, I'm coming back and dressing you myself."

She leaves then, and I stare at her wake for a few seconds before pulling myself together and doing what she says. I've never seen her like that and I really didn't want her to come back for round two. Maybe if I just go to this stupid movie with her, she'll leave me alone. I release a frustrated breath. I'm beginning to remember why I thought friends were a bad idea. I should have just gone for a run.

CHAPTER ELEVEN

Hallie

"Please, Hal. We'll have so much fun."

I groan inside and open my eyes, trying my hardest not to snap at her. *You like this girl*, I tell myself over and over again. She'd come bounding in here 10 minutes ago, full of excitement, and disturbing what was sure to be an incredible nap. She's got this ridiculous idea about me going home with her for Thanksgiving. It isn't happening. I'm planning on spending the holiday right here, possibly in this very position. I bend my knees and let my feet rest against the wall, frowning at the chipped black polish on my toe nails. I should fix that.

"Codie, I can't," I say quietly.

She lets out a huff and slumps down on the bed next to me. I shift and allow her more room. She moves beside me and copies my position, lay on our backs with our legs up the wall. The Ramones – Psycho Therapy begins to ring out from the speakers I bought last week, and I can't help but laugh a little at the slight grimace Codie pulls. She is so different to me musically. Codie likes all the cheesy pop songs that radio stations play on constant repeat. I prefer real music, made with real instruments, and not computers.

"Your taste in music needs some work," she comments, causing me to turn my face full to her and arch an eyebrow.

"My taste in music is just fine, thank you."

She laughs softly, and turns her head up to face the ceiling. Codie and I have gotten closer over the past couple of weeks. She's dragged my depressing ass, somewhat reluctantly, back into reality, and I'm not sure whether or not I'm grateful yet. Still, it was kind of nice to have a friend, even if she is forever trying to take 'selfies' with me. The girl is picture crazy, snapping them of just about everything. She's made it her mission to battle against the constant rumors about me, taking the majority of her fight to where it had originated – Facebook. I learnt that, like me, she isn't a fan of social media, and though she does have a profile or whatever, she only rarely uses it. I told her to ignore the things people were saying, not wanting her to be tarred with the same slut-brush as myself, but she deadpanned, telling me to just accept it.

My hand slides from its resting place on my stomach and lands on the bed between us.

"Hallie I don't want to leave you on campus by yourself. If you're not going home, then please come with me."

I sigh inwardly. My dreams of blissful solitude are burning in the distance. This isn't a battle I'm going to win, I can already see that.

"Why do you care so much what I do?" I laugh.

Her hand lands on mine, and I try not to show my confusion when she curls her little finger around my own. Her head falls to the side and she settles her gaze on me.

"You're my best friend, Hallie."

Her response is simple, but still leaves me dumbfounded. What the hell am I supposed to say to that? I've never been anyone's best friend. Even when I had friends at high school, I was always kind of the misfit. I never quite gelled with the rest of them. I see the world differently to other people - black and white, no shades of gray. Things are either right or wrong, and my mind leaves no room for humanity. Basically, a person is either an asshole or they aren't. I'm cynical, and don't believe in anything until I see it with my own eyes. Codie is different. The wonder at the world, and crazy optimism, literally shines through her eyes. You can see it, feel it coming off her in waves. She's always smiling, infecting every room she walks in with her contagious laughter. We are a stark contrast from each other, two sides of two very different coins, but it works. Kind of. I pull my eyes away from hers and fix my stare back on my feet. I release a long, defeated breath.

"So, what color nail polish does a girl wear in Ohio?" I ask.

Codie is silent for a short second before squealing beside me, loudly. I wince from the noise.

"Oh my God, Hal. This is going to be so fucking fantabulous. Like literally A-fucking-mazing!" She turns to face me fully. "I really want to hug you."

"No."

"Please."

"Codie," I warn.

"I'm going to."

"You're not."

I barely get the words out before she pounces on me, her arms flying around my neck as our legs tangle together. She presses her lips against my forehead and kisses me, making an over-exaggerated lip smacking sound.

"I love ya, bestie," she laughs.

"Don't call me that," I groan in reply, pushing her off me.

"Oh, hell no! I'm only ever going to call you bestie from now on." She smiles wider. "Hallie and Codie – BFFs forever."

Oh dear God.

She climbs off the bed, her face still stretched impossibly wide in a grin. I watch her as she pulls her cell from her pocket, taps the screen, and holds it to her ear. Her smile doesn't falter as she talks quickly and animated down the line. I can hear Codie's mom faintly in the background, as my roommate informs her that she's managed to 'convince' me to make the trip with her. I tune her out, and reach to the cabinet beside my bed. In the bottom drawer I find my little bag of nail polishes and some cotton wool. I pull out the small bottle of polish remover, and then begin the boring procedure of removing the chipped black from my toe nails. Codie ends her call as I'm just finishing up and jumps down on the bed.

"So, do you wanna road trip it, or get a plane?" She asks.

I hesitate. I have money in my account, but I'm reluctant to use it as I know it came from sperm donor. He is high on my list of assholes and I have no plans to bump him down. I turn to Codie, weighing up the options. Cleveland is less than a three hour drive away, so the 'road trip' wouldn't be so bad. But then, the girl is chatty. Three hours in a confined space with her talking nonstop about her sex life with Ryan might blow my head off. It's bad enough that I have to hear it myself. Ryan is a moaner. The choice is simple; my pride or my sanity. Which did I value more? *Yeah, right.*

"I'll drive."

Codie smiles at my response. What she doesn't realize is

that in my car, I control the stereo and the music choices. There will be absolutely no Taylor Swift on this trip. That preppy bitch is banned.

By the time we're pulling up in the drive of Codie's house, I'm regretting my decision to come completely. It's not that the drive had been hideous, or that Codie's out of tune singing had been unbearable. It wasn't that at all. In fact the whole, should have been 3 hours but instead took 5 hours, trip had been actually quite amusing, fun even. We'd played the music in my Focus impossibly loud, and laughed along with each other as we told stories of our high school days. I'd told her some of the lighter, more amusing, rumors from back home, and she'd told me some of the things her and her family used to get up to. No, the reason for my sudden distaste is the dark blue truck parked in Codie's open garage. Well, not the truck so much. I wasn't all that offended by *that*. The owner, however, is a colossal dick-head, and with the current state my mind was in, I'd completely forgotten he lived here too and was likely to be home for Thanksgiving.

Jace Barnes isn't someone I wanted to spend any holidays with, or any time at all, period. As if sensing my unease, Codie places her hand gently on my shoulder.

"Don't worry about him, Hal. He'll be too busy trying to persuade his ex-girlfriend to put his penis in her mouth."

Despite my annoyance at the situation, I laugh. Codie sure has a colorful way with words sometimes. I mentally square my shoulders, and with a simple nod of my head in reply, I climb from the car. Codie meets me by the trunk, and we haul our stuff out. Me with one bag and my guitar, her with a suitcase and two extra bags. This is her house. Why did she need all this stuff? I glance up at it, the door open wide as a woman stands beaming at us.

"Oh, Hallie, it's lovely to finally meet you," Codie's mom gushes at me as we reach the front door.

I stand awkwardly in the threshold of the door, clinging to my bag as if it will somehow save me. Codie has told me a little about her family over the last few months. They are all super tight, which is weird in my eyes. Apparently her mom is super nice and tries to 'mother' everyone so much, that all of Codie's and Jace's friends call her 'mom' too.

"It's nice to meet you too, Mrs. Barnes," I reply finally.

Her brows furrow in what looks like distaste. Did I offend her already?

Jeez, that was quick, Hallie.

"Please, call me Sarah." Her smile is back in place now. "Mrs. Barnes is my mother in law."

I glance at Codie who just rolls her eyes and moves further into the house, beckoning me to follow her. There's definitely a story there. I let Codie lead me through the house and up the stairs. She stops outside of a door and turns to me, a big smile on her face.

"This is where you're staying. My room is just down the hall." She pushes the door open. "Do you want to freshen up and settle in whilst I go call Ryan real quick?"

"Yeah, that'd be good, thanks."

She smiles and assures me that she'll be back in a couple of minutes then dashes down the hall. I laugh to myself. A couple of minutes, my ass. I've heard their phone calls before, several times. They are rarely less than an hour long. Shaking my head slightly, I push open the door. I'm greeted with cream walls, covered in floral portraits, and the soft smell of lavender. There's a double bed in the far corner of the room, filled with an excessive amount of decorative cushions. I let my bag drop to the floor at the foot of the bed and look around once more. I can hear Codie's parents laughing down stairs, and the sound claws at my insides. *What the hell am I doing here?* My eyes catch the small picturesque window and I glance through it, moving closer. Children run around the garden opposite, smiling wide as their parents chase them around. A sigh catches in my chest, making it ache. I never had that, and I never will have that. I drag my gaze away, not wanting to witness the perfect family image anymore. How is it that I can miss something I never had? It doesn't make sense. I shake off the dull resentment and pull my guitar from off my shoulders, slumping down on the floor with it, my back to the bed. I dig the ancient red pick from my pocket and flick it over the strings, with my guitar resting on my knee. I strum softly, careful to disturb Codie's family downstairs. I play out the tune that has been spinning around the back of my mind all day. It's deep, dark even, and suits my current mood completely. No matter how hard I try, or Codie tries, I just can't pull myself out of the funk I've gotten myself into. I'm choking on my own misery, but unable to let anyone share the burden. I know all of this best friend bullshit with Codie won't last. It never does. People never stick around, they change and turn their backs on what doesn't work for them. It's just the way the world works. Codie re-enters the room after at least an hour has passed, just like I predicted. She beams at me from the door, the smile reaching her eyes.

"Let's go bond with the family, they're all dying to get to know you!"

I take a breath and stand. Here we go.

CHAPTER TWELVE

Hallie

Well, that was the longest week of my life. Holy crap. Maybe not having the happy family life isn't so bad. I mean, jeez all those people. I thought it would have just been Codie, Jace, and their folks but, half the town turned up for thanksgiving dinner. Apparently, Sarah invited their entire family. I was like a sitting duck. It didn't help that Jace kept on insinuating that we were an item, putting his arm around me and sitting super close. *Personal space, dude.* He tried to apologize a bunch of times, asking if we can start over. I didn't even respond. What was the point? He was one of *them*. One of the campus followers, a sheep in the 'Hallie Is a Whore Brigade', and a complete idiot.

I drop my bag on my bed flick my speakers on full blast. Fuck the neighbors if they can hear it. I need my music, and I need it loud. Freak on a Leash – Korn vibrates off the walls of my room and I smile. This in an awesome song. Out of the corner of my eye I see my phone light up, so I begrudgingly pick it up from its home on the bed and open the new text.

Kian: *U coming down today? The old man is asking for U...*

I laugh. Kian works at one of the homeless shelters in the city. I found the place a few weeks ago and have been visiting as often as I can. The old man, is one of the regulars in there, Howard. He's a gentle giant of a man, at least 500 years old, and a complete sweetheart. I tap out a quick message.

Me: *Just got to shower then I'm on my way. Tell Howard I'll be by with his pie soon.*
Kian *Oh, he'll love that. See U later.*

I leave my cell on the bedside unit and head into the bathroom. I switch the shower on full, and begin to strip off my clothes as the water heats. A solid three bangs sound from the main door of the suite. I roll my eyes. Here come the complaints. I look down at myself as the door bangs again. I've only managed to get my jeans and panties off. The faded Beatles shirt covers my ass so I guess I'm good. I stroll out, not bothering to rush for whatever miserable asshole is at the door. As I walk through the kitchen, the door swings open, and an annoyed looking Nate stands in the threshold. I halt my steps, pushing down the urge to wrap myself around him. I've been fighting that urge a lot lately. Luckily, I didn't see him as much. He finally started to take the hint and is leaving me alone, for the most part. Now though, we seemed to have entered a silent battle of wills. Who could piss off who the most. I'm winning, I think.

Nate walks in further, his eyes glaring into my own. I hold his stare, mildly fascinated that I'm seeing this whole new side to him. It's actually kind of hot to see him all riled up.

"Are you fucking kidding me with this music, Hallie?" He all but growls at me.

I suppress a smirk and ignore him, walking over to the refrigerator and grabbing a bottle of water.

"Oh sure, Nate. Come on in, please," I say, with sarcasm that could choke a horse.

I jump up on the kitchen counter and watch as he slams the door shut, before walking over to me. His glare deepens, and if I was anyone else, I'd probably be a little intimidated. But, alas, I am me, and I'm not worried. Just amused.

"I'm serious, Clarke," he seethes.

"What's up?" I ask. "Don't you like the song?" I flash him a smile. "I can always change it for you, just gotta ask nicely."

His eyes narrow on me, studying my face as I pour some water into my mouth. I shouldn't be toying with him like this, I know that. But it's just so much fun. And he hasn't exactly been playing fair, walking around our dorm shirtless, and flashing me panty melting smiles. He's no innocent party. It's just easier to be this way, to ignore my actual feeling towards him, and be the bitch everyone thinks I am. This way makes him hate me, and hate I can handle. What I can't handle is when he looks at me like I'm the only girl in the world. It's too much pressure to be perfect, especially when everyone around you is telling you you're not.

"Just turn it down."

I pretend to think about this for a minute, looking up to the ceiling, before bringing my focus back.

"Nope." I jump down off the counter. "Is that everything? I'm about to get into the shower."

I don't wait for him to respond, and walk back down the

hallway. Nathan follows me into the bathroom. I almost laugh, this is entertaining. I turn to him, arching my brow in this direction. He looks from the shower to me, then back again.

"Look, I already know I sound like an asshole so you can stop looking at me like that," he says. "But between your roommate fucking mine, and this fucking noise, I can't hear myself think."

A part of my amusement dies. Codie and Ryan can be pretty freakin' loud, so I guess I feel for him there. But I'm not gonna cave. He'll just have to deal with it. His roommate is the reason mine is so damn loud. Ha! I mentally high five myself for my inner joke.

"I'll be out of here in less than an hour, so chill. I'm sure you could go and see your girlfriend or something until then."

Why the hell did I say that? To hide my regret, and embarrassment at opening my mouth, I pull off my shirt and bra, then step into the shower. I hear him curse as the water rains over me, then the sound of the main door banging shut alerts me to his departure. I smile to myself.

I think I won that one.

"So you just stripped off and jumped in the shower. Naked."

I laugh at Codie. I've just walked in from the shelter, after a long afternoon of reading lessons with Howard, and am now telling her about my latest altercation with Nate. She's been harping on at me for a while now, ever since it came out that I spent the night after the party with Nate, about us being together and how perfect we are for each other. I ignore her for the most part, and force myself not to get annoyed about it. Codie is all about romance, and fairy tales, and happily ever afters. She doesn't get reality. At all. I hand her the box of candy I picked up on my way back to campus and slump down beside her on the couch.

"You got another note today," she says.

I frown and hold my hand out. She doesn't pass it over though, instead she unfolds the small square of paper, and reads it aloud in what I can only assume is her best stalker voice.

"Dear Hallie." She offers me a bored eye roll before continuing. "I'm so glad you're back from your trip. I do hope you enjoyed the holiday. Maybe next time, you'll be spending it with me. Yours always, JC." She flicks the paper at me and shoves a handful of the sugared candy into her mouth. "Sounds like a right creeper," she comments.

"Oh, definitely." I smile. "Makes for great reading material though."

"Sure does! Are you running tonight?"

"Yeah, going to head out in a minute. You here for dinner? Or seeing Ryan?" The smile on her face tells me I won't be seeing her for most of the weekend. I laugh. "Never mind."

"Don't judge me!" She chuckles. "I go away again soon for Christmas."

"Yeah, yeah," I say, standing. "Gotta get your fill, right?"

"Exactly right!"

I leave her in the lounge and head to my bedroom to change. Once I have my running stuff on, I leave the dorm, and make my way to the park. I keep my music volume high to avoid hearing the not so hushed whispers of people on campus. I've become a social pariah, thanks to Tami and her team of morons, and people have begun to hurl abuse at me wherever I go. I'm living high school all over again, and I'm not enjoying it. But, it will take more than mindless name calling to penetrate my ice walls, so good luck to them.

I hit the trail hard, pounding my feet into the ground. I'm desperate for the numbness to take over. Desperate to punish myself into blissful oblivion. White Snake - Here I go Again blasts through the speakers in my ears, the beat urging me forward. I concentrate on the music, pushing the burn I already feel to the back of my mind. Some nights I can come out here and feel the welcomed mind numbing within minutes.

Tonight is not one of those nights.

CHAPTER THIRTEEN

Nate

As awesome as the break from college was, I'm so glad Christmas is finally over. That was a long couple of weeks, which had included a long ass series of bullshit charity functions with Dad, a strange Christmas day with my grandma in Florida, and a stiff formal New Year's party with my dad's firm.

"Dude I'm gonna go pick Codie up from the airport, you wanna come with?" Ryan calls to me from the kitchen.

Getting used to my lady slayer best friend being tied down for more than one night is hard. I spent the first couple of weeks just waiting for him to fuck up and cause a massive fall out, but it never happened. They seem to balance each other out. As for our other neighbor, she's been freezing me out or riling me up since the day I showed her the damn Facebook page. I only wanted to make sure she was okay. I couldn't believe what I read. Is that what she was really like? Everything I know about her pointed in the opposite direction. Of course, I don't exactly know that much about her. It had been Tami that showed me; I bet she fucking enjoyed that. I wanted the ground to swallow me whole after Hallie walked up the hallway and caught me talking to her at my door. Tami just showed up dressed like a street corner skank moaning about some Halloween party she wanted me to go to. After I caught the look Hallie threw at me when she called Tami my girlfriend, I was floored. I set Tami straight. Told her I wasn't interested and that I'd been with someone else the night before. She knew straight off it was Hallie. She then proceeded to tell me all about the things she's supposed to have done. I slammed the door in her face then went straight to my laptop to look. Once I'd seen it I had to talk to her. I wanted to know if it was true. I was mad, sure, but not at her. Whoever made this page had brought out a rage in me I couldn't describe. My poor Hallie. That's right, I said *my* Hallie. Whether she knows it or not, that girl is mine. We connected that night in my bed. She'd let go, and I saw how much she wanted me. I don't care how much of a pussy I sound by saying it.

I planned to talk to her that night. I wanted to tell her how much I wanted to be with her, how much I couldn't stop thinking about her. I didn't get my chance though. She left that night for a run only returning hours later practically crawling and silent. She didn't say a single word to any of us as she came through the door. I hadn't meant to stay there that late, but after telling the other two about the whole thing over dinner, we decided we'd all wait for her and check she's alright. Didn't happen though. She walked in and went straight to her room, not looking at any of us. It was decided then that my best friend and I would leave it to Codie to talk to her. Ryan mentioned later that week that Codie eventually managed to get through to her but that his girlfriend refused to go into any details about it, saying only that most of it was bullshit from heartless idiots. I tried texting her and talking to Hallie but she's completely closed up, icier than ever, and giving only one worded responses and non-committal replies. That's if she even bothers to say anything at all. Then all of a sudden she is talking, only she's a total bitch. And my traitor dick loves it, loves the fire in her eyes because at least she's showing something. She walked into the shower butt naked a few weeks ago, just to get away from me. Granted, I probably shouldn't have followed her into her bathroom, but damn it I wanted her to talk. And to turn her fucking music down. She was all legs and sass, and I'd had to work my dick furiously to get the sight away.

The guys on campus have started shouting things out to her, but she barely glances their way, and I don't see her at any parties. The Facebook page has taken off immensely, and is becoming some sick, twisted game to people, guessing what she will do next. People are constantly posting stories on there of things they are claiming she's done and several guys have put that they've slept with her. They don't even try and make it believable, often saying it happened when even I know she has a class. Tami is leading the charge on that one, determined to make sure that Hallie is never seen in a good light again by spreading vicious rumors that she's sleeping with half the campus, professors as well as students. She's turned out to be every bit as psychotic as I figured she was. She managed to convince most of the campus that I was drunk, and Hallie took advantage of me the night I fucked her. Apparently Tami and I haven't got back together as I'm 'dealing with personal issues' because of it. Of course I told her, very loudly and in front of several people, that we were never together to begin with, and I'm dealing with issues. I just don't have the slightest interest in her. Plus, I made sure she knew that I fucked Hallie because she's hot as hell and I liked her. Still like her actually. Haven't been able to stop thinking about her. We've had a few awkward encounters over the last few weeks. And by awkward, I mean we have either avoided each other, or we've snarled at each other. I even waited outside her English class at one point to try and force her into talking to me but she closed up. She's put up walls that need a bulldozer to take down. I'm at a loss on what to do.

I tried talking to my dad about the whole Hallie thing over the break. He's usually pretty good with stuff like that having had several girlfriends in his life, but the only advice he could give me was to stay away from it. Apparently I don't need the drama and baggage of a girl with a past, no matter if it is all lies. Unfortunately, as much as I try, that just doesn't sit right with me. I know there's more to her than what people say. I know there's a side to that story I don't know about, that I doubt anyone knows about. She's not the heartless bitch she's being made out to be. I just know. The way she made a point of making sure Ryan and I ate properly. Who does that? Plus I see the way she is with Codie. She cares about her. That isn't the girl that the assholes here are describing.

I tell my best friend that I'm going to stay here at the dorm, and then offer him a small wave from my perch on the couch as he leaves. Thinking about Hallie, and all the crap surrounding her, has put me in a serious funk now. I wonder what she'd do if I just turned up at her door, refusing to leave until she talked to me. HA! She'd probably rip my nuts off with her bare hands, and then make me swallow them. All without saying a goddamn thing. Maybe Dad is right. I need to just stay away from her. Not that she's making it difficult for me.

I stand and grab my keys from the table. I need out of this dorm suite, the fucking walls are driving me insane. I pick my jacket up from the back of the couch and leave through the front door, deciding a long drive to absolutely fucking nowhere in the dark should fix it. I'm met with the sounds of sniffing and turn abruptly to see Hallie walking up the hallway towards her dorm, her arm clinging across her stomach. Holy fuck. Her head is down and she's covered in dirt and mud. Her hair is falling out of the hair tie she has in, and as I look closer, I can see a small tear in her shirt. What the fuck has happened to her?

"Hallie?" I call, and she looks up suddenly.

Her tear stained eyes widen a fraction before she turns away, wiping frantically at her face and hair. She's not quick enough. I saw the fresh bruising there.

"Hey, are you okay?" I ask, walking closer to her.

Her hand is shaking as she desperately tries to get the key in the lock. I cover her hand with mine to still it and she tenses.

"I'm fine," she whispers, and I wonder if she's saying it more to herself than in reply to me.

"Yeah, obviously. Here let me," I say, taking the key gently from her.

She immediately pulls her hand away, choosing to hug herself tightly, watching me with obvious impatience. I open the door easily then step inside before she can shut the door in my face. There is no chance in hell I'm going to leave her in this state. Something has obviously happened to her. When I don't hear her following me, I turn and find that she's standing in the doorway, staring straight ahead as small silent tears fall down her face. The image is heart-breaking and I'm at a loss at what to do to help her.

"Hallie talk to me. What's happened?" I urge as I take her hand and gently lead her into the suite.

She looks at me for a while, before a humorless laugh snorts from her.

"You know," she says, her voice detached and hollow. "I always knew people could be assholes and I've never expected anything less. But jumping a girl when she's got her back turned, is fucking cowardly and low."

I try to walk to her but she spins on her heels and limps towards the bathroom. I follow her, determined to find out who has hurt her. I'll fucking kill them. Actual murder, with my bare hands. No one gets to hurt my girl. *No one.*

"Hallie, who did this to you? Do you want me to call the cops? I should take you to hospital," I tell her, but she shakes her head slowly and she leans over to start the water for a bath. I notice her wincing as she moves, so again I use my hands to still her. She looks so broken and sad right now, its gut wrenching.

"Please let me help you," I plead and I watch as she purposely blanks her face and turns to face me.

"Why?"

She doesn't give me time to answer though, as she turns and leaves the bathroom, walking straight to her bedroom and closing the door. Well shit. What do I do now? I turn back to face the tub that's slowly filling with water. Surely she isn't going to just leave it like that. After a while I can hear her grunting and cursing from the other side of her bedroom door, so I shut off the water and go over, knocking quietly on the door.

"Hallie, do you need some help?"

"No I'm... fuck! I'm fine," she calls back, a loud bang separating her words.

"I'm coming in there, so if there are things you don't want me to see, then cover up."

I wait two beats before opening the door. She's sat on

the edge of her bed in just her panties and shirt. Her jaw clenched as she stares at the ceiling, her left arm wrapped around her stomach.

"I can't get my shirt off," she murmurs, and I walk over and sit down next to her.

My eyes roam over the room. It's painfully tidy with pale green walls, the same as mine, only she has littered the walls with pictures and posters. An acoustic guitar stands perfectly in the corner of the room. I had no idea she played.

"I can help you if you let me," I tell her, hoping she hears the sincerity in my voice.

I study her, and can see the internal battle happening in her head. Why won't she just give in and let me look after her? I stand and hold my hand out to her, patiently waiting for her to take it. She brings her big eyes up to look into mine and tilts her head slightly, staring at me for a few seconds before carefully putting her hand into mine. I almost smile. The head tilt thing is something I've noticed she does when she's reading someone, or thinking too hard. I gently pull her up to stand, ignoring the sharp anger I feel when I see her wince from the pain it causes her.

I lead her into the bathroom then close the door behind us. I know Ryan won't be back with Codie for hours yet, but I don't want to take any chances that they will come busting through the door any minute. I move over to where Hallie is stood staring at the tub and turn her to face me.

"I'm going to take these off now," I tell her, gesturing to her torn clothes. She takes an audible breath so I continue. "I will look at your face, and nowhere else I promise, okay?"

I exhale softly at her small nod, before gently easing her arms out of the short sleeves of her shirt. I lift it over her head and her arms immediately go to her stomach, covering it, but not before I see the large bruises beginning to form across her side and ribs. Fucking assholes. It looks as though they were kicking her whilst she was lay down. I turn her gently so her back is to me and unclip the clasp on her bra, slipping the straps off her shoulders. She quickly discards it on the floor below us then crosses her arms over her chest. She was so confident and sexy the last time I saw her naked, and now she's hiding herself away. This isn't right. I've been so desperate to see her again, to feel her skin on mine, but not like this. My hands go to her hips and I hook my thumbs in her panties, whispering for permission in her ear. She nods agreement so I carefully pull them down her shaking legs, bringing my hands up quickly once it's done in order to not delay the ordeal. I have to help her. My arms reach around either side of her, taking both of her hands and stretching them so her elbows sit in the crook of mine.

"I'm going to help you into the tub now, lean all of your weight on my arms," I tell her then wait for her to step one foot into the water.

She does as I instruct and leans back on me as she brings the other one over the side of the tub. I help her to sit gently then walk over to the bathroom door to give her some privacy.

"Could you, um, maybe get me some water?" She asks me suddenly and I smile, safe in knowledge that I know she can't see me. I can only imagine how much that must have hurt her to say. The damn girl never asks for help with anything. This only makes me worry more. Something serious must have happened to have her asking for things.

"Sure. I'll be right back," I reply, then head straight out into the kitchen.

I pull a bottle of water out the refrigerator then pour some into a glass. After some more digging around, I manage to find a box of painkillers so push two out then head back to her. She's trying her best to wash her hair when I enter the bathroom, and if it wasn't for the circumstances, I'd probably laugh. It's not going so well for her but I don't want to push it by offering help.

"Here," I say walking over, handing her the water and pills.

"I don't take painkillers, but thank you," she responds quietly and I do laugh then.

Of course she doesn't. I take the pills from her, not wanting to force her out of fear she'll turf me out.

"I'll wait in the lounge for you," I say, making sure she knows that I'm not planning on leaving.

I can hear her sighing softly as I shut the door on my way out. Okay. Shit. How do you cheer a girl up that pretty much hates the world? I'm thinking ice cream and a fucking chick flick isn't going to cut it. My cell ringing distracts me so I hurry to answer it.

"Yeah?"

My best friend's voice greets me back. "Sup man."

I smile. If anyone can help me, this guy can. He's a fucking expert at groveling to girls. Maybe I can convince him to take Codie over to our place and sleep there. I don't think Hallie needs people seeing her right now.

"Hey Ry, you still at the airport?"

"Yeah. That's why I was calling. Codie's flight got delayed. It's going to be another 3 hours before she's here. Can you believe that?" He laughs now. "She'd left me a voicemail but I hadn't bothered just check it. She called 10 minutes ago as she was boarding." That sounds about right. Ryan never checks his damn messages. It's why I never leave them. This is good news though.

"Yeah no worries bro," I reply, forcing my tone even. I

stand and walk aimlessly over to the kitchen as he rambles on.

"Gonna book us into a hotel room so I don't have to drive back when it's late."

I laugh now. Does he think I'm an idiot?

"Plus you're not sure your dick will hold out long enough for you to make it back," I comment and he sighs.

"It's been a long Christmas break my friend." I laugh again as he continues. "So you're cool? You looked pissed when I left before."

"I'm fine." Maybe he can help. He's been with Codie for a while now so maybe he knows more about Hallie. There's only one way to find out. "Hey! Random question – how do you cheer a girl up that has a massive problem with people and things and, well, fucking everything?" I ask, my voice hopeful and he chuckles a couple of deep beats before replying.

"So Hallie then?"

"Um..." Shit. Do I tell him? I'm pretty sure she'd punch me in the face, hard, if I did. I don't have time to consider as he speaks again.

"Don't worry bro my lips are sealed, so to speak. But if it helps I happen to know she has a weakness for hot chocolate and Channing Tatum. They have all of his DVDs on the television stand."

At his words I glance over and see a stack of DVDs by the TV. Channing Tatum, really? I never had her down as a chick flick kind of girl.

"Thanks bro. I'll catch you later," I say already moving towards the DVDs.

"Good luck!" He mocks back.

I end the call laughing then go in search of the mentioned movies.

Channing Tatum. *Fucking hell.*

I set the TV up, pushing in the first disk I find with his face on then get to work on hot chocolate in the kitchen. I may be doing this all wrong but it's the thought that counts, right? I hear the bathroom door open and then Hallie bedroom door close as I'm placing the drinks on the small coffee table. I sit down on the couch facing the screen, putting a blanket I found next to me ready for when Hallie comes in. This is assuming that she doesn't walk in, hit the roof, and throw me out. I wait patiently, my fingers tapping nervously on my knees until I hear her door open and close. I force myself not to look up straight away and keep my gaze trained on the screen in front of me.

"Is that hot chocolate?"

"Um yeah, here sit down," I reply, patting the seat beside me as I finally look up to see her.

She's wearing a loose pair of sweatpants with a white tank that shows off her midriff a little. If it wasn't for the blank expression on her face, she'd look fucking adorable. Her sweet honey scent fills the air as she sits carefully beside me. I lean forward to get her drink and pass it to her then bring the blanket over her knees.

"You didn't have to do all of this," she comments, as I point the remote at the TV to start the film. Her body is still tense as she brings her knees up to her chest.

"I know. Now hush, Channing Tatum is on the screen, and I just love this guy," I joke and I'm rewarded with a soft laugh.

Fuck. I could listen to her laugh all day. I have to get her to do it more often. I was stupid to think I could walk away from her. Just hearing her name over the past few weeks has drove me crazy. I haven't been able to go near another girl, spending my nights furiously getting myself off to the memory of her. Pathetic, I know, but I can't help it. I need to have her again. I need to know everything about her. *I need her*.

She brings the blanket tight around her and I let it hang loosely over myself as we settle down to watch the movie.

CHAPTER FOURTEEN

Hallie

My eyes flick open as the sunlight rouses me gently from sleep.

Oh jeez. Everything hurts. I slowly lift my sheets off me only to realize that they aren't my sheets. They are in fact a blanket and I'm not in my room. I'm on the sofa, my head resting on Nate's hard chest.

"Shit."

I sit up abruptly and he groans from beside me causing me to freeze. This will be the second time I've bolted from this guy before he's woken up. But where am I supposed to go? Just to my room? He's in my fucking dorm. What the hell was I doing? It's not like I can just leave. Not like this. My mind flashes back to last night - the punching, the kicking, and the name calling. I'd decided to walk to the store as it was only a couple of blocks from campus. Hell, I only wanted some fucking candy to drown my sorrows after watching Nate return to the dorms. The sight of him had caused the ache in my stomach to intensify. Which is again, pathetic. I thought I'd gotten a handle on my unnatural feelings for him. But spending the Christmas in a dorm room, alone, has a way of forcing you into wading through your thoughts. And almost all of mine were of him.

I had made it to just outside of the school gates, last night, when I felt the first hit. I'd heard the voices calling things behind me as I walked, but after the last few weeks I'd learnt to tune it all out. I barely managed the walk back home, my ribs feeling like they were about to crumble. The stairs were difficult, and my head was a mess as I cried out of pain and sheer fucking exhaustion with everything. That's why I didn't notice Nathan standing there watching me. I almost peed with embarrassment when I heard him say my name. I forced myself to stay as far away from him as possible. I couldn't risk being around him. I like him too much, and he makes me feel too much. I can't risk that. I can't risk getting in too deep with a guy like that, a guy that's bound to hurt me, or get hurt *by* me. I'm too self-destructive.

I tried desperately to get into the dorm, but my damn hands were shaking all over the place so he took the key from me and strolled right in. I was in shock. I couldn't believe what had happened to me. Never, in my short 18 years of life had I been subjected to violence of any sort. I mean sure, the girls at high school would push past me in the corridors, and Timmy Green did push me down once when I was in kindergarten, but never anything like the assault I endured last night. It scared me, and a small part of me had been happy to see Nate, which only scared me more. Anger begins to stir in my stomach as I remember. Five of them and one of me, yet they still took me from behind, making sure I didn't see their faces. Doesn't matter. I know who was behind all of this. I just wish I cared.

Nate stirs beside me and my whole body tenses. Maybe I'm thinking too loud. Carefully, I slip off the sofa and walk (limp) to the kitchen. Of all the people to witness my humiliation, it had to be him. Shit, he even undressed me. I was too numb last night to feel mortified but holy fuck, I'm feeling it now. He'd been so gentle with me, his hands soft on my beaten skin. His scent had filled the room, comforting me with the familiarity. I tried to hide away from him, wanting him to remember my body as what it was when we had our night together, and not what it is now – bruised and broken. I searched his face, looking for disapproval or distaste but all I'd found was concern and contained rage. It scared and soothed me all at the same time causing me to spend my bath trying to organize my conflicting thoughts. When I walked into the lounge and saw that he'd made me hot chocolate and had the screen set on to my favorite Channing Tatum movie, I almost melted. I was determined to go in there and kick his nosy ass out so I could wallow in self-pity privately but the way he just sat there, nerves radiating off him, I couldn't. I just couldn't bring myself to do it, and I know that's because a part of me wanted him there, needed him there. We watched a couple of the movies before apparently both falling asleep on the couch together, my head resting on his chest and his arms draped over my shoulder, pulling me close to him. I hate admitting this, but I actually liked it. Thank god Codie isn't home. I'd never hear the damn end of it. With everything going crazy on campus she's been like a rock. Arguing with anyone that dared to say something whilst she was with me, including her own sleazebag brother. I've tried to push her away but she hasn't stood for any of it, forcing her way into my life one way or another, so eventually I caved and we've become half decent friends.

I carefully pour the coffee I hadn't realized I'd been making into two cups and carry them over to the lounge. So apparently I'm not running away from him, I'm making him a fucking drink. I suppose he did help me last night so it's the least I could do. Should I make him breakfast? Pancakes maybe. Nothing says thanks for bathing me like coffee and pancakes.

"Hallie, can I smell coffee?" Nate suddenly croaks, almost making me drop the cups.

I place them carefully on the small table to avoid minor accidents.

"Uh, yeah," I answer, then sit at the edge of the seat.

He leans forward and picks up one of the cups, gulping at the contents.

"How're you feeling?"

It would be useless to lie to him. The man saw me naked last night, bruises and all. Oh jeez. If only he knew the inappropriate thoughts that had been going through my head as he wrapped his arms around my naked body, helping me into the tub. My mind had flashed back to that one wild night we had. I've been thinking about it a lot since it happened, unable to get him out my mind. I trained myself to think that it was just sex, nothing else. That was until last night. He'd taken care of me. No one else in the world ever had. I'd enjoyed it. I'd enjoyed being with him, hanging out with no pressure.

"Sore," I answer simply and he nods thoughtfully. "Thank you, by the way. You know, for last night," I add, mentally scolding myself for the pathetic stuttery delivery of my words.

Picking my coffee up from the table, I lean back on the seat.

"That's okay. Are you ready to talk about it yet?" He asks, putting his arm over my shoulders.

I exhale a long breath, ignoring the instant comfort I get from his touch. Does he feel it too? I turn my gaze to him briefly, letting my eyes study his face as he looks back at me. His features are soft but I can still see the barely restrained anger behind them. The same I'd seen last night.

"I didn't see their faces."

I knew exactly who it was, but I never actually saw them. So, technically not a lie.

Nate pulls me closer to him, his scent and warmth surrounding me, making me feel slightly dizzy. My eyes dart around the room, the urge to go running suddenly consuming me. How am I going to manage without my run today? We sit silently and sip at our coffee as my mind begins to reel, desperate to run or be away from here. I know exactly where I need to go.

"Do you think maybe we should tell the cops, Hallie? Whoever they were, what they did to you was wrong."

I stand, offering him no answer, and take both of our now empty cups away to the sink. I'll just leave campus for the day. Leave it all behind just for a little while.

"Hallie," he whispers, coming behind me. I flinch as he places his hands gently on my hips. "Hey, it's just me. I'm sorry," he adds quickly, his breath on my neck. I'm desperate to lean back into his embrace but I force myself to stay put, focusing only on rinsing out our cups. A noise distracts me and I shift uncomfortably, trying to move from Nate but he tightens his hold.

"Please," he breathes into my ear as I listen to Codie and Ryan entering the dorm.

Why is he doing this? They're going to get the wrong idea.

"Nate," I whisper, scolding him as he presses his mouth against my neck.

He kisses me there softly and I tense, desperately trying to ignore the feelings that are beginning to stir within me.

His body moves closer to mine, his hard chest pressing at my back.

"Hallie, I want you. All of you. I've been trying to tell you for a while then I tried to stay away, to give you the space I knew you wanted but I can't. I need to be with you," he murmurs quietly into my ear before pulling away from me and turning to the new arrivals.

I don't move, instead I keep my gaze on the sink and rinse out the cups for the twentieth time. What does he mean he wants all of me? He needs to be with me? Holy shit.

"Well well well. I go away for a couple of weeks and this happens. Ryan why didn't you tell me these two were *finally* hooking up." Her laughter fills the room. "I was getting sick of listening to you two bitch at each other."

Oh Jesus, Codie. I turn then, careful not to make any sudden movements. My body aches from its recent assault.

"Holy shit, Hal, what the fuck happened?" Ryan shouts as he spots the fresh bruising on my face.

I don't need a mirror to know how bad it must look, I can feel it. Codie turns then, and I watch as concern tortures her features as her eyes roam my face.

"Hallie," she starts but I cut her off.

"I'm fine."

I don't wait for them to say anything else and walk down the hallway to my bedroom, closing myself in there. I can hear Codie shouting at Nate trying to find out what has happened but I tune it out, not wanting to listen to him recount the events of last night. How the hell am I going to get out of here? I can't stay here all day, it'll drive me crazy. I fling open the doors of my wardrobe and dig out a pair of black leggings. I find a long white tank and then dress as quickly as I can manage before adding my denim jacket and dark brown boots. I grab my purse from the cabinet beside my bed then head out the room. I don't stop to talk to any of the others and just continue out the door, walking as best as I can. I don't want their pity. Nor do I want to think about how it made me feel to have Nate so close, telling me he wants me. Shit.

I hurry down the stairs, ignoring the looks I get from people as I pass them by, and head straight out to my car. I climb in and then lower my head on to the steering wheel in defeat. Why couldn't he just leave me alone? Why couldn't I just throw his ass out last night? Why did he have to see me all messed up? I've been so careful to avoid him over the past few weeks. He's texted and called, stopped me around campus but I've managed to brush him off, the same way I managed to brush everyone off. Things have gotten crazy over the Facebook bullshit with UM's head sorority bitch leading the charge. Apparently I'm fucking the entire school, professors and girls included. I'd been hauled into the Dean Vincent's office just before winter break to answer to some rumors that had been filtering about my accused relationship with my English professor. I'd almost lost my shit at that one. Mr Cooper is an awesome guy and an amazing teacher. Sure, he's a lot younger than most of the others and he's helped me a few times with projects and hiding but nothing sinister. He's obviously heard the rumors about me too and is always asking if I was okay and helping me to focus on my projects instead of campus bullshit. I hate that these assholes are dragging him down with me. Don't they realize this is the kind of shit that could ruin his career?

The passenger door opens on my car and I turn quickly, fear consuming me for a second before I realize it's only Nate. I've got to stop being so damn jumpy.

"Where are you going?" He asks me, looking at me curiously.

I stare back, searching his face as my stomach does flips. What is he doing in my car? Also, why am I happy about it?

"Away," I answer eventually and he flashes me a panty melting smile.

"Awesome, let's go."

I stare at him dumbfounded as he leans back, fastening the seat bell across him. I spent all night cuddling him, he watched me cry and helped me to get into the fucking bath and now he's sat in my car refusing to let me disappear on my own. I don't know if I'm angry with him or relieved. I turn my head back to the road and with a silent breath, I start the engine. I guess I'm having company today.

CHAPTER FIFTEEN

Hallie

We don't talk for the entire twenty-minute drive. Instead, silence and unspoken questions fill the space. It suffocates me and so as soon as I pull up in the car lot I burst out the door, desperate for the clean air. I take deep breaths of it, forcing composure on myself.

Fuck Hallie, get it together. He's just a guy.

Nate comes around the stand in front of me as I lean against the car. My eyes look up to him and again he gives me *that* smile. I chew the inside of my lip to stop myself from saying something stupid and move past him, heading out the small side door to the street. He falls in step beside me.

"So this is *away*," he muses as I lead us down the familiar street.

I found this place a few weeks earlier and fell in love. I'd been looking for a place to buy some posters for my room when I stumbled across the small town called Dexter. I parked, drawn to the simplicity of it, and strolled around, stopping at a music store. Inside, I found old music records and even older band posters littering the walls. The woman who owned the place, Willow, had been kind and helpful, offering me coffee and showing me the best things in there. Now, I made of point of coming out here a few days a week to see her and help out at the store.

"Otherwise known as Dexter," I answer him, smiling inside as I push open the old wooden door. The musky scent fills me, soothing my mind in an instant. I glance around me, spotting Willow dusting the drum kit in the corner. Nathan stops beside me and I turn, laughing a little at the confusion on his face.

"Hallie!"

I smile and spin around to meet Willow's face. She runs over and hugs me tight causing me to wince from the pain that radiates through my entire body.

"Oh, Hallie, what the hell happened?" She cries as she pulls back and notices my face.

I smirk at her. "I guess there are a few people out there that don't appreciate my fuck it attitude, huh?"

She laughs at this, shaking her head slightly. It was her that referred to my manner as a 'fuck it attitude'. We'd been sitting in the back having lunch one day when she'd asked about my family and friends and why I wasn't going home for the holidays. I'd told her a little about how I didn't have friends and wasn't close with my family and she'd told me that was because I exuded an attitude that made it obvious I didn't care. I watch her now as she turns to Nate, her eyes roaming him fully as he stands there uncomfortable.

"Willow this is Nate Harris, stalker of the day. Nate this is Willow. She owns the store," I introduce and they both smile at each other.

I leave them stood there awkwardly and head into the back to make coffee. Lord knows I need it. I can hear Willow questioning Nathan and I chuckle, she's quite the character. I'd been genuinely terrified of her when I first met her. She'd forced me into trying everything out in the store then when she noticed me checking out an old Johnny Cash record, she'd put it on and danced around. There was something about her though that put me completely at ease. Still, she does take some getting used to.

I make the coffee and walk back into the store carrying the cups on an old tray. The sight I see almost has me folding over in fits of hysterical laughter but I refrain. Willow has managed to get Nate to go down on all fours whilst she stands on his back and reaches for something on the top of one of her shelves. I stand, watching for a minute before clearing my throat so they both know I'm there. Willow turns then jumps down excitedly clutching a record in her hands as she rushes over to me. I raise my eyebrow at Nate, his response only being an embarrassed shrug.

"Hallie I found it, finally!" Willow shouts as she thrust the record into my hands.

I look down and gasp slightly as I stare down at the signed Bon Jovi cover. *Oh my*. I've loved the band ever since I caught my mom dancing around to them when I was just a kid. The memory has stuck with me and now I owned nearly all of their original records. Born to Be My Baby is the only one I don't have and now here it is in my hands. Emotions overwhelm me as I reminisce dancing around with Mom to it, laughing with her as she put bright red lipstick on me. All of that was before the men, before they took my number one priority spot in her mind.

"How much?" I ask Willow keeping my eyes on it, my finger brushing over the fading signature. She leans into me and kisses my forehead lightly before telling me that there is no charge, it's a gift. I stare at her shocked. This record alone is worth a fortune; I can't take this for free. I tell her as much but she ignores my pleas and rushes for her coat, asking me to watch the store whilst she runs some errands. I agree as she dashes through the door, coffee cup in hand.

I stroll over to the long couch at the far end of the store, picking up my favorite acoustic guitar on the way and sit back, letting my fingers strum against the strings lightly. I'd always loved music, finding peace in it when my world became colorless. The sweet sounds add a delicate hue to the harsh black and white of my life. Showing me the beauty beneath the ugly and helping me to see that even though the lights don't always shine, I can still find my way in the dark.

I feel Nate sit beside me as I idly play out an unrecognizable tune. My fingers still as I look over to him. His gaze levels with mine, looking through me and seeing me behind the walls of ice I so carefully forced up to keep him away. I wanted to keep them all away. I trained myself in how to be alone, in how to rely on nobody but myself then last night I let him take care of me. I let him see me at my most vulnerable and now an internal battle plagues my thoughts. How do I take back the control after he's seen this? How do I put that ice brick with his name on back up and block him out?

"Our game still stands, right? The twenty-one questions thing?"

His lips twitch into a smile. "Of course."

"Why are you here?" I ask, suddenly desperate to know what he wants from me.

He lets out a breath before placing his hand gently on my knee, his eyes never leaving mine.

"I told you, I want you. I want all of you. I let you walk away from me once and I'm not about to do it again."

His answer throws me off. I was expecting him to tell me it was all pity and that he felt like he owed me because we hooked up but I can see the sincerity in his eyes and it scares the hell out of me. I nod once, unable to form any words then resume the soothing dance of my fingers over the strings letting a gentle tune play out.

"I didn't know you played guitar," Nate comments and I smile at him gratefully. He knows I'm done talking about us.

"I don't, not really."

He laughs. "Sounds like you do," he states and then it's my turn to laugh.

"I don't play the guitar. That would mean I wanted people to hear it. I just strum a few strings to make myself feel better. It fills my silence," I tell him softly as I close my eyes.

"Where did you learn?" He asks and again, I laugh remembering Bobby and our odd friendship.

I bring my feet up onto the seat and let the guitar rest on my knees.

"One of my mom's old boyfriends was in a band. He used to bring his band mates over and Mom would make me sit with them all whilst they practiced. I didn't mind, I was 13 and excited at staying up late. I love music and they weren't half bad. Derek, Mom's boyfriend, was the bass player. The lead guitarist was his younger brother. He taught me to play on electric and then I taught myself to play on acoustic."

My thoughts drift to Bobby. He was a good friend to me for the longest time, even after Mom and Derek broke up. He'd pick me up in his truck and then we'd drive down to the lake to hang out. We didn't talk much, but he introduced me to his music. He showed me how I could use it to heal myself, something I will always be grateful for. It had almost killed me when he moved away.

I rise then, placing the guitar back in its stand and turn

to Nate. He smiles up at me, then joins me standing and takes my hands in his.

"I don't know if I can be with you, I don't know how. There's so much bullshit surrounding me right now and I can't bring you into that. The things they will talk about will be awful. I'm used to it, but I don't think you are," I say quietly and he releases one of my hands, using his fingers the brush back my hair from my face gently.

"This is new to me too, but I need you baby. I can help you through all of this, it doesn't matter what anyone else thinks. I don't give a shit. The way I feel when I'm with you overshadows everything they could possibly say."

I melt at his words. Damn it. Why did he have to be so hot with a sweet mouth to match? I don't say anything as Willow returning distracts us causing me to breathe a small sigh of relief. I'm not good with this. I have no reply for his last comment. Do I want to be with him? I don't know. Yes?

We stay in the store for a few more hours before Nate forces me out and over to a small diner for lunch. People watch as we enter and I mutter curses quietly to myself. I'm not one for caring what people think of me, I'd drive myself crazy if I did, but it doesn't mean I like it when they openly stare. I caught a glance of my face in a reflection at the music store so I know the cut and bruising above my eye is bad. Now, here with it all on show, I can't help but feel exposed. Taking my hand gently, Nate leads me over to a small booth at the back of the diner. He takes the side which faces the rest of the space and I sit opposite, where only he can see my face.

"Thank you," I say, knowing he's done it for my benefit.

Why is it he can always sense my unease? It's like he can read my mind and see past the bullshit I portray. I don't know how I feel about that. He nods softly then hands me a menu from the stack at the end of the table. I glance over it, the words blurring into one. How am I supposed to concentrate on what I want to eat with him opposite me?

"Hi guys! My names Wendy and I'll be your waitress today. What can I get you?"

I look up at the voice. An older woman with kind eyes frowns down at me and I know it's because of the bruising. I look down quickly, not wanting to see her disapproval.

"I'll take an ice tea and a grilled cheese sandwich. You want the same baby or something else?" Nate asks me and I'm forced to look over and meet his gaze. His eyes are soft as he shows me a reassuring smile. I look back to the waitress and almost laugh out loud when I see her glancing between Nate and me. She's assuming he's the reason I have bruising. Oh that's hilarious. Well maybe not hilarious, but pretty funny.

"Are you okay, honey?" The older woman asks and I smile small in her direction as her eyes flick back to Nate.

"Yeah I'm okay. I'll have the same as him."

She scribbles in her little notebook then dashes off quickly towards the main counter. I put my menu back on the stack then lean back in my seat. The diner is quiet, not too many people are here. I know Willow comes in here a lot. She lives in the small town and knows everybody here. The place is perfect, low key and not a lot of people. Coming from Des Moines, I'm used to the busy city life. Small towns have always appealed to me.

"Ten bucks says the police are here within the next 4 minutes to arrest me. She definitely thinks I hurt you."

I laugh, looking over to see Nate's worried face. Maybe I should have corrected her, but it's not like she came right out and asked me. I glance around the booth, spotting the waitress talking with a man who looks equally as old as her. Time to go win ten bucks.

"Be right back," I say then stand from the booth. I walk over, my face impassive as customers glance my way.

Wendy smiles as I reach her and I prop myself, painfully, onto one the tall stools across the counter from her. I can feel Nate watching me but I brush it off, bringing my gaze solely on the woman in front of me.

"I know what you're thinking but it wasn't him," I say as I incline my head discreetly in Nate's direction. Her gaze flickers that way then back to me and I laugh before adding, "And now you're thinking I'm just saying that because he's right over there."

She smiles small. "We can keep you safe here until the cops come if you want, honey," she half whispers to me and I fight the urge to bang my head against the counter. Maybe I should have just left it. Let the cops come for the entertainment alone. Watching the calm and full of swagger Nate Harris sweat it out might have been amusing, but after last night I can't do that to him. I owe him, I know I do.

"No honestly, it wasn't him. I got jumped last night and he actually helped me. We go to college together, his dorm is actually next door to mine. We're friends? Maybe. I don't know what we are actually as things are a little awkward," I ramble before clamping my mouth closed. Good grief I need to learn to keep my trap shut. What the hell is happening to me? I'm normally a vault.

She smiles wide now, her eyes twinkling as she looks over to Nate again. I follow the gaze and bite my lip to stop from laughing when he flashes a nervous grin and gives a small wave in our direction.

"Oh Sweetie you know what you are, you just haven't accepted it yet. I'm sorry you got hurt last night. People can be so cruel sometimes but don't you let it get you down. You have that man over there and young love is a beautiful thing. Go on, get back over to him. I'll be over with your drinks soon." She turns away then, effectively dismissing me as I sit there dumbfounded.

Young love? God that's gross and so very far from truth. I shake off the thought and stroll back over, sitting down carefully on the seat.

"You owe me ten bucks," I say to a very confused Nate. He laughs before pulling a note and tossing it on the table. I smile and move to grab it but his palm falls flat over it.

"You cheated, you went and spoke to her."

I smirk. "You never said in your wager that I couldn't." His eyes narrow a fraction before he releases his hand and leans back on the chair.

He shakes his head. "I don't know if I should be appalled or impressed," he comments and I laugh, his eyes lighting a little as I do. I tell him I don't care how he feels as Wendy brings our drinks over shortly followed by our food. We spend the next hour talking idly and I'm surprised to find myself at ease. Even after we've finished eating, we continue to sit there asking each other questions and I find that Nathan is so much more than I originally thought. In fact, he's actually a bit of a geek. A hot geek, but still a geek. I'm trying my hardest not to laugh as he gushes about his massive interest in Star Wars when his cell rings distracting us. He looks at the caller ID before bringing it to his ear.

"Hey, what's up? Yeah I'm with her. Um sure, hold on." He looks at me as he passes me his cell. "It's Codie, you left your cell in the dorm?"

I shrug and take the phone from him. "Hey Codie."

"Hi Hal! Having a *good* day?" Wow. I can practically hear her eyebrows wiggling. I don't even want to know the thoughts she is bound to have running through her little mind right now.

"It's okay. What's up?" I answer, hoping to steer the conversation is another direction.

She laughs. "You know I'm gonna want all the details when you get home right? And I mean *all* of them. Like last night for a start." Her voice goes serious by the end of that sentence and I automatically tense. Do I tell her about being jumped? Or do I play it off? She's a friend, I think. Either way I'm in for an inquisition when I get back. Just perfect.

I sigh, "Is that why you're calling?"

"Oh God no," she laughs. "I just wanted to check you're alright and ask where the hell you are. I was worried, but then we noticed Nate was missing too and so I wanted to definitely call and see what you're doing." I hear her telling Ryan to be quiet at the other end of the call then a door closing as she begins to whisper into the cell. "Sorry, Ryan wouldn't stop asking me questions and I know how you feel about people knowing your business but I'm your best friend so I get to know everything." She chuckles again as my mind registers her words. *Best friend*, she called me her best friend. "I have to know Hal, are you and Nate... you know?" She continues and it's my turn to laugh. Like I can answer that. I don't even know myself, besides he's stood right in front of me.

"Sorry, I can't tell you. You aren't the only one with ears in front of you. I'll be back soon," I answer, noticing the way Nate's eyebrows raise. He absolutely knows we're talking about him.

"Yes! Good plan. We'll kick the boys out, get pizza and talk. Don't even try and get out of it," she scolds and I laugh again. I'd never admit it but I was secretly over the moon that my roommate constantly forced me into friendship. If she didn't, I'd never have tried.

"Yeah okay. Later Codie," I finish then hand the cell back to Nate narrowing my eyes as I watch Wendy walk away with our bill.

The fucker has paid for lunch whilst I was on the phone.

"Don't look at me like that. If I pay, I can pretend this was a date," he winks then stands and waits for me to join him.

"This was not a date," I reply and walk past him and out the door. He falls into step beside me and links his fingers with mine. I stop abruptly and turn to him. "What are you doing?"

"Holding your hand, you moron," he smiles before turning and practically pulling me along. I walk with him, his simple touch sending waves of comfort through me, despite the fact that he just called me a moron. I'll have to store that in my brain for when I'm capable of kicking his ass.

I keep his hand entwined with mine and lead him down the road. I really did love this little town. Rain begins to fall as we reach a little park and I turn to him, smiling before I let go of his hand and run over. I hear him calling to me as he chases and I laugh. I stop at the swing set and sit on the black rubber seat, kicking my legs to it begins to move. I loved the swings when I was a kid, I'd push my legs out as hard as I could to go higher. It felt like I was flying and I loved it, feeling so free with the wind in my hair. Nate is laughing as he joins me.

"The swings, really? Hallie it's raining."

I laugh softly. "I know," I reply simply and push off as he sits down on the one beside me.

I cling on to the chains either side and let my head fall back, my hair blowing around my face as the water soaks it. I turn my head, watching Nate as he pushes gently on the swing. His shoulders are hunched as he faces the ground in an attempt to keep the rain from drenching him. I on the other hand revel in it. The cold drops covering me as I push harder and swing higher. My ribs ache from the recent onslaught but I ignore it, pushing down the pain to experience the simple euphoria letting go is giving me.

"You're insane," Nate comments, his eyes watching me full of amusement.

I let my legs dangle loosely as the swing slows to a stop. Insane – yeah I'd say that was about right. I've been called a lot worse I suppose. The thought has me laughing out loud as I place my feet firmly on the now wet floor.

"I guess you have a point," I say as I stand and lean back against the frame of the swing set. Nathan stands and moves towards me and despite the cold rain, my body heats from the look in his eyes. Lust. Want. Need. My gaze follows a bead of water as it falls seductively down his face, landing on his shoulder. His black jacket blows open and I get a glimpse of his blue tee clinging to his broad chiseled frame, showcasing every line a ridge of his body. My mind dances back to our one night together, I know that body well. The way it moved, his muscles tensing as I rode him. The thought causes me to press my thighs together as I feel a familiar pressure between my hips. A slow knowing smile spreads across his face as he stops in front of me, his shoes toe to toe with mine.

"I love seeing you like this," he says as his arm reaches over my head to rest on the cold mental behind me. The movement brings him closer to me and I lose all coherent thoughts. It really isn't fair for a guy to be *this* hot.

I smirk, desperate to gain some composure and control. "What? You mean wet?"

He laughs now, and kisses the sensitive spot just below my ear. "As much as I love seeing you *wet*, that's not what I mean." He turns slightly, using his arm to gesture to the swings we've just vacated. "Over there, just then. You look so free, unguarded." He continues and I lean back, the cold rain on the mental beginning to seep through the denim of my jacket. My eyes move up to his, an uncontrollable force stopping me from looking away, from moving at all. "I see you Hallie, all of you, and I'm not going anywhere," he finishes, his words piercing my soul. Why does he always know the right things to say?

He brushes his fingers lightly over the cut above my eyebrow before pressing his lips softly to it. "I hate that someone hurt you and I can't fix it," he mumbles as he twist his finger around the dripping ends of my hair. Goose-bumps begin to pimple on my skin from the contact.

I lean in closer, letting my emotions control me as I wrap my arms gently around his neck and bring my lips to his. It doesn't take him long to react, his hands griping my hips and sparks igniting around us. My mouth parts and his tongue begins to explore, massaging softly against my own as I push my body against him, ignoring the sharp pain shooting through my ribs. I forget everything as he surrounds me, clouding the pain and sorrow with lust and want. My need for him grows rapidly and I force myself to pull away after a few short seconds. He rests his forehead against mine as we both fight for breath. My arms fall from his neck to hang loosely by my sides.

"Not everything can be fixed," I say quietly then move away from him.

We walk back to my car and I let him drive as the pain

in my ribs has increased. My body throbs with every bump in the road. I watch Nate's profile as he steers my car into the lot on campus. His eyes are focused on the road in front as he absentmindedly pushes his hand through his messy hair. I guess that's my fault, the messy part anyway. I touch my own, already knowing how difficult it's going to be to get the knots out. I don't care though, not really. I actually had fun today, more than I've had in a long time. It's just a shame it can't happen again. Not with Tami around. The rumors are out of control, at the point of physical violence. I'm finding myself questioning why I'm still here more and more every day. If I just left, Tami would get over herself. She could get her claws back into Nate because I'm not stupid enough to not know that he is the biggest reason for her strong dislike towards me. The girl is deluded. All of this is because I slept with him one time. How much worse will it be if I was to date him? For that reason alone, I know I can't. Sitting with him in that diner today I'd let myself wonder about it, wonder what it would be like. I'd be lying to myself if I said I didn't want it. I'd never wanted it before, but with Nate things are different. He sees me, I know he does, and that speaks to me in a way that is indescribable. My body is tuned in to him, I know the second he's nearby and my eyes will immediately lock onto his. Yet, I don't think that's enough. It's not enough to pull him through the gutter of lies and rumors that I face every day.

He parks up and turns to me, smiling wide and ending my negative thoughts.

"So... question time," he begins. I roll my eyes dramatically and he laughs. "I have 19 left and I do plan to use them all." He gives me a pointed look and I laugh softly.

"So, are you going to let me take you out this weekend

or will I have to hijack you in your car again to get another date?"

I smirk. "By saying another date you are implying that we have had one already, which we haven't. I think I'd remember if we had."

I climb from the car and he follows me out laughing.

"You're not an easy woman to please, are you?"

"No, I'm definitely not."

CHAPTER SIXTEEN

NATE

"I suggest you just tell him what you know, asshole. He's isn't going to let go until you do."

I nod my agreement to Rye's words in case the moron whose throat is in my hand doesn't quite understand. I know he knows something about who hurt Hallie, and he's going to tell me. This guy always knows what's going on in campus life. He's worse than the fucking girls.

"I don't know anything," he splutters.

I raise my eyebrow to Ryan who just shakes his head and then steps back. I release my grip on Harvey Carsen and take a small step back.

"So you don't know anything, huh?"

I hate being this much of a dick but people need to realize that they can't mess with my girl. It's been an entire week and so far I've managed to find out who two of the guys were, but Hallie said there were five of them. Fucking pussies. Harvey's hand flies to his throat immediately as he sucks in air. Somewhere inside me I feel bad, guilty even for doing this to him, but then I see her. I see my Hallie broken and deflated after being attacked and the anger returns. It consumes me until all I can see is red. Without thinking I rear my arm back and smash my fist straight into Harvey's jaw. The impact causes him to fall back into the metal fence and to the floor. Ryan moves in front of me and crouches down as he lifts his head up.

"Know anything now?" He asks, in his usual sarcastic nature.

My knuckles throb but I swallow it and watch as Harvey shakes off the hit, locking his eyes square with mine.

"Look all I know is that Andrew Pike and a few of the other Delta guys were huddled with QB at the welcome back party Jace Barnes threw," he shifts himself into a sitting position and shakes his head. "When they came back a few hours later, Jace practically dragged them into the Frat meeting room and he was pissed about something."

I step to him and hold my hand out, pulling him up when he reluctantly takes it. "Look, I don't know for sure if the two things are connected, but it's suspicious you know? Everyone knows QB has it in for Hallie, and with Jace's sister being Hallie's roommate it's obvious he'd be pissed about the whole thing."

I nod soberly. I had a feeling it would all connect back to that psychotic bitch. This is going to be messy to try and fix. Very messy. I fix my hardest stare on Harvey.

"We're gonna need names."

~

"So now you have the information, what are you gonna do with it? I mean, you gonna tell Hal?"

I raise my eyebrow to Ryan. "She'd kill you if she heard you calling her that."

He beams. "Nah, bro. She loves it."

"Uh huh," I chuckle. "Anyway, I dunno. I feel like I should probably leave it, you know? She's not in a great place right now. It's only been a week and she'll be pissed that I'm doing this when she asked me not to. But I can't just let them get away with it."

I shake my head in frustration. I've tried over and over again to get her to deal with this, to press charges or at least tell someone on campus but she's not interested. She just wants to forget it all and it's eating me up inside. She shouldn't let them get off so easily. "She might be okay with letting it go, but I'm not."

Ryan holds his hands up. "Hey, you know I'm with you, bro. But I think you're right. We should keep both the girls out of it. This is too close to Jace for Codie to get messed up in it," he laughs. "She'll go off the deep end if she finds out his connection."

"Yeah. We'll keep them out of it. Besides," I smirk. "Hallie's gonna be pissed enough when she sees what I left for her this morning."

"Yeah, you're getting your ass kicked."

I laugh as we climb the steps of the Business Building. She is going to be more than pissed when she finds the tickets I left for her. I've been on at her to come with me to see my cousin's band play all week. They're at a U21 club in the city and I know she'd love them, but she's just so stubborn and reluctant to be seen in public with me. So, I've bought the tickets anyway and I'm going to drag her ass in there next month whether she likes it or not. She needs to get out more. She needs to stop letting the assholes on campus stop her from living her life. I refuse to let her be ripped down by them. I can be strong enough for both of us if I have to. That reminds me, I should probably check my cell to see if she's started blowing it up with her complaints yet. Or maybe she'll wait until I get back to the dorms so she can really tear into me. She's going to absolutely hate that I've done this. It takes all the control away from her, but it's about time she relaxed the reins a little. It's for her own good. *I hope.*

I follow Rye into our business class and take my usual seat three rows back. Professor Bridge starts his usual monotone lecture, but five minutes in the door bursts open. I whip my gaze there in time to see Hallie stomp through the door. And she's mad, real fucking mad. My dick stirs at the sight, fully appreciating how hot she looks in ripped jeans, biker boots and a painfully thin band tee. Her signature leather jacket hangs loosely from her body as she stands staring holes into the faces of my classmates, the familiar tickets clutched tightly in her hand. I flick my glance to Ryan who greets me with a knowing smile. I thought she'd at least wait until after class to bitch me out about the tickets. I guess we're doing this with an audience. Awesome.

"Can I help you?" Bridge asks.

She glances at him briefly before finally finding me. Her deep amber eyes burn like fire and I have to fight back the smile that wants to split my face. *Finally*. Finally, I'm seeing something other than emptiness and hopelessness in them.

"You," she all but growls.

I sit up straight and ignore the sniggers coming from around me, specifically from my best friend.

"Hey baby, what's up?"

I didn't think it was possible, but I could swear her eyes just got darker. Meaner. Definitely hotter. She walks towards me with purpose and flings the tickets at me. I look at them and then raise my eyebrow at her as she practically vibrates with rage in front of me.

"*What's up?* I'll tell you what's up. What the fuck

is this?"

"Excuse me, miss," Bridge says, raising his voice. "But you need to leave now."

I lean around her and smile at him. "We're just having a bit of a domestic. Shouldn't take too long."

The class laughs, but not Hallie.

"They're tickets to a show, babe."

"This isn't funny, Nathan."

I love it when she uses my full name. I stand and walk around the desk to face her, leaning back and perching on the edge. I tilt my head the way I've watched her do so many times. Her eyes narrow so I know she notices.

"You'll like Badger and the guys. They're *your* kind of cool."

"I don't give a fuck," she says through gritted teeth. "Wait. What the hell is *that* supposed to mean?"

She shakes her head. "I'm not going. I told you I didn't want to go so why on earth have you bought these and then left them for me with a lame note." She pulls the small square of paper I left for her out her pocket. Oh shit. *She wouldn't...*

"Can't wait to show you off to my cousin baby," she reads, causing half the class to laugh. "Are you fucking serious with this shit?"

I force the embarrassment down. I guess Hallie and I need to have a conversation about what can be disclosed and what can't be in front of people.

"Why can't you just leave me be, huh?" She continues. "I don't wanna go out, I don't wanna meet people, and I don't want to make plans that are an entire month away."

I take the note from her before she can recite the rest of it and grip her hip, forcing her closer to me.

"Are you about done?" I ask, letting my smirk show.

Her mouth parts perfectly when she realizes what I'm about to do. I don't give her chance to stop me as I pull her against me and press my mouth to hers. She tries to pull back but I grip her tighter and soon she relents. She melts against me and allows my tongue entrance to taste her. Her lips are soft as we move together in a rhythm only we understand. Cheers erupt around us, but I barely register it. When she's here with me like this, it's like no one else exists. It's just us, no matter how much that makes me sound like a chick. All too soon she's pulling away from me and resting her forehead against mine.

"People are watching," she whispers.

"All I see is you."

The corner of her mouth twitches, a tell she has when she's fighting a smile. Pride and straight up fucking joy fills me. I've missed her smile over the past week. She has such a perfect smile.

"You're an idiot," she says, then pulls away from me. "Why do they call him Badger?"

It takes me a moment to gage what the hell she's talking about. I'll never get used to the way this girls mind works. I think back, trying to remember where the ridiculous nickname for my cousin came from but come up empty. His real name is Kai but I've always known him as Badger. Since forever.

"I really don't know," I answer.

She shakes her head. "Weird. Okay, I'm out."

I wait until she reaches the door before I call out to her. "Can't wait to see you later, baby."

She turns, and smirks. "Yeah? You can *see* yourself later."

The people around me laugh and mock as she exits but all I do is laugh along. My girl is fucking amazing.

CHAPTER SEVENTEEN

Hallie

"Hallie you look amazing!"

I smile nervously at Codie. God, why am I doing this? I should absolutely not be doing this. I tug nervously at the navy dress my roommate has forced me into. I shrug into the black blazer she holds out for me and push my feet into the black ankle boots on the floor by my bed.

"I feel stupid," I sulk and she rolls her eyes.

I've been dead set against going on this date with Nate. I never date. *Ever*. He won't stand for it though, and even enlisted Codie's help in getting me to agree. I didn't even know where we are going but Codie knows, hence why she's dressed me tonight. A knock at the door causes her to squeal in excitement and me to groan out loud as she dashes out of my room to answer it. I look in the mirror for the hundredth time in the past twenty minutes and smooth down an invisible strand of hair. What the hell am I doing? It's just a stupid date. I can do this. I square my shoulders and take a deep breath before walking out and into the lounge area where I can hear Codie talking animatedly with Nate. They don't notice me straight away and I take the time to check him out. He's dressed in dark fitted jeans with black chucks and a black dress shirt under a grey sweater. He looks panty melting hot and I shift uncomfortably as his green eyes find me. *I can do this.* He's silent for a moment, his mouth hanging a little, before jumping up from the couch and walking over to me. My body heats, the way it only does when he's around, as he takes my hand and pulls me close.

"You look beautiful," he whispers into my ear, his breath hot on my neck. I wonder if we can skip dinner and just go back to my room. No? *Damn.*

I push my sultry thoughts aside and let Nate lead me out the door, waving goodbye to an over excitable Codie. Nerves radiate through me as we make our way down the stairs. There are solid reasons why I don't date, one of them being this nervous crappy feeling. There is no need for it, this is just Nate. I spent almost every day with him since he found me walking back from being attacked. The thought causes my hand to touch where I'd been cut above my eyebrow. The skin is still tender, but luckily the bruising on the rest of my body has begun to fade. Not here though. The small cut above my eye is still noticeable to everyone.

I've made Nate wait two weeks before taking me out. I wanted my injuries to be less painful so I could move more freely, you know, in case I need to run away. And honestly, after the shit he pulled with the band tickets and his inappropriate PDA in class, the need to run is already there. It doesn't help that Nate has been holding out on me, refusing to move past making out until everything is better. The guy is hot, painfully so, and my body is hard-wired to his. When I'm with him, I'm aware of his every movement. When I'm not with him, my eyes find him immediately. I feel him before I see him, it's unexplainable and I need that connection between us. It's how I know everything's alright. It's the only thing I know how to do properly.

Tami and her equally bitchy followers stand by the entrance watching as we approach. Nate takes my hand and squeezes it as she steps in front of the door, blocking our exit.

"Hallie Clarke."

I groan inside. I really don't want to deal with her right now.

"Great, you know my name. Now how about you choke on it," I snap at her as her eyes burn holes into where Nate's hand clings to mine.

She's been a complete nightmare since word spread that I'm dating Nate. It's pathetic and I've almost had my fill of it. The taunts and rumors around campus are becoming too much. Everywhere I go people whisper comments in my wake about the multiple men I'm sleeping with, not to mention the professor I'm apparently hooking up with too. The idea leaves a sour taste in my mouth and renders me awkward whenever I have his class. Even Adam the Friendly Psychopath now avoids me in our English class, apparently believing that I am in fact having some illicit affair with Professor Cooper. The very thought is laughable. Luckily Cooper doesn't shun me; he still helps with my assignments and actually offered me good advice on handling everything. I turn my attention back to the creator of all these rumors.

"Tami get out the fucking way," Nate says, his voice laced with boredom and exasperation.

"Well you move on fast, Hallie, don't you? Poor Mr Cooper. And oh no, what happened to your face? Did you fall? That's so clumsy. You should be more careful," she smirks and the fist of my free hand clenches. God I'd love to smack that look right off her smug preppy face.

"Bite me."

I pull my hand from Nate's and push past her, not caring one single bit if I hurt her. Actually I kind of hope I did. I also kind of want to go back out there and make sure I did. I don't. Instead I ignore the fiery looks aimed at the back of my head and march over to Nate's truck, throw the passenger door open and climb in. He moves in beside me and looks over with an amused stare. I turn to face him and can't help the short laugh that leaves my mouth. Nate has been witness to more than one of my interactions with Tami, much to her distaste.

"Well now that you've had your daily dose of Tami, shall we go?" He asks from beside me, barely containing his laughter. I roll my eyes then nod as he pulls out of the lot.

Twenty minutes later he's parking up outside a small, secluded bistro. Light shimmers through the red veils covering the windows, inviting me inside. I watch as a middle aged couple leave the building, his arm around her as he steers them both over to a black Mercedes. A fur coat drips seductively from her arms and she laughs full heartedly at something her companion whispers in her ear. He brings his face close to hers, a knowing smile tugging at his lips as his hand cups the side of her face. I smile to myself at the sight of them. They look so happy; it's hard not to let their bliss ignite hope in myself, hope that I could be her one day.

The door opens beside me and I jump, startled. My head whips around, coming face to face with Nate causing him to smirk at my obvious fright as he holds his hand out to me. I take it, ignoring his smug look, and climb out the car whilst trying my hardest to appear graceful in the dress I'm wearing. He links his fingers with mine, my mouth parting in a silent gasp at the electricity of the contact, and together we walk inside.

The smell of smoking grills hits me instantly, my stomach stirring in appreciation as Nate asks for our reservation. A waiter shows us to a small table at the back of the restaurant, cream fabric draped across it. Red candles light the center and I try not to gape as the leather backed chair is held out for me. I sit carefully and smile small when a menu is handed to me. My eyes widen at the price of everything in here causing me to recite a silent prayer that I've saved up so much cash. I'm going to need it if these are the kind of places Nate likes. I watch him as he talks to the waiter, completely at ease with the formal surroundings in here. I know he has money, comes from wealth, but I don't know much about his family. He mentioned his father a couple of times, and I think they're close, but he's never delved into his family history, not that I can comment on that. This guy knows next to nothing about me. That's probably a good thing.

He turns to me when the waiter leaves and smiles wide.

"Well, Hallie, as this is our first *official* date I think we should do it properly. So, hit me with your best small talk."

I raise my eyebrow as the amusement grows on his face. He knows I'm not good with small talk, or talking in general. We had a conversation about this very subject two nights ago! I think back to it.

"You know, for some reason people seem to think you're not a big talker," Nate says, his face completely serious.

I laugh a couple of notes, noticing the sarcasm for what it is.

"Really? How strange," I muse then throw in a sly wink for good measure. "So do I conform and go with the standard

red UM jersey, or dare I brave wearing this blue shirt?" I ask showing the clothing in question.

He snorts. "Hallie Clarke conform? Has hell frozen over?"

"As always, you make a very good point Mister Harris," I laugh and toss the jersey back into my wardrobe. "So why are you questioning my conversational skills?" I turn to face him as he sits on my bed, his long frame covering it.

Nate leans forward and pulls me to him, kissing at my stomach as I stand before him in just jeans and a bra. The touch sends heat down my body I sigh inside. Maybe he'll finally let me have him. As soon as the thought enters my mind he pulls back and again leans against the wall. I stifle a groan.

"Well, I'm just curious about you, baby. You really are pretty quiet, but not shy."

I laugh, "Is this one of your questions?" We've been playing our silly game constantly over the past few days since I took him to Dexter. So far he has 11 questions remaining and I still have 17. He's asked light things, like my favorite color and favorite band whereas I've asked him things about what he wanted for the future and why he is so convinced we are meant for each other.

"Definitely. So, Miss Clarke, tell me. Why don't you talk much?" The cute smile on his face is almost impossible to ignore so I distract my thoughts with pulling my shirt on.

I shrug, "I don't have a lot to say."

Nate laughs then makes an obnoxious buzzer sound before telling me that he doesn't accept that answer. This is something else he's started doing. Whenever I give him vague responses he drags a longer explanation out of me. It's both sweet and annoying at the same time.

"Alright, alright. I don't know really. I never really had a

lot of friends or whatever so never really needed to have long meaningful conversations with people. I guess now I'm just used to not having to talk a whole lot. I don't really know how to small talk," I laugh.

He stands and wraps his arms around my waist. "I'm gonna teach you."

"Earth to Hallie."

I look up, snapping out of my flashback and smile at the memory.

"Sorry, totally spaced. Small talk... right," I say and laugh under my breath. "You were supposed to teach me how."

Nate laughs now, the almost dreamy look on his face telling me he's re living the same memory.

"We're gonna learn on the job." I swallow hard as he continues. "So, baby, what's your star sign?"

I laugh out loud at the purring quality to his voice. *Seriously?*

"You're an idiot." His only response is a shit eating grin.

The waiter returns a few minutes later and we order our food. We spend the next few hours eating and talking. Nate has decided that during our date, the question game is halted so he's using his free pass to ask me as much as he can. He tells me about his family, how he hasn't seen his mom since he was 6 and how his dad owned a law firm with Ryan's dad back in New York. I ask about Ryan and what he was like when he was younger and Nate laughs, telling me he has always been the same.

"What about you, Hallie. What's your family like?" Nate asks when he finishes telling me a story about his dad having to apologize to a nanny he had hired to take care of 8 year old Nate. Apparently, this certain 8 year old spent an entire day jumping out from behind doors and scaring her.

I laugh. My family...

"Well, my mom raised me on her own. And my dad, um, my dad and I have a difficult relationship," I offer. Nate smiles reassuringly and gestures for me to elaborate. I sigh, "We don't really gel. Clashing personalities maybe? I don't know. He's formal, stiff and focused far too much on his image whereas I don't care. The rumors about me back home hit him hard I guess, and we've never really come back from that."

Nate reaches across the table and takes my hand softly, his eyes staying fixed on mine.

"How about your mom?"

I smile. My mother is useless, but I love her because of it. She never tries to be anything else and when I was growing up, she'd always be there in her own messed up way. We just lost our way, that's all.

"We were close when I was a kid but as I got older she began dating more and became less active in my life. She's there but not at the same time. I guess the best word to describe her is flakey," I laugh. "I get my interest in music from her. She used to play these really old records and make me dance around the living room with her. She was the one who bought me my beat up old guitar."

"She sounds great. My dad was always too busy with work or women half his age to do anything like that with me," Nate says and his face drops momentarily. His usual smile is back within a second though, making me question if I actually saw his face change at all. "Hey, I've just had an idea. My dad is coming up here next month and I want you to meet him."

My eyes widen. *Is he crazy?* "Nate, I don't think that's a good idea. I mean come on, you told him my name right?"

He nods so I continue, "Which means he's probably searched and found that page..."

I watch him tense. We don't talk about the rumors or the Facebook page much because it makes him mad and makes me close off. It doesn't mean it isn't there though. The more people see me with Nate, the nastier the lies seem to get. Nate is constantly telling me he doesn't care but I know deep down it's only a matter of time before he will. Rumors are vicious and can rip apart anything good. I know that first hand.

"That Facebook page is bullshit and you know it. In fact, my dad can probably help with it. I bet he can get an order to close it down you know," Nate suggests and I shake my head.

There's no point in fighting it, they'll just find new ways to taunt me. At least with it being online, I don't have to see it. I'm not connected on Facebook and couldn't care less what they write. I haven't even looked at it since the first time. I also haven't spoken to my dad since that day. Sensing my unease, Nate drops the subject and moves on to ask about other things which include the shelters I help at. By the time he drives us back, it's late and my eyes are beginning to feel heavy. I yawn as he opens the door for me which causes him the chuckle. I glare at him playfully and together we walk into the building. His arm snakes around my waist at the top of the stairs as he halts me. I turn and look up at him, his eyes burning into mine.

"Nate what are you look-"

I don't get to finish my sentence as his lips crash onto mine, kissing me hard. His hands grip my hips as he forces my back against the wall. I moan into his mouth as my desire for him rises and he takes the opportunity to slide his tongue in.

How does he do this? How does he fill me with so much need so fast?

We kiss full of passion, clinging on to each other with our mouths dancing in a rhythm only we understand. Seconds turn to minutes and too soon it's over and Nate is walking me the rest of the way to my door. He watches as I pull the keys from my purse and I turn to stare at him.

"What are you waiting for?"

He laughs, "For you to go inside."

"Why?"

"So I know you've got home safe, obviously."

I smirk. "What if I wanted to watch you get home safe?"

"Do you?"

I smile wide. "You bet, go on."

He laughs a little then when he sees I'm not about to move he shakes his head and walks to his door. He opens it then looks over and salutes before walking in. I laugh a little then sigh as I put my keys in the door, not prepared in the slightest for what greets me on the other side.

I close the door quickly and back step until I hit the wall opposite the front door. Oh God, I can never un-see that. Please let them have not noticed me. That is not a conversation I want to have with either of them. I shudder. What now? My eyes flick to the door that Nate has just walked through. Should I? I mean we *are* dating so surely letting your girlfriend stay over because she just caught her roommate being bent over the couch is in the rules, right?

I take a deep breath and walk over, knocking on quietly before I lose my nerve.

"Well well well, Miss Clarke. Can't get enough I see," Nate smirks, his now bare chest sending ripples through my body.

Why is the man always topless? Doesn't he realize what

he's doing to me? My libido screams for me to take charge, to show him just how ready I am but I push it down.

"Hilarious," I say sarcastically. "Your friend has my roommate in a position I'd rather not disturb."

His eyes widen as he pulls his lips inside, an attempt to stop from laughing.

"I'm serious, pal," I scold.

His obvious amusement causes the corners of my own mouth to twitch as I try to keep from laughing. Damn it.

"Stop it! It isn't funny," I moan.

His strength breaks and a loud laughs erupts from his mouth.

"It is a little funny," he comments a few seconds later when he's calmed down.

"Maybe. So, you gonna let me in or what?"

He pushes the door open wider and I brush past his unmoving body and into the dorm. I stroll over to the couch and sit down as he closes the door.

"Why are you sitting there? It's bed time," he asks.

"I know. You got a blanket?"

He looks at me confused, his eyes darting from the couch to me. I know what he's thinking. He's wondering why I'm not just going to stay with him. But that just isn't something I do. Then again, dating isn't something I usually do either but here we are. Still, I'm not sure I can lie next to him all night when he isn't going to touch me. The frustration may just kill me.

"You're sleeping with me," he says finally.

I let out a long breath. "No I'm not. I'll be fine here on the couch."

"Hallie." His eyes touch the ceiling briefly before coming back to me. "You're not sleeping on my couch. Come on, bed."

His hand reaches and grasps my own then he pulls me from the sofa, practically dragging me to his bedroom. He closes the door behind us and then finally releases my hand. I watch him as he rifles through a drawer, my mind dancing over the memory of the things he did to me on them. *Oh boy.* I chew on my lip to stop from speaking my sultry thoughts aloud. After a few seconds, Nate throws a t-shirt at me and tells me to put it on. I smirk at it, the thought is almost too cheesy and cliché to bear. He questions my look but I just shake my head and kick off my shoes and drop my purse. I excuse myself to the bathroom.

Chapter Eighteen

Nate

My dick twitches at the sight of her when she walks back through the door.

There is definitely something about a girl wearing your shirt that does things to a guy, especially when that girl is Hallie Clarke. I've been dying to have her, to hear her moaning my name, but worried she'd take off again. It's the reason I haven't touched her since we started dating. That's not the excuse I give her though. I've made out I'm worried about hurting her. The injuries she got when she was assaulted are still faintly visible, so it's not exactly a lie. I really don't want to hurt her. I know who attacked her that night. I have all their names, every last one, but I'm keeping the information to myself. Hallie isn't the type of girl that dwells on things like that, she won't want me 'defending' her. She just wants to forget it all, move on from it. Doesn't care one bit that they are getting away with assault. The damn girl is too independent and too stubborn. I will defend her though, she just won't know about it. All five of them will get their punishment and Hallie will get her

. Somehow. She is *my* girl, and no one has the right to her in any way.

I watch her now as she pulls a small black hair tie from her purse. Her arms reach up as she pulls her hair back, my shirt rising up her legs, teasing me and causing my dick to strain against the rough fabric of my jeans. Damn, the girl is crazy hot! It is definitely taking every single ounce of self-restraint I have not to pull her down on the bed and have my way. But I need to know she'll stay, I need to know she wants all of me even if that makes me sound like a chick. I push down my jeans and climb into bed before she notices the boner I'm now sporting, motioning for her to join me. She hesitates a little, an inner battle visible on her face. I know this was new to her, I know she isn't used to having a boyfriend, but she is getting better. Hell, I finally got her to come out with me tonight. I've never had to try this hard for a girl. She's worth it though, I'm sure. Eventually she slides into the bed next to me and I pull the comforter over us both.

"You're going to stay here all night, right?" I ask.

She's quiet for a second before replying with a soft nod. I let my body relax and rest my hand on her hip. Her tiny frame molds perfectly to mine, her back plush against my chest. Her ass moves against my crotch so I push my hips back, not wanting her to feel the activity happening in my boxer shorts.

She lets out a long breath before speaking, her voice as soft as silk. "Can I ask you something?"

"Of course."

She waits a beat, then spins so she's facing me. She stares at me carefully and I just know that if it wasn't for the way she was lay, her head would be tilting in concentration.

The thought causes a smile. Only with Hallie have I ever noticed the little things about a girl.

"So, what do you want to ask? By the way, this takes you down to 16," I say.

"It's still better than your 11. You're running out buddy," she laughs then turns so she's facing the ceiling, her back flat on the mattress. "Nate," she starts and I pull my eyes away from where they'd lingered to her breasts. She really does have great tits. "Is there any particular reason that you won't fuck me?"

A laugh bursts from me but after one look at her unimpressed face, I'm in silence.

"I'm serious, Nate. You haven't touched me since we started dating. I'm not sure how I feel about that," she says. Her voice falls a little and she pulls her arm over her face to cover it. "I mean, if you don't find me attractive, then why are we even doing this?"

Oh. She's serious. Is that what she thinks? I have to fix this.

I sit up slightly and lean on my elbow so I'm looking down at her. Her arm is still over her eyes but I know she can sense me watching by the way her body reacts, her thighs pressing together as I run my free hand softly up her leg and under the hem of the shirt. I lean in close to her, whispering into her ear.

"I find you more than attractive, baby." My hand cups her breasts. "It's taking everything I have to not sink myself inside you."

Her breath hitches, a small gasp escaping from her lips. I rub my thumb over the thin lace of her bra, her nipple hardening through the material instantly.

"Why?"

I smile small, my hand traveling back down her legs.

"Because..." I let my finger brush gently between them, her arousal evident. "...Last time, I woke up and you were gone."

Her breathing stills and I rest my hand on her hip, my thumb hooked into the edge of her panties. She slowly removes her arm from over her face and sits up, forcing me up with her. She rises to her knees and places a hand softly on my cheek. Her eyes glisten as they search mine before she leans in and places a chaste kiss on my lips. The gesture is sweet and so *not* like Hallie that it leaves me momentarily speechless. Not that it matters as she speaks before I can regain composure.

"I'm not going anywhere."

Still unable to form words, I do the only thing I can think of. I kiss her. Not sweetly, and definitely not chaste. I command her mouth, pushing my tongue inside as she moans around it. With all self-restraint gone, I pull her so she's straddling me. My cock strains beneath her and I grip her hips, pushing them down so I know she feels me.

"This is what you do to me," I say against her lips. "Every. Fucking. Time."

Her teeth clamp down on her bottom lip causing me to groan. Fuck, she's hot. I push her back, climbing on top of her so my body dominates hers. I tease her with my fingers, rubbing over her clit through the thin lace of her panties. Her wet response is glorious as she begins to shift beneath me.

"Do you want me, Hallie?" I ask as my lips graze at her neck. Her response is a slow nod. I nip at her ear, my fingers moving her panties to the side.

"Say it," I demand.

"Yes," she gasps as I push my finger inside her. Her

voice is almost a moan and the sound makes me harder than ever.

"Tell me you'll stay with me."

I quicken my pace with my finger, my thumb pushing on the nub of her clit. Her back arches and I know she's close.

"Tell me," I repeat.

"I'll stay."

I commandeer her mouth again, kissing her hard. She gives it to me back with equaling want and need. Her hips push against my hand and my dick pulses, desperate to feel her. I withdraw my finger, reaching over to pull a foil packet from the drawer beside the bed.

"Take your panties off," I order as I remove my boxer shorts and roll on the condom. She does and I smile at her obedience. She has no idea what that does to me. She pulls at the hem of her shirt but I stop her.

"Leave that on. I like you wearing my clothes."

I don't give her time to answer. Instead I grip both of her wrists with my hand, forcing them above her head as I hold them against the mattress. She squirms below me, her hips bucking. I pull her legs further apart and move so the tip of my length is sitting at her entrance.

"Nathan please," she begs, her voice rasp with lust. "I need you."

I groan and push inside her, her tight walls welcoming me. This is where I want to stay, with her, always. Her labored breath comes in pants as I thrust, turning me on more and more. Her eyes are closed, her neck exposed so I take full advantage and press my mouth against it. She moans as I suck at the little spot just behind her ear where I know she likes it. I can feel her getting closer to climax, feel her tightening around me. I can barely hold on myself. Her hands fight to get free so I release them, groaning when they go straight to my back. Her nails dig in, causing me to pump into harder. I rear back, demanding her to open her eyes and lock my own with them. I could get lost in the deep embers, searching forever for what she hides behind the impassive look she always has.

"Give it to me, Hallie," I growl when I can no longer hold on.

She does. Exploding around me, calling my name and milking me for everything I have. I collapse beside her, pulling off the condom and disposing of it in the trash. She lays still, staring up at the ceiling with a blank look on her face. For a second I worry that she's about to get up and leave but instead she surprises me for the second time that night. She turns, rests her head on my chest and her arm across my stomach. I pull the comforter over us and wrap my arm around her. She sighs softly, her fingers tracing the small stars I have tattooed across my hips.

"Goodnight, Nate," she says quietly.

I smile. "Goodnight, baby."

CHAPTER NINETEEN

NATE

She's beautiful. Stunning actually, and she has absolutely no idea. I watch her now as she mindlessly fingers the strings of her guitar whilst holding a conversation with Codie. I don't even think she realizes that she's doing that. It's an automatic reaction whenever she's close to her instrument. She has to touch it, feel it. I can understand that. I feel exactly the same way about her. As if on cue, her eyes catch mine. A rare smile touches her lips before she turns her attention back to Codie's rambling. I chuckle inside. Hallie still isn't one hundred percent, so we've all piled into the girl's dorm suite and ordered far too much pizza. My Saturday nights suck without her anyway.

She tried to force us all to go out without her tonight. There's a big party just off campus but none of us are interested, especially considering all the assholes that I know will be there. I'm still holding onto information that a part of me wishes I didn't have. I'm still trying to figure out what I'm going to do with it. Do I go to the cops? Do I deal with it myself? All I know is that I can't let her discover that I know. I promised her I'd let it go, but there isn't a chance that's gonna happen. She has to understand that. There is never going to be a point where I think it's okay for people to hurt her, and I'm never going to be okay with them getting away with it if they do.

I glance back to Hallie as she tries and fails to hide her amusement at Codie and Ryan arguing. She'll never admit it, but I can tell she's happy we're all here. It's amazing to watch her with people, with *our* people. Outside of the four of us, she's a different person. She's closed, unwilling to accept anyone else. She hides behind a wall built so high, that it's almost impossible to climb over. But we did. Hell, I'm all but bulldozing my way through and taking Codie and Ryan with me for the ride. She needs us, even though she the strongest person I know.

With one last look in her direction, I jump up from the floor and head to the kitchen area. I laugh as they all start shouting their drink orders to me.

"I'll get you two one," I say, pointing to Hallie and Codie. I turn my eyes on Ryan. "But you can fuck yourself, bro."

"Bro!" He protests, then laughs and stroll over to join me. He claps me on the back then says in a low voice, "What's with the frown, big guy?"

I fix him with an annoyed look, but he shrugs it off. I shouldn't expect anything less. This is Ryan. He doesn't care what he says, and seriously lacks a brain to mouth filter. It's what gets him in so much trouble.

"I can't let this shit go with the guys that hurt Hallie," I answer, making sure to keep voice quiet enough to not be heard. "I don't know what to do. I wanna tear their fucking heads off."

Rye nods. "Yeah, me too man. But you gotta be smart here. If Hallie finds out what you're doing, she'll flip," he passes me two sodas from the fridge for the girls. "And you can't keep threatening half of campus. It'll get back to her eventually. Let me talk to some guys I know, yeah?"

I exhale heavily. I should have known Ryan would have people in his back pocket. It's just the way he is. Always a man with a plan. Relenting, I nod my agreement and we head back to the living room. I drop myself onto the floor beside Hallie, letting my hand touch her knee. She still from the contact, only for a second, then relaxes into it.

Progress.

"So," Ryan starts, his eyes on Hallie. "Are you going to actually play something we know?"

She laughs, reaching for a slice of pizza. "Your taste in music is pathetic. There is nothing I can play that you will know."

He mocks pain at her. "That's harsh, Hal."

All she does is raise her eyebrow in reply.

"Oh I know!" Codie interjects, almost knocking the soda out of Ryan's hand. "What's that band with the guy from School of Rock in? Shit. What's his name?"

"Jack Black?" Rye offers.

"Yes!"

"Tenacious D?" Hallie laughs. "You want me to play Tenacious D?"

Ryan is practically jumping up and down in excitement whilst I sit here in my usual confusion whenever the topic of music comes up.

"Who the fuck are Tenacious D?" I ask.

I'm met with three faces of disbelief. I can only offer them a shrug. Music isn't my thing. At all. It's why I'm dragging Hallie to see my cousin's band play next week. He's been on at me to go see them play for years, but I haven't really had any interest. I know Hallie will though, even if she's refusing to admit that.

"That settles it," Ryan says. "You have to play. His ass needs educating."

He beams. "Can you do Hard Fucking?"

What the...? Is he asking my girlfriend if she can fuck hard? When I'm sat right fucking here? I narrow my eyes at him. He laughs in my face.

"Calm down, Bruce Banner. It's the title of the song."

Hallie chuckles, shaking her head slightly, and begins to strum her guitar in a long slow tune. Her voice follows it, smooth as silk over the notes. We all stare in shock. Hallie playing the guitar isn't anything new, but Hallie singing definitely is. She's incredible. I listen in to every word, despite it being probably the most offensive song I've ever heard. It doesn't matter though. All that matters is the way her voice carries over the tune like silk.

Too soon, Ryan ruins the whole thing by joining in, followed by Codie.

The rest of the night is spent mostly the same way - the four of us screwing around on the living room floor of the dorm. It's after midnight when Codie and Ryan slink off to her bedroom.

I stay on the floor with Hallie, pulling her over to straddle me. She laughs a little and tries to escape but I hold her tight. I need to feel her, be with her. It's crazy, and terrifying, but she's fast becoming my most favorite thing on this planet. I'm in way too deep with her, I know this, but I'm not drowning. I'm letting it consume me, letting *her* consume me. She looks down on me now, her eyes bright and happy for once, and just like that I feel it. I feel the fall. It's not a light, gentle float. It's a hard hitting, in your face free fall from a mountain.

I'm falling in love with Hallie Clarke.

"What are you looking all serious about?" She asks.

I smile, shaking the thoughts away. She's not ready. Hell, I'm not ready. "Just about you."

"What about me?"

"Just how I want to know everything about you."

She exhales a long breath. "Ask me anything."

So she's in a sharing mood? Perfect. "And you'll answer properly?"

She laughs at my stern look and then hold three fingers up. "Scouts honor."

I smirk. "You were never a scout."

"No, not even close," she laughs. "But go on. I'm an open book."

"Uh huh. Sure you are," I roll my eyes dramatically. "Tell me something I don't already know."

"I hate the color green."

I snort a laugh. "That's deep. Now try again."

She sighs, but it's not in exasperation for once. "When I was sixteen, I ran away from home."

My eyebrows shoot upwards. "Really?"

"Yeah. Not for long, mind. I stayed two nights at this shelter I used to help out at."

"Shit. What did your folks say?"

"You're kidding, right?" She laughs. "When I went home, my mom asked how my school field trip was."

Ouch. "Wow... I thought you and your mom were close?"

"We were, but not so much now. She discovered dating,

and my mom is a free spirit. A hippie, basically. She barely knows what day of the week it is. Besides, I hit high school and didn't want to be best friends with my mom anymore," she laughs. "Because that would be lame."

"Babe," I whisper. "You are lame."

"Oh!" She hits me on the shoulder. "Thanks for that."

I laugh as I rub my thumbs across the bare skin of her hips where her shirt has risen. She wriggles from the action. "Ticklish?"

Her eyes widen. "Don't do it."

I smirk. "Do what?"

"I swear to Go-"

Her words become laughter when I suddenly push her back and begin to tickle her on the floor. She tries to wriggle free from me but I'm relentless, loving that I'm witnessing this rare, care-free version of Hallie. Her laughter is like music to my ears, making me want to record it so my creep-ass can listen to it over and over again.

"Nathan, please," she begs, changing the mood drastically with that plea.

There's just something about the way she begs that gets me all hot and horny. Hell, I'm practically walking a fine line of surprise erection avoidance whenever she's around as it is, but when she says my name like that. Like it's a promise that's just for me. I just can't. I stop my torture and move my hands up to brush the hair from her face. She stills, the brandy of her eyes darkening with lust and obvious want. My body is covering hers almost completely so I know she can feel my dick, can feel what she does to me, what she always does to me. The inches between us suddenly fill with anticipation and need, the air around us sizzling under our heat. She runs her hand up my body, letting it slide under my shirt and over the ridges of my stomach. Every cell inside me ignites, a fire that burns only for her.

"Why do you look at me like that?" She whispers.

"Like what?"

"Like I'm the only girl in the world."

"To me, Hallie, you *are* the only girl in the world."

CHAPTER TWENTY

Hallie

It's filthy, smoky and littered with emo-rockstar wannabes.

I love it.

I don't tell Nate that though. I'm more than willing to let him believe I'm still mad that he's dragged me here against my will. I can't give him everything.

"Are you smiling?"

I turn to him wide eyed, sucking my lips into my mouth to hide the tiny smile he's caught. "What? No," I clear my throat. "Don't be ridiculous."

"You are!" He laughs and I fight the urge to kill him on the spot. "You love it here already."

"Shut up. *If* I am smiling, which I'm not, then it's in protest."

I pull my hand from his and head over to the bar. He follows me, but I pretend to ignore him as his amusement is practically smacking me in the face. I absolutely refuse to give him anything here. Not happening. I have principles, and he should respect them, even if they are a bit ridiculous.

Nate places his hand on the small of my back and leans over the bar to order us both a bottle of water each. He presses his body completely against mine in an obvious attempt to disarm my thoughts. It works, and for a few short seconds I forget who the hell I am. I forget everything but the feel of him, the way his hand stays possessively on my back. He pulls away and I miss him immediately. *Get a grip, girl,* I scold myself, frowning a little. When did I get so pathetic over this guy? When did I get so *emotional?*

I thank him and then turn to face the crowd that has gathered, putting some much needed distance between myself and Nate. I have to get a hold on my feelings. Every day I spend with him, I feel my need for him run even deeper. With every lingered stare across campus, every instinctive touch because we can't stop ourselves, every surprise fucking latte just because he's thinking about me, one of my carefully guarded ice bricks crumbles to the ground. It's unnerving as much as it's thrilling, and I haven't got any idea how to stop it. *It's too fast,* my subconscious whispers, but my heart is in direct disagreement. My heart wants me to jump in two feet first and to hell with the consequences. My heart is obviously having a meltdown.

I sneak a glance at Nate as he watches the people around us. He really is beautiful, which is a pussy word for a guy, but somehow it just fits for him. It should be illegal for someone to be as hot as he is. As if sensing my look, he moves his head to face me and offers me a wink before turning back. *Buh-dum.* My heart beats just for him and the realization of that is suffocating. There is every possible chance that I could fall for Nathan Harris. There is even more chance that I already have.

The thought knocks the wind from my lungs but I somehow manage to keep it together on the outside. It takes everything I have to squash down my feelings, but I'm not ready to analyze them right now. *Or ever*. He reaches for my hand, linking his fingers through mine. I let him, but don't move my focus from the club.

It's not overly packed in here, but all the tables are taken, with a few wannabe groupies lining the worn-out stage. They scream as an obvious heavy metal band take the stage. I turn to face Nate with a raised eyebrow, shutting out all my inner emotional ramblings. He laughs and shakes his head, answering the silent question on whether that's his cousin or not.

The lead singer roars down the mic as he rips his shirt off, revealing a heavily tattooed torso which could do with a burger or two. The girls up front don't seem to mind his lanky physique as they squeal anyway. Gross. The music starts heavy and loud, a thick drumming polluting the space. I wince at the harshness of the electric guitars, forcing back the urge to go up there and confiscate them. They obviously aren't ready.

I like all music, but I'm not sure this comes under that category. All I'm hearing is noise.

I turn to Nate and lean in close to his ear so he can hear me.

"What time is your cousin's badger band on?"

He chuckles into my neck, snaking his arm around my waist and pulling me close. "Badger band. Really?" I nod as he smiles. "After these I think."

"These are awful," I laugh and then motion towards the crowd. "Why are they screaming for them?"

"Girls scream for anything."

I push him playfully and he flashes me his perfect smile that makes me want to drag him into the bathrooms and do unspeakable things. Woah. I *really* need to get my emotions in check. In my own defense, he looks all kinds of hot in his low riding jeans, tight shirt and hooded jacket. *Is he trying to kill me?* I almost died when he picked me up and I saw him. I feel a little inadequate in my skinnies and old Beatles shirt, but I'm not about to dress up fancy for a band gig. Besides, this is my comfort zone. He's in my world now and that thought pleases me greatly.

We're interrupted when a guy cruises over to us, clapping Nate on the back. He's a direct contrast to Nate, sporting crazy tight jeans and a loose hanging vest. His hair falls over his eyes in a side fringe that would make Justin Bieber weep, which I notice he constantly brushes back as he talks animatedly. They both turn to me a few minutes later and I'm pulled into a hug.

"Hey, I'm Badger," he says into my ear. "But feel free to call me Kai."

He releases me and I smile, more nervously than I'm willing to admit and a little uncomfortable at the impromptu hug. "Hey, I'm Hallie."

He smiles wide and then ushers us through a door to the right of the bar. Nate takes my hand and somewhere inside I breathe a hard sigh of relief as we're lead down a long corridor and into a dusty room. I don't care if I'm being clingy, I do not trust wherever the hell we are. I look around the room; curious faces look back.

"Can actually hear in here," Kai/Badge says. "Blood Sugar are insane."

He shakes his head. "Come on, meet the rest of the guys."

Nate walks further into the room and begins to do that guy handshake pat on the back sort of thing with the other band members. I stand and watch the interaction from the safety of doorway.

A wave on envy falls over me when I see how easily it is for Nate to just converse with people he doesn't know. I wish i could be that way. I wish I could loosen the shackles on my personality long enough to meet new people. That's not how the world works though, not my world anyway. Letting people see you only gives them ammunition to destroy you.

"Babe!"

Nate's voice pulls me out of my head. He's sitting on a sofa and beckoning me to come over. I walk slowly, raising my eyebrow when he pats his knee. He shakes his head in response, laughing quietly. It's about time he realized I was never going to be the girl who fawns all over it, despite the way my hormones want me to rub against his leg. I drop myself onto a lone chair between the sofa and an arm chair, then turn my attention in the direction of Kai as he begins to speak.

"Hallie, this is the band, Charcoal Dreams," he points to them all one by one. "That's Tyke. He's our lead singer. Cole plays bass. And that miserable fucker tryin' to work out how to play the guitar is Juice. He's supposed to be our lead guitarist."

Kai laughs as Juice looks up and glares. "Fuck you, man," he strums and I wince from the sound. "One of you fucks have been screwing with it."

Cole coughs. "Juice has a bit of an issue with paranoia." When the guy in question growls in response, Cole adds, "and aggression."

He offers me a two fingered wave. "It's awesome to meet you. I knew Nate back in middle school."

I nod. "Yeah, you too."

The sounds of Juice's playing cuts me off and causes me to wince again. Fuck me. So this guy is obviously an asshole. I look at Nate and try not to groan when he gives me the "leave it alone" look. He knows I want to tell this moron off, and fix his damn guitar, too.

"Juice!" Tyke shouts. "You need to get that shit sorted before we go on in twenty. Not even my voice will drown out how awful you sound."

He turns to me. "Hey Hallie, nice to have you here," his gaze drags over my body then flicks to Nate. "You're one lucky bastard that's for sure."

Nate laughs. "You got that right."

Juice strums his guitar again and the sound gyrates my eardrums. I cringe. *That's it.*

"Hey asshole," I say, fixing my eyes on him. "You got your strings too tight."

His eyes widen. "Are you talking to me?"

I roll my own in response then stand from my seat and walk over to him, snatching the poor instrument from his hands.

"Hey, what are you doing?" He protests.

"Oh quit being a baby. I'm gonna fix it for you so you can stop your whining."

I twist at the blocks holding the strings, loosening them just enough to be able to re-tune. When I'm happy with it, I run my own fingertips across, smiling to myself when it sounds smooth.

"It's a nice guitar," I say, standing to hand it back from him.

"Yeah," he murmurs. "Thanks. Shit. Do you play?"

CHAPTER TWENTY-ONE

Nate

She's nervous. She doesn't think anyone can tell, and they probably can't, but I can. It's in the way she's pulling at the hem of her shirt as Juice fires question after question at her about guitars and old bands or some shit. I don't know, and I don't care, I'm just happy that she's here. Apart from the nerves, she's enjoying herself tonight, despite her reluctance to come. It took three solid days of begging, bribing and pestering to get her to finally agree. I know I was right to make her though.

I look at her now as she enters a conversation with Cole about famous bass players and the music that the band play. I couldn't be any less interested, but at least she's happy. Badger knocks my arm, causing me to look at him. The smirk he gives me is all knowing and makes me want to punch him in the eye.

"What?" I say, keeping my voice low.

He chuckles. "You got it bad, haven't ya?"

I snort in reply, offering no confirmation or denial. I barely know what's going on myself, never mind him. He laughs and shakes his head.

"Come on fuckers," he calls to the rest of his band mates. "Time to go save the poor bastards out there from Blood Sugar."

A chorus of cheers erupts and they all grab their instruments and get ready. Badger shows us the way back out to the bar, and I laugh as they all force a kiss on Hallie's cheek before heading to the stage.

"Fucking musicians," she mutters, then offers me a side look. "I need a drink."

I take her hand and lead her over to the bar. It's gotten busier since we've been in the back, a larger crowd gathered in front of the stage. I buy us some water each and hand hers to her. She smiles almost coyly in return as Tyke announces the band.

"Are you ready for this," she shouts to me.

I shrug and she laughs, obviously knowing something I don't.

I find out soon enough.

Juice strums hard on the guitar, causing it to almost squeal. It echoes around the room only to be met with the screams of the people in there. Badger begins to pound the drums and I realize why Hallie was asking if I was ready. I look at her and she leans in close to my ear. I try to block out the way her warmth breath on my neck sends shivers right to my cock.

"They're a hard rock band. This is going to be loud."

I smile at her, noticing how her eyes have completely lit up with the music. This is where she's comfortable. I move closer and press my lips against hers. She accepts them instantly, molding against me. My tongue sweeps her bottom lip, urging her to part them for me. She does, and I waste no time in exploring her mouth, tasting her. She pulls away after a few second, but I can feel her reluctance with it.

"Kissing me won't make them quieter," she says, laughing.

I rest my forehead against hers. "Worth a try."

She turns in my arms, pressing her back to my chest and pulling my arms tighter around her waist. I feather two small kisses against her neck, reveling in the shudder of arousal that I know she feels. She twists to face me, her gaze as soft as the small smile on her lips.

"Thank you," she mouths, before turning back to face the band.

I smile inside.

I'm so getting laid tonight.

"Make sure you come check out our practice. We'd love to hear you play with us."

Hallie laughs at the words of my cousin. "Maybe. You guys were great."

"Why does it feel like we're getting the one night stand slip, guys?" Tyke says.

I laugh at that. If Hallie was planning to ditch them all, she wouldn't give them a compliment first. Hell, she wouldn't give them a single word. I know that shit from first-hand experience. We offer our goodbyes and then leave them to head for my truck. The club doesn't have a car lot, so we had to park up near some crappy twenty-four hour diner. The smell of the grease makes me realize that I'm hungry so I drag Hallie in with me. She groans in protest but then her stomach rumbling at the scent of fries gives her away. We grab a table near the back.

"What do you want?" I ask.

She looks up from the laminated menu. "Okay don't judge me, but I kinda want pancakes *and* fries."

I laugh. "Is that it? I'm about to eat half of this menu."

She shakes her head and opens her mouth to speak again, but a group of people barreling through the door distract us both. I turn to face them, frowning slightly at the way Hallie retreats.

The new arrivals are around the same age to us, but I don't recognize any of them from campus. They have on bright blue wristbands so I know they've been at the same U21 club as we have. I guess it makes sense that they'd come here, especially given how drunk they look. Their laughter travels through the diner as they pile into two booths up near the front. One of the guys, an obvious moron, wolf whistles one of the waitresses. His face seems familiar, but I can't put my finger on where I know it from. Maybe they are off campus.

A chair scraping back behind me averts my attention. I spin to find Hallie pale as a ghost and pushing back from the table.

"Babe?"

"I... I've gotta go," she mumbles, then hurries from me.

What the?

I follow in her wake, ready to drag her back inside, but she stops short as the obvious moron stands in her way.

"Excuse me," she mutters, keeping her head low.

He smirks and crosses his arms. "Well well, I knew it was you I saw in there. Hallie Clarke. How the fuck *are* you?"

She knows this guy? Oh god. This can't be good. My fists tighten at my sides and I step right beside her. She flinches slightly, but thankfully doesn't pull away from me. I slip my arm to the small of her back and raise my eyebrow in the direction of the guy in front. He smiles wide in return and sticks out his hand.

"You must be Hallie's guy for the night. I'm Jason Evans, and old friend."

Hallie's entire body tenses as though she's turning to stone right next to me. *Jason Evans.* Why do I know that name? Wait. That's the guy Hallie gave her V Card too. The bet guy. Piece of shit. I contain the growl trying to break free from my throat and narrow my eyes.

"Can we just go?" Hallie asks me, her voice quiet and almost pleading.

"Yeah," I grunt. "Let's go."

I push Jason out the way and pull Hallie so she's standing in front of me. She walks through the door and shivers when the cold air hits her, so I pull my hooded jacket off and wrap it around her shoulders.

"You don't have to do this," she says, attempting to shrug away from me.

I grab her hips firmly. "I know I don't have to. I want to. Stop being a pussy and wear my jacket."

She laughs. It's hollow, mind, but it's something.

The door chimes behind me, and it doesn't take a genius to know that Asshole Evans and his band of merry morons have followed us out. I groan into Hallie's ear, not really reveling in the fact that she's about to see how much of a dick I can be.

"Please just leave it," she whispers.

"Not a chance, baby. Don't let him get to you."

Surprisingly, she doesn't fight me on it. Just sighs and turns to face them with me. I grip her hand in mind and step forward a little.

"Can I help you?" I ask, keeping my voice stable.

I'm far from stable though. This is the guy that turned my Hallie into what she had to become. This is the fucking asshole that turned her most intimate gift into a joke. This, mixed with the rage I'm still harboring from her recent attack, bubbles under my skin. I clench my fist.

"I'm just hoping to catch up with my girl."

My girl. Who the fuck does this guy think he is? His girl, my fucking ass. *Stay calm, Nate.* I raise my eyebrow, forcing myself to seem unaffected. Hallie tightens her hold on me, but I know she won't be showing them anything but absolute nonchalance.

"Your girl, huh?" I glance around. "Sorry man, I don't see her."

He snorts a laugh. "Come on. We both know I mean Hallie, and we both know I got there first," his eyes crinkle in a cocky smile. "And let's be honest here, *man.* I'm pretty sure I could get there again."

It's Hallie's turn to snort a laugh now. "Dream on, pal."

There are a few snickers from the people surrounding him, but he doesn't seem affected. If anything he looks more interested and determined. I almost laugh. The Hallie he left broken so many years ago is not the Hallie standing beside me now. She'll tear him to pieces.

"Baby, you know I like a challenge," he purrs, stepping closer to us. "Which you're not. Everyone knows how easy Hallie Clarke is."

"Funny that," she laugh and shifts herself so she's standing almost side-on with a hand resting on my shoulder. "Have you ever sat and wondered why despite how easy I am, I never went *there* again."

She finishes on a pointed look at his crotch and I almost want to applaud her when I see his face redden. She makes a good point though, and she's apparently not done making it as she sighs loudly.

"I mean, it's not like you never asked. I'm pretty sure you asked me to hook up at least three times a week," she yawns. "I guess I was just too busy fucking all those other guys, huh?"

His eyes narrow and the snickers around him get louder and multiply. I snake my arm over her shoulders and nestle her into me, pressing a kiss into her hair. I'm so fucking proud right now. I know she'd normally hide away or try and ignore guys like this, especially *this* guy. I think he's shocked by her too, as he's currently standing with his mouth slightly hanging.

"What's up, Jason?" I ask, my amusement evident in my voice. "Got nothing to say?"

His eyes dart from Hallie to me before huffing out a breath and spitting a "fuck you" in my general direction. He storms back into the diner, his gaggle of followers running after him. I turn to Hallie and laugh.

"That guy? Really?"

She shakes her head before resting it against my chest. "I was young and stupid, don't judge me."

"Oh I'm judging alright." I lift her chin and kiss her lightly on the mouth. "Come on, let's grab a pizza on the way home and you can tell me all about how superior my sexing you up is."

She raises an eyebrow. "Who say's you're superior?"

CHAPTER TWENTY-TWO

Hallie

Something is wrong.

He's acting shifty, and he keeps glancing at me every couple of minutes whilst he's on his cell to Ryan. They've been having these secret little conversations for the past few weeks now. Whatever it is, Codie doesn't have a clue either. She glares at Nate's back from beside me in the booth of the diner.

"It's driving me crazy, Hal. What the hell are they planning?"

I offer her a sideways glance. "I don't know," I say through gritted teeth. "But it can't be good."

She nods her agreement. "Something is definitely going on. I was in Starbucks with Ryan yesterday and the weirdest thing happened. Three guys, who I think are in Jace's frat, looked right at him and then practically ran out of there."

That gets my attention. I turn to face her completely. "What three guys? Do you know their names?"

"Uh," she screws her face up with trying to remember then clicks her fingers. "Okay, one of them was definitely

Andrew Pike. You remember him from that party right? Guy with the creep hands."

I freeze. Yeah, I remember him. From more than just the frat party. I distinctly remember his foot connecting with my ribs. My hand faintly brushes over the recently healed skin. I can still feel the sting as though it's happening all over again.

Why would he be scampering away from Ryan? Unless... My eyes dart back to Nate as I curse quietly. How the hell does he know? Maybe I'm being paranoid. He promised he wouldn't do anything, but now I know him better I can't see him being able to let it go. That's not who Nate is. He's a protector, he's the nice guy who wants to fix everything. He's *my* nice guy. That doesn't change the fact that I told him to leave it be, though.

Codie places her hand on mine. "What's up?"

I smile tightly. "I'm gonna kick his ass, that's what's up."

"Okay," she says on a long breath then stands and pulls on my hand. "Let's go to the bathroom and you can tell me what I'm missing."

I follow her through the diner and shake my head as she bangs on all the cubicle doors to check for any signs of life. At least she's thorough. When she's done searching, she turns back to me and hits me with a sharp look.

"Okay, you need to tell me what you obviously put together out there."

"I don't know what you're talking about," I say, the lie tasting bitter on my tongue.

"Bullshit."

A short laugh bursts from me from the pouty look on her face. "Fine," I exhale. "I didn't want to tell you because I don't know how involved your brother is."

"Jace?"

"Yeah," I stretch out my neck then lean back against the sinks. "Remember the night I got jumped?"

"Of course," she says, then widens her eyes. "Wait! You don't think Jace had anything to do with that do you? He wouldn't Hal. I know he can be a dick, but he'd never hurt a fly. At least I hope not. Holy shit. I'm gonna kick his ass if he had anything to do with that."

I place my hands on her shoulders and shake her a little to stop the verbal vomit before she gives herself an ulcer.

"Codie, relax. No, it wasn't Jace. But, it was five of his frat brothers, Andrew included," I sigh. "I haven't told anyone about it. Not you because of your brother's ties with Delta. I didn't want you to be stuck in the middle of something."

Her eyes round out, the warmth there almost startling. I don't think I'll ever get used to the way Codie's moods can change so quickly. She's like a bipolar sufferer on steroids. But she is my friend, my best friend whatever that means. All I know is that I'm finally thankful that I have her, even if she is a little bit nuts.

"You should have told me, but thank you for trying to keep me out of it all," she says softly.

I smile in reply.

"So, I'm assuming you told Nate and then he'd obviously tell Ryan," she rolls her eyes. "And of course they're both trying to play white knight now."

I shake my head. "I never told Nate. I have no clue how he knows, *if* he does know. But it would make all these secret conversations make sense, huh? I'm gonna be pissed if that's the case, because I specifically told him to leave it alone."

Codie snorts a laugh. "Fuckers. I hate to break it to you

though, babe, but there was never a chance he was gonna let it go."

Now I roll my eyes. "Yeah, I know."

She smiles wickedly. "Doesn't mean we get them back for keeping secrets though."

I arch my eyebrow. "Oh yeah?"

She nods. "Fancy a girls night tonight?"

"Aren't we supposed to be going out with those two?"

"Uh huh. And we can. We'll dress super sexy for them too, but after dinner we'll go home and ditch them both."

I laugh. "Codie Barnes, that's a little bit evil."

She winks. "I know."

"Fuck," he breathes, dragging his gaze all over me.

I smirk inside. As the day wore on, I'd been losing confidence in Codie's revenge plan, but the doubts disappeared the second he put his eyes on me. Nate Harris is going to suffer tonight, and he deserves every last bit of it.

I've been silently steaming all day at the knowledge of what he's been planning. Codie and I knew we needed evidence before we executed our mission - code name: Blue Balls - so we paid a little visit to Harvey Carsen, the keeper of all gossip. A flutter of eyelashes later, we found that not only had Nate gone looking to him for answers, but that's also where his black eye came from.

"He's doing it all for you, Hallie," he'd said. Not that it made a difference to my annoyance.

I squash down the urge to strangle him, and smile over at Nate.

"You like it?" I ask, smoothing down the creases in my incredibly tight dress.

"Uh huh," he mutters, stepping closer to me and putting his hand on my hips.

I look over to Codie and smirk. She'd received a similar greeting from Ryan when he caught her in the shorter than short red lace dress she has on. He's drooling over her now.

"Are we ready to head out then?" Codie asks, a bright smile on her face.

"Yep," I step out of Nate's hold and stroll over to Codie. "Guys?" I ask, raising my eyebrow at them both.

Nate visibly shakes his head and smiles, elbowing Ryan in the stomach to get his attention.

"Yeah yeah, we're ready."

"Awesome," I smile, then let Codie link my arm. "Let's go."

She pulls me ahead of them and out the dorm door. We laugh silently as we hit the stairs. These aren't the sort of game I enjoy playing, but it was incredibly awesome seeing his face like that. It really helps with the anger.

The guys follow behind us, mumbling away to each other as we head to Nate's truck. I'd normally sit up front, but I climb into the back with Codie. Nate's eyes connect with mine in the rear view mirror, so I force a smile and wink at him. His eyes widen a fraction before he clears his throat and says, "Alright, let's do this."

Yes, I think. *Let's.*

CHAPTER TWENTY-THREE

NATE

Thank fuck that's over, is all I can think when we pull up back on campus. That has to have been one of the longest dinners of my life. I glance over at Rye in the front passenger seat of the truck. By the tortured look on his face and the way he keeps rearranging his jeans, I'd say he's struggling as much as I am. At least I'm not in this alone.

I don't know what's got into the girls, but they're acting different. Hallie has been overly affectionate, stealing little touches at every possible chance. Not that I'm complaining, it's just different. I'm not sure how I feel about it really. It seems off.

Rye nudges my in the arm as the girls climb from my truck. I look over as he turns his cell to face me. It shows a text from Dan, one of his guys. All it reads is *It's Done*. I nod and then jump from the truck. For the past few weeks, since we found out who has hurt Hallie, we've been planning a way to bring the fuckers down. As much I want to, I can't go to the cops with my knowledge as Hallie doesn't want to press charges. I can screw up their pathetic little lives with bullshit though. The first one, some lame ass sophomore who should know better, will see what I mean tonight when his parents get a visit from the drug dealer he owes money to. It's all lies, but his folks don't know that, and as they're both youth workers I can't say they'll be pleased. It's petty shit, but it's about all I've got.

My eyes find Hallie's ass as she walks into the building in front me, Codie by her side. Ryan groans next to me.

"Fuck me, man," he says. "This is like torture."

"I know," I mutter, watching my girl as she turns back to face me at the door. She bites down on her bottom lip and offers a smile that promises so fucking much for my dick. I curse. "Okay. Which dorm do you want tonight?"

It seems ridiculous to be having this conversation, but we decided months ago that if we were both staying with the girls, then we'd obviously go in separate dorms.

"I'll take Codie to ours. I need her to help me with my assignment tomorrow morning," he replies as we enter our building.

We clap hands and fist bump, the way we have since we were kids, and rush after Hallie and Codie. We catch up with them as they hit the top step. Hallie is laughing at something Codie is saying, the musical sound of it wrapping around my bones and squeezing. There is nothing in the world that sounds better than my girl laughing. Nothing.

Ryan snakes his arm over Codie's shoulder and whispers something into her ear as we approach the girl's door. She giggles and then pulls away from him, using her key to unlock the door. Ryan looks slightly taken aback as she steps into the threshold. I guess I'm sleeping in our dorm tonight. I place my hands on Hallie's hips and turn her to face me. Her hand moves up my stomach and clutches in my shirt. She pulls on it, forcing me towards her, and presses a hard, hot kiss on my lips. She moves desperately against me, pressing her entire body into mine. Heat ignites, brutal need for her crawls up me and pollutes my blood. I have to have her now. I groan into her mouth when she bites on my lip and pulls away.

"Thanks for dinner," she winks, then joins Codie in the doorway. "But it's girl night now, so see ya."

They go to shut the door, but Rye sticks his foot out to block it. I'm glad he's on the ball because I'm still reeling from that kiss. He cocks his head to the side and smiles in the same way I've seen him do over and over again.

"Baby," he pouts. "You can't tease me all night and then ditch me."

Codie smiles. "Awh, babe. I'm sorry. We just figured you two would be busy tonight so we made plans."

"Busy?" I ask, watching the way Hallie's stance changes to one of defense. She no longer looks as carefree as she has all night. She looks ready for battle now. "What do you mean busy?"

"You know," Hallie says, but there's an edge to her voice. "Other things to do."

"Like what?"

It's Codie now. "Like, I dunno," she looks to Hallie for inspiration. "Maybe a football game."

"Or a guy's night," Hallie offers.

My head whips between the two. This feels like we're being double teamed by a two headed snake. I look to Ryan. He looks just as clueless as me as the girls continue to take turn in suggesting ridiculous shit that we could be doing.

"Oh, I have it," Hallie clicks her fingers then hits me with a look that could floor the devil. "Maybe you want to completely ignore your girlfriend's wishes and go behind her back to find information that she kept to herself for a damn reason."

Oh shit. She knows. I open my mouth to speak, but Codie pulls her back and slams the door in our faces. Rye curses but I stay silent, unable to get the look of betrayal on Hallie's face out of my mind. I knew she wouldn't be happy when she find out, and she was always going to find out, but I wasn't expecting that much hurt in her eyes. I wasn't expecting to feel like shit about it. I don't even know what I was expecting.

"How many?"

"Eight texts and five calls. What about you?"

Ryan sighs. "Looks like I have you beat. Eleven texts, two calls, and three hang ups. Yay me."

I laugh humorlessly. We're fucking pathetic. We've gotten to the point where we're tallying up how many texts and calls the girls are ignoring from us. They're fucking next door.

"Why am I being punished?" Rye asks. "This is between you and Hallie. It has nothing to do with Codie or me."

I shake my head. Idiot. "They're girls. If Hallie is pissed at me, then Codie is pissed at you by association. It's just the way it works. And I know, before you even say it, it's stupid and makes no fucking sense," I stand from the sofa. "I'm not about to mope here about it. Time to go deal with this shit."

"Your funeral," he calls after me.

I head out the door and to the girl's dorm. I bang on their door.

"Hallie, open the fucking door."

Nothing.

I bang louder, not giving two fucks when people on the

corridor start opening their door to witness us. It wouldn't be the first time we've put on a show, I don't think it'll be the last.

"Hallie!" I shout. "I swear to fucking God I will put a hole through this fucking door."

It swings open and she stands there, looking sexy as hell in tiny shorts and my UM shirt. *Fuck.* Her arms are crossed over her chest, her hip jutting out slightly to the side. She looks every bit the pissed off girlfriend and my dick is fucking loving it.

"What?" She grinds out, narrowing her eyes on me.

I swallow hard. "We need to talk about this."

"So talk."

I glance around me at all the assholes watching on and squash the urge to tell them all to fuck off. As much as I hate it, I can't blame them for wanting to witness. Hallie is something of an enigma on campus and they will all crane their necks at the chance of seeing her, especially seeing her half-dressed and tearing me down.

"I'm only doing it for you," I say, hoping she'll understand what I mean.

"No, Nate," she arches her brow. "You're doing it for you."

"What the hell is that supposed to mean?" I take a step towards her. She doesn't move an inch. "Hallie?"

"I told you to leave it, Nathan. I told you to let it the fuck go because I didn't wanna deal with it. You promised, and yet you did it anyway. You did it because *you* needed to deal with it, not me. Don't come here and dish out the nice guy all for you babe act, because it won't work."

Her words hit me in sharp jabs. How can she not see that what I'm doing is justified?

"So I'm the asshole, huh?" I ask, feeling some of my own annoyance.

She's calling me out on my shit, yet the crap her and Codie have pulled tonight is supposed to be okay? I'm supposed to just accept that she can fuck around with my emotions like that whenever I do something she doesn't like? Fuck no.

"Yeah, you're the asshole."

"What about you? You're not exactly innocent party here."

Her eyes widen. "Me? What the fuck have I done?" She takes a step towards me so we're both practically toe to toe now in the corridor. "Whats up? Feeling a little sore that I teased you with a short dress all night and then chose not to fuck you? Feeling a little screwed over? A little betrayed? Hurts, doesn't it?"

Okay, so yeah. She sort of has a point, but she still should have just talked to me about this. Playing games like this doesn't solve anything. I just wish she didn't look so cute right now. It's making it a lot more difficult to make my case.

"If you were so hurt, then why didn't you say something?"

"I did!" She replies, raising her voice. "When it fucking happened. I told you to leave it, and you said you will. I only found out you've been lying through your teeth this afternoon."

She lets out a groan in frustration and because I'm a smart guy, I choose to stay quiet. Instead I silently watch her as she continues to rant on at me about how I'm awful, and interfering and whatever. A small smile curves on my mouth when her arms start flapping around her. I don't think I've ever seen her show this much emotion in anything. She notices my smile and stops mid-sentence, fixing her eyes in a glare.

"What the fuck are you smiling at?"

"You," I place my hands around her hips. "You look so damn cute when you're angry."

She gasps when I pull her against me. I whisper into her ear, "But it's time for you to stop bitching me out now."

She pulls back from me but before she can call me an asshole, I kiss her. I kiss her hard, I kiss her fast, and I don't stop. Cheers erupt from the people watching and she laughs into my mouth.

"I'm still mad at you," she says, her voice much softer than before.

"Yeah, I know. I'm sorry."

"That's okay."

CHAPTER TWENTY-FOUR

Hallie

Absolute confusion.

That seems to be the emotion I've settled on when it comes to trying to deciphering how I feel about Nate. The guy has me seeing things I never thought possible. It's like I'm hallucinating. Suddenly the grass is greener and I swear I was actually looking at the stars last night. The actual fucking stars.

What is he doing to me?

My usual anger at the world disappears when I'm with him. Replaced by love songs that make sense and feelings I never thought I'd have. We've been 'officially' dating for two months now. It's not been easy but every day that passes, I relax a little more into him. He doesn't let me brush him off, thawing my ice with his warmth. He sees me, he really sees me. Past the bullshit and the image of myself I created back home. I'm a different girl here with him, stronger, and I don't exactly hate it which I think is what confuses me the most.

He filled me in on his plan for the guys that attacked me. To be fair, it isn't a bad plan, and it can't be tied to me.

Phase one of the plan happened the night I found out about it. News of Garrett Child's embarrassment at being pulled from a frat party by his mom filtered through campus the day after and a part of me did feel good about it. Okay, I was over-fucking-joyed, but I didn't tell Nate that. More of the same is expected to happen to the others, and it is a lot less than they probably deserve, but it's the perfect justice in a strange kind of way. I hate that he's doing all of this for me, but then a small part of me loves it. A small part of me loves that he cares enough to do it.

I groan inside at the conflicting thoughts and new sunshine disposition I seem to have adopted and push through the door to the English building. Mr Cooper emailed me yesterday, asking me to go and see him. Something about my paper maybe, I don't know. I can't say I mind, the guy is awesome. He handled the rumor shit like a pro, not bothered at all that he was being subjected to them. I'm bothered though. It isn't fair to him. Stuff like this could ruin a man's career. Don't they realize that? I walk down the long hallway to his office and knock on the door when I reach there. His smooth, southern voice calls through, inviting me in.

"Ah, Hallie," he pulls his glasses off and gestures to one of the tatty chairs facing his desk. "Thanks for coming."

Cooper is a great teacher. He's young, and so seems relates to us a bit better than the others. It's like he knows exactly what we want to listen to and the exact moment our minds switch off. Plus, he's funny in a sarcastic way which we can all get on board with. He's been almost a friend to me since Tami started her mission to destroy me, always making sure I'm fine. He even offered me extensions on my assignments and one-on-one support. I didn't accept, obviously, but it's nice to know he understands.

Cooper stands, pushing his sandy brown hair from his face as he looks down at me with a brilliant smile. I was surprised to learn a couple of weeks ago that he wasn't married or involved. He's hot in a smart guy with a man bag kind of way. Not my type, but definitely someone's. Plus he has a killer sense of humor and you just know he'll go the extra mile.

"I just wanted to check how you were doing," he says, moving closer to me. A small sigh escapes his lips. "I know it can't be easy dealing with all the things people on campus are saying about you, about *us*."

He moves to sit on the chair beside me. "It must be causing problems with your boyfriend."

I shift in my seat and cringe. Something about the way he said 'us' seems off. I mean, as professors go, Cooper is cool, but calling a meeting just to ask how I am is more than a little unnecessary and maybe crossing some teacher-student lines. I shove down the doubts. It's probably just because he's been brought into the rumor bullshit. Yeah, I'm sure that's it. All of this affects him too, I suppose.

"I'm fine," I reply, shrugging slightly.

"And your relationship? Everything is okay there?"

My tone is weary as I respond. "Um... Yeah, Nate and I are okay."

Why is he so concerned about Nate? What did he care if I was having relationship problems or not? Did he think my English work wasn't good enough? Is he seeing if that's why? I mean, since Nate got together I haven't studied as much but I still get everything done on time and I never miss class.

His mouth presses in a hard line, brows creasing as he studies my face for a few seconds. "I see," he muses then sits up and places his hand gently on my knee.

I flinch from the contact but he either doesn't care or doesn't notice as it stays there whilst he speaks again.

"I just want you to know that I'm here for you, for anything."

I stand, desperate to move away. The air around us has shifted with that one little touch, now still and stifling. I need to go. This is getting weird.

"Thank you *Professor* Cooper," I say and re-shoulder my purse. "But I've got to get back. My *boyfriend* will be waiting for me."

I walk towards the door, hoping that the not so casual mention of his profession and the fact that I'm not single will deter him from making this worse. He follows me, placing his hand firm on the door to stop me from opening it. I glance at him, confused by the expression gracing across his face. He looks almost predatory as he rakes his eyes over my body. Every inch of me burns in the wake of his stare, unease settling in my stomach.

"Why are you with him?" He asks.

I blank at the suddenness of his question. Should I answer that? How do I answer that? I can't even begin to explain what makes Nate and I work, we just do. Kind of.

"I mean, do you love him?" He continues, his frown now prominent.

Again, I blank. Is he serious? Now this is definitely crossing some very distinct lines.

Do I love Nate? Maybe... I mean, I do like him, a lot, and he makes me feel things I never thought I could. He makes me think I can do anything I want, that what other people say about me doesn't matter because he still wants me. No one else exists when I'm with him. Is that love? I shake off the thoughts. Now is really not a good time to be analyzing my inner feelings.

"I really do have to go," I answer eventually and breathe a silent sigh of relief when he shifts his stance and removes his hand. I brush past him quickly and head through the door.

"You hesitated," he murmurs, his voice barely audible and causing me to halt. I don't get to respond to that as he talks again.

"I want your paper on my desk by Wednesday," he says.

I turn to face him, again confused. "I thought it was due Friday."

"Now I want it Wednesday," he snaps then slams the door shut behind me.

I'm a statue for what feels like hours, unable to fathom what just happened. Where the hell did that come from? Like, what the fuck? Somehow, I manage to pull myself together and leave the building. I walk straight over campus and into my dorm building, luckily bypassing Westley on the way up to my suite. When inside, I slump down on the couch and let my head fall back. Maybe he's just lost his mind for the day? I sure hope so. I don't need another crazy person in my life. No, definitely not. I have enough with my folks.

Dread fills my stomach. I still hadn't spoken to my father since I found the crappy page online dedicated to me. I know I'll have to deal with him at some point, just like I did with Jason, but I'm enjoying myself too much to care about his disapproval right now. I don't want him to ruin it.

Banishing all thoughts of George Clarke and The Nutty Professor from my mind, I head into my bedroom and change into my running clothes. After a morning like this one, I definitely need to let off some steam. Then apparently I needed to write up this stupid paper. Which also means calling Nate to cancel our date tonight as I'll have to spend all morning tomorrow on it too. Man, this sucks. I grab my water, plug my earphones into my cell then use the hands free to call Nate as I head out the suite.

"Hello?"

I can't help but smile inside at his voice. I'm becoming obsessed with this guy, not good.

"Hey."

"Hey, babe, you alright?" He asks.

"Yeah, well kind of. I dunno," I shake my head, annoyed at myself for being affected like this. "Weird morning. Anyway, I'm calling because I need to bail on tonight," I say, pushing the main door of the building open a little bit too harshly.

"That sucks! What's happened?"

I sigh. I wish I knew. "I don't really know. I went in to see Cooper today," I pause, my speech and my walking. Do I tell him about what was said? No... he'd only get the wrong idea. But then is he going to get mad if he finds out and I haven't told him? It's not like anything happened... because I left. But will he see it that way? Do I really want to start more drama after we've been doing so well for so long? No, no I do not. I kick at an empty bottle in frustration before continuing. "Well I had a paper due for him on Friday, but now he wants it Wednesday."

His voice is suspicious. I can't blame him, this is totally out of Cooper's character. "Seriously? Why would he do that? Has he changed everyone's?"

"I don't know, I mean, I assume so. He was in a weird mood, not himself at all," I say and technically not lying.

That's great, Hallie. I'm sure if (when) it all turns to shit, a technicality is going to save your ass.

He laughs. "I wonder what crawled up his ass," his

laughter dies, replaced by a sigh. "So, are you working on it tonight? I mean can't you finish it tomorrow?"

I scoff and begin to walk in the direction of my favorite trail. "I haven't even started it. I thought I had until Friday!" I laugh a little now. "I'm just heading to the trail now, then will start when I get back. I'll have to spend all morning tomorrow and then after my afternoon classes too."

He groans. "Well Cooper just made the official asshole list," he's quiet for a second. "Okay, I have to see you tonight. How about I come over later and help you? I won't stay long I promise."

His voice is hopeful and, annoyingly, I find myself agreeing. I'm laughing when I hang up the call a few minutes later.

My body relaxes the second I hit the trail. I waste no time in setting off, starting my pace at a comfortable jog. I force the reality of the day away with every step, pushing the doubts and Professor Cooper to the back of my brain. My mind is blank as I get further into the park, expertly navigating the now familiar trail. I've been here almost everyday since I started college. I know this place like the back of my hand now, just like I know that coming now means there are less people around. I hate it when it's full. It's hard to lose yourself when all you can hear are preppy students around you. Today though it's nice and quiet, perfect even.

I stay out there for longer than I expected, only returning to my dorm after three solid hours. My legs are numb as I slump onto the couch beside Codie.

"Good run?" She asks, her eyes lifting from her book and shining with amusement as she takes in my obvious discomfort.

"Yeah, I needed it," I tell her then consider a little if

maybe I should talk to her about Cooper.

She laughs. "Yeah I saw you marching across campus earlier like you'd just witnessed a crime. Did your meeting with your professor not go so great? I thought everyone was in love with the guy?"

I snort, unable to stop it. "You could say that," leaning back, I let out a long breath before looking at her. "I think he came on to me," I say quietly.

Her eyes bulge, practically busting out the sockets as she launches forward in her seat, the book she was holding flying across the room.

"He did fucking what?"

I can't help but laugh at her dramatics. Who knew that my first ever friend in forever would be someone so unlike myself, someone so over the top and out there.

"Yeah... I dunno. Maybe?" I sigh.

"Hallie you're gonna have to give me some deets here. Did he try to kiss you?"

My head shakes quickly. "No, no nothing like that."

I sigh again before telling her the whole story of what happened this morning. She nods along, offering a few explicit curses as I talk.

"Holy shit! Hallie that is super not good. Maybe you should go to The Dean or something? I mean, he shouldn't be doing that or asking you those things. It's really, *really* wrong," she says when I'm finished.

I laugh. "Yeah because they'll believe the rumor girl right? Especially after I made such a big fucking deal to the dean the first time about how it was all horseshit."

My mind drifts back to that day. I'd been furious that the rumors about Cooper and I had even started, and even more annoyed that The Dean believed it enough to drag me into his office for a lecture on the whole thing. I assured him though that it was garbage, but I know he hadn't fully listened to me. Why would he? It was his own damn daughter leading the bullshit parade.

"Well, you should still be really careful around him," she says bringing me back out of my head.

I nod and assure her I will then head into the kitchen. My eyes find the small white scrunched up bit of paper that I'd thrown on the counter this morning before heading out. I pick it up, unfolding it and looking down at the words. I've already read it, but still find myself soaking in the scratchy scribbles.

Hallie,
I'm on your side, remember that.
One day, all of this will be behind us, and we can live our lives free from the judgment of others.
We can be together, I know it.
Always,
JC

I've been getting these notes for a while now, always along the same lines as this one. I have no idea who JC is, and no desire to know either. He (or she) is clearly on the rumor band wagon and is either messing with me, or worse, falling for the bullshit. Either way, I'm not interested. Nate almost blew a gasket when I told him about them, demanding that we find out who it is. It has taken me forever to calm him down. He can't understand why I don't care. But I'm used to this. The notes, hushed whispers, stares. It's nothing new, and definitely nothing to stress out over. I deposit the note in the same place I put all the others - the trash - and head into the bathroom for a shower. After that I'll make a start on this paper.

CHAPTER TWENTY-FIVE

Hallie

A knock on my bedroom door causes me to pull my gaze away from my laptop screen.

"Come in," I shout as I try to re-focus my eyes. Staring at a screen for the past five and a half hours has seriously had an effect, I feel like I've been taking drugs.

Nate strolls in and takes a seat on my bed.

"Hey, baby. How are you getting on?" He asks.

"I'm seeing red dots. That can't be normal, right?"

He chuckles. "Looks like I came at the right time. You need a break," his hand pats the bed next to him. "Come sit with me, just for a little while."

I hesitate, knowing just being close to him will cause my body to beg for him which will definitely not be a productive way to get this paper written. I watch him as he watches me, his emerald jewels searching my face. He leans back against the wall and stretches his solid frame across the mattress. The way his muscles move under the white tee he's wearing has my stomach doing summersaults. The guy isn't just hot, he's sizzling. *And all mine.* That thought has me rising from my desk chair and joining him on the bed, leaning my back against the wall beside him. Nate reaches down the end of my bed and pulls my old battered guitar from it's even older stand.

"What are you doing?" I ask him, eyeing him curiously as he beings to pluck the strings clumsily. The sounds coming from it cause me to wince.

"Playing guitar."

I laugh and take it from him. "That's not playing, that's torturing it," I position it across my knee flat. "Here let me show you."

I move his fingers off the strings and reposition them, showing him where to strum. We play around like that for a few minutes, laughing along with each other before I take full control. I let my fingers brush softly, a sweet tune echoing out as I lean my head back against the wall.

"What's that you're playing, I don't think I recognize it," Nate says.

I laugh a little under my breath. "No you won't, it's mine."

"You write your own songs?" His voice doesn't hide his surprise and I smile.

"Not really, I just get a tune in my head and sometimes add some words."

He deadpans. "That's called writing a song, Hallie."

My eyes roll. He'll never understand it. I love music, but it's not something I'd ever do for a job, which I know is his next question. I don't have dreams of being famous, nor do I want my songs out there for the world to hear. I just do it to relax, I do it for me. Just like running. I don't respond to his comment, instead I just stop playing and place the guitar down. I lie back on my bed and stare up at the ceiling, working hard to try and forget my day. Nate's face appears over me.

"Everything okay?"

I release a frustrated breath. "Yeah, just this paper," I lie.

That isn't why I'm frustrated and annoyed. Cooper has riled me up today. At some point during the day, I've gone from being confused to just plain old angry about the whole thing. He knows what the rumors are doing to me, how much they are hurting me. He knows that, he can see it, and yet he's trying to make them come to life, make them real. Does he even realize how wrong that is? I'm fighting them day in and day out because I'm scared he'll lose his job and there he is making it worse. What if someone saw? I'd never be able to convince The Dean it was horseshit if they had. He'd lose his job and I'd lose my scholarship.

"Anything I can help with?" Nate asks, pulling my attention back to him.

His bright green eyes bore into me and a familiar feeling begins to stir inside. I've never been so strung up by a guy. Just one look and I want him screwing me to Sunday and back. It can't be healthy, surely. I pull my bottom lip between my teeth, lust clouding his eyes instantly.

"Well there is something..." I say quietly.

A lazy smile forms on his mouth. "Is that right?"

I nod slowly then ignoring the knot of hesitation in my stomach I get every time we're close, I bring my hands to either side of his face and pull his lips to mine – Spiderman style. It isn't long before our sweet kiss turns to something fueled with passion and need for each other, my body reacting to him in ways I could never describe. It's always like this with us; always hot, heavy and completely satisfying.

He pulls me up, his mouth still slanting perfectly on mine as he moves our position. Before I know what's happening, he has me trapped beneath him. His hand tangles in my hair, the other roaming my body lightly. His fingers are barely brushing against my skin but my body still ignites to his touch. My legs naturally part for him and he moves his hips until his body is between them. I can feel him pushing against my core and the low seductive grumble of arousal begins to light in my lower stomach as our mouths become more desperate. One of my hands wrap around the back of his neck, pulling him closer to me and I thrust my hips forward. The need for more over taking my mind, clouding my brain and banishing all thoughts of anything that isn't us.

My other hand slowly moves under his shirt and up his stomach, reveling in the feel of every ridge. The guy is a God, with the body to match.

"Hallie," he says, his mouth moving to my neck as he begins to feather light kisses along the length of it.

I squirm, enjoying the sensations that are rippling through me from his touch. "Hmm?"

"I have a question."

I laugh and push my hips against him. "I'm not sure now is the right time to play the question game," I say, completely hating the whiney undertones of my voice.

"Now's the perfect time," he smiles against my neck and a shiver of anticipation runs through me. His mouth moves to my ear, the hot breath coming from him sending my senses on overdrive. "If I told you I loved you, would you run away?"

My body freezes, a metaphorical bucket of ice dousing the flames that were roaring inside me just seconds earlier. Nate moves from over me and sits back, his eyes burning holes into my face as he watches me. I sit up, bringing my knees to my chest and wrapping my arms around them. I rest my head on my legs and turn to face him as his words crash over me again.

It's not like he actually said it, but would I run? Could I let him love me? The very idea of that has my mind going on a confusing tailspin. I take a deep breath and study him. Our eyes lock, the way they always do, and we sit there staring at each other. Not one of us breathes a word, both caught in the spell of our connection, a connection neither one of us can understand. I can see the regret of his words flashing through his mind and disappointment courses through me. The realization slamming into me like a bulldozer to my emotions. *I want him to love me.*

My psychosis rattles as I try to pull together my words carefully, an inner battle of the old Hallie and this new unfamiliar Hallie waging a war inside my mind. I want so desperately to say the words, to tell him exactly how I feel and spill it all out, but the tiny voice inside me that clings on to the rejection of my high school years blocks the words.

Nate sighs loudly before standing from my bed and walking silently out the door. His sudden absence is enough to drag me from outside my own head. Before I know what I'm doing, I'm off my bed and pulling the door to my room open. His slumped shoulders are just turning the corner into the kitchen. I follow him, my mind blank to everything but him. I can't let him leave, not like this.

I call his name as he pulls open the main door to the suite. He looks back, his eyes hooded and weary as I walk closer to him. Without thinking I fist my hand in his t-shirt and pull him closer to me, reaching up and kissing him hard on the mouth. He hesitates for a second but is soon kissing me back, his emotions readable through the connection. I pull away and rest my forehead against his, taking a minute to catch my breath.

"I have to get this paper done," I say and he nods slowly before pulling back from me completely. My hand reaches for him and I tug him back to me before he can walk through the door.

"Nate," I start and bring my eyes level with his. I need him to know I mean this. "I wouldn't run."

I catch the small smile on his lips before I turn and walk away, back to my room. Whether I liked it or not, I had to get this paper finished. Then *Professor Cooper* can fuck himself.

CHAPTER TWENTY-SIX

HALLIE

I keep my head held high as I march across the campus to the English building. I spent two days solid on this paper and he better had freakin' well appreciate it. I learned from one of my classmates yesterday that they haven't had their deadline changed meaning, and I'd already assumed as much, it's just me. Added the fact I had another goofy note slipped through my door this morning, I'm pissed. Real pissed.

The note has told me that the mysterious JC can't wait to see me on campus today and that it won't be long before we can be together properly. I snapped a picture of it and sent it to Nate before throwing in the trash and storming out the door. My phone immediately blew up with calls and texts from him but I'll deal with that after. Right now I need to focus on this. Codie has given me one of her 'famous' pep talks on my way out which has done nothing to help my mood in the slightest, but I smiled tightly and hoped that would pacify her enough to let me walk out the door. Luckily, it did.

I take a deep breath as I approach the steps of the English building but before I can enter, I pick up a faint wolf whistle to my left and turn to find Jace and his pervert friend Toby staring at me, a funny smirk on their faces. My eyes narrow. Jace might be Codie's brother, but he's still an asshole.

"Looking mighty fine, Hallie," Toby shouts over and his tongue traces along his bottom lip.

The gesture has my stomach recoiling and I respond with my middle finger before continuing up the steps and into the building in front of me. I'm in no mood to deal with horny frat boys today.

I rush down the long hallway to Cooper's office with every intention of slamming my paper on his desk and walking straight back out. The hope of that is quickly squashed though as I almost walk right into him as I round the corner.

"Hallie, in a rush to see me?" A strange smile plays on his face as his amused eyes glance down at me.

I straighten my shoulders and hold my folder out for him.

"Here, my paper. Done, like you asked," I say.

He looks at it, then back to me and smiles. Not his usual friendly smile, but something indistinguishable, darker even.

"Well come on into my office and I'll take a look at it."

He walks ahead and into his office before I can respond, leaving me stood with the folder hanging pathetically from my hand. I groan inwardly and then follow him through, unable to see any other options. He stands at the door as I walk past, and shuts it firmly when I've entered. I glance back, the hairs on the back of my neck alerting me to how wrong this feels. A week ago, I never would have thought twice about this situation. But now, now it doesn't feel right. It feels sordid.

"Sit down, Hallie, we can use this time to discuss..." a smirk plays on his lips as he pauses for a second. "...your assignment."

I eye him warily then place the folder on his desk and sit carefully on the seat opposite, praying that he takes the leather office seat on the other side of the desk. He doesn't, and I sigh inside knowing that prayer was never going to be answered. I lean as far as I can away from his position on the chair next to me without making him aware. The last time I pissed this guy off I lost two days from my assignment. I'll be damned if that's happening again. He picks up my paper and sits in the chair beside me, turning so his whole body faces me.

"Let's have a look then," he muses as he begins to flick through the pages.

A ball of dread bottoms in my stomach as I watch him read. He makes noncommittal noises and nods a few times as he comes to the end.

"As always, Miss Clarke, it's perfect. I'd maybe elaborate on a couple of points but it's an A without it," he says. He leans forward and places my folder on the desk before turning back to me. "I forget how smart you are sometimes. You're my best student."

I clear my throat a little, my nerves causing me to stutter. "T...Thanks Professor Cooper."

He laughs. "Oh Hallie, please just call me James. After some of the things the campus have said we've been doing," A dark gleam stains his eyes and a knowing smile spreads across his face. "I think we can call each other by our first names."

His gaze locks on mine, rendering me unable to move as

he peers down at me. I cross my legs, wishing I'd worn something a little less revealing than my denim shorts. His eyes dart there then back up to my face, his expression changing to a look of lust within a second.

Oh no.

Noise at the window startles me, and I stand and look over. Cooper walks across and peers out before turning to me and shrugging. I take the distraction as an opportunity to leave and excuse myself. He meets me by the door before I can open it though. He places a hand on my arm and looks down at my body again, my legs burning from his stare.

"You look very nice today, Hallie. Although I'm not sure how I feel about how much skin you're showing."

I snap my eyes to him. In what universe did what I wear have anything to do with him? He places his hand on the side of my face and I freeze. *What is he doing?*

"You're so beautiful," he murmurs before crashing his lips on mine. It takes me a second to register but when I do, I place my hands on his chest and push him away from me with as much force as I can muster.

"What the hell are you doing?" I hiss.

His eyes turn to stone as moves back towards me, I open the door before he can reach me though and run from the office. Luckily I don't see anyone as I barrel down the hallway and out the door. I round the corner of the building and lean against the wall, placing my hands on my knees and bending over. What the hell was that? And how the hell am I supposed to face my English classes now? It's too late to transfer out, which means I'm going to have to drop the class. Which then means changing my damn major. My head begins to spin with all the stress and so I take a couple of deep steadying breaths before straightening myself up and heading back to the Trisler Building. As I reach the car lot I spot my car and make an impromptu decision to ditch my afternoon classes as I drive to see Willow. That woman always manages to cheer me up. I send a quick text to Nate and let him know I won't be meeting him for lunch then throw my cell on the passenger and make the drive to Dexter.

Willow is busy with a customer when I arrive, so I throw her a quick wave then head over to the couch, pulling my favorite guitar with me. I lose myself in the music quickly, letting the emotion pour out of me through the chords. This is the only way I know how to express myself, this is where I can be me with no judgement. Rumors, college, none of it matters here. Because here I'm alone with the music, just me and the sounds that soothe my senses. I don't know how long I play for, but at some point I notice Willow staring at me which causes me to still my fingers on the strings.

"Have I ever told you how talented you are?"

I laugh at her words. "Every time you hear me play."

She smiles. "Just checking. What's on your mind, honey? You don't look very happy right now. In fact I'd say you look about as lost as you did the first time I met you."

I scoff. I feel about as lost as I did then too. "Just college stuff."

Her eyes turn sympathetic as she regards me carefully. "Still being harassed by those silly kids at school? I told you not to let them get to you," she scolds.

I smile sadly. "It's taken a dramatic turn."

She looks at me expectantly, so I continue. "You remember me telling you about my English professor and the rumors right?"

When she only nods I let out a breath and inform her of what happened this morning. I don't know how I expect her to react, but the way she just nods thoughtfully has me confused.

"Hallie, people in life will always test you and you will find yourself in situations where you think a solution is impossible. What you have to remember is that everything has an expiration date. Things can be tough for a while, but eventually the drama fades and things become nothing but a bad memory. Only you can decide whether you let it drag you down or not," she smiles. "You're a fighter. I see it your eyes, in the way you play your music."

She pats my hand gently. "You'll be okay honey, I don't doubt it."

She stands then, and makes her way to the back room to get us both coffee. I place the guitar back in its stand and look around the store as I consider her words.

Am I fighter? Can I move past this?

My thoughts drift to Nate. I can only imagine the reaction he'll have when I tell him. I push those thoughts aside. I came here to get away from it all, thinking about it is just going to be counter-productive. When she returns I smile gratefully as she flips the 'CLOSED' sign on the door and together we curl up on the couch and talk. Willow tells me stories of her childhood and I tell her a few of mine from back home.

It's at least two hours later when frantic knocking at the door distracts us. Willow rushes over as I take our cups out to the kitchen at the back of the shop. I rinse them through as she lets in whoever was at the door.

Probably a customer, I muse.

I stroll back out, figuring I should probably let her get back to working. I stop short, my eyes landing on Nate as he talks to Willow. His eyes land on mine immediately, locking me in the intense emerald gaze. He watches me, eyes roaming from head to toe before coming over to me and pulling me into him. His scent surrounds me and I allow myself to be comforted by it.

"I've been looking everywhere for you and trying to call you," he says against my hair.

I pull back and smile apologetically at him.

"I left my cell in my car."

He laughs and raises his gaze to the ceiling. I can see the frustration on his face. Not surprising considering I just took off without a word. But I couldn't be there, I needed to get away. I watch as he brings his eyes back to mine, the green of them slightly darker as he studies my face. I bring my hand to his cheek, reach up and plant a soft kiss on his lips. His arm wraps around my waist as he relaxes into me. He drops his head to my shoulder and murmurs against it.

"Hallie, we have got to stop with the disappearing acts, okay?"

I laugh. "I'll work on it," I step back so he has to move his head and take his hand. "Come on, I'll buy you a milk-shake to make it up to you."

He chuckles as I pull him out the store, waving goodbye to Willow on our way out. We make the short walk to the diner and take a seat at our usual booth. I smile at the memory of the first time we were in here. I'd been bruised and broken and the owners had assumed Nate was the reason. He'd known then that I didn't want to be seen so he'd choses this booth at the back and made it so I could sit facing only him.

Wendy appears at our side and takes our order before dashing off.

"So, are you going to tell me what happened today?"

I dart my eyes away from him and stare at the street outside. How the hell do I tell him? Without him going postal? *Gah!* This is all too much stress.

"Hallie?"

I bring my eyes back to him as Wendy places our milkshakes down on the table. I flash her a grateful smile and then stare into my drink which looks about as appealing as a firing squad right now.

"So... something happened today," I start but before I can continue his cell begins to ring.

He looks down at the caller ID, curses and then brings it to his ear. I sip at my shake as I listen in.

"Hey man what's up? Yeah I'm with her now. What do you mean? Shit! Alright yeah okay. Find out and get back to me. I'll figure something. No it's probably best she doesn't. Okay man I'll call you later."

I watch him drop his phone on the table before cursing again and looking up at me. His features are now tortured as he eyes me carefully. It's the same look he was giving me right before showing me the Facebook page so whatever is about to come out of his mouth can't be good.

"Hallie..." he starts then shifts uncomfortably in his seat.

"Just spit it out," I snap.

"Okay. Professor Cooper has just been fired for having an inappropriate relationship with a student."

My face hardens as my rage over the familiar rumor intensifies. Are they fucking happy now? In their efforts to ruin me, they've destroyed a man's career. I'm out my seat without a word to Nathan. I pull a bill from my back pocket and throw it down on the table before walking out. The air chills around me as I walk briskly towards the parking lot. As always, I feel him before he speaks.

"Hallie, wait up! Where are you going? Damn it how do you walk so damn fast?"

Despite my mood, I laugh a little. "I don't know, and back to campus."

His brows furrow as the corners of his mouth turn to frown, his jaw twitching. I wonder if he knows that he gives every feeling away with his face. I always know what he's thinking.

"Hallie you can't. People are going crazy over there. They've assumed it's you. Baby I could get us a hotel and we could stay away for the night," he says softly as he links his hand with mine. I ignore the comfort and pull my hand away before continuing towards my car.

"This isn't right Nate," I say as he falls into step beside me. "This shouldn't be happening. Was jumping me not enough?" I mutter to myself. Nate doesn't reply.

We reach my car and I climb in as my cell begins to ring. I groan then pull it from the passenger seat frown at the name flashing on it. One guess what this is about.

"What?"

His voice is harsh. "Hallie don't speak to me like that, I've just heard some very disturbing news. Luckily, I'm in town so I'm on my way to your dorm whilst we try and straighten this out."

I hit at my steering wheel before climbing back out the car and pacing. "No. I'll handle it myself."

"You will not. You've gone too far this time, Hallie," he lets out a long breath. "The Dean is meeting me there so I suggest you get here. Now."

I lean my free hand on the car and lean against it. Letting my head rest on the metal as I mentally talk myself out of screaming. Of course. This is all my fault. It doesn't matter that it's not actually fucking true. I feel my tough exterior cracking as I fight to regain composure. Why can't he just for fucking once be there for me? Why can't he just tell me everything is going to be alright instead of making me feel an inch tall? I don't bother to force my voice even as I reply.

"Oh I have, huh? If that's what you think then stay the fuck away from me."

I hang up before I have to listen to him say anything else. I need to get back to the dorm, pack my shit, and get the hell out of here. I never should have even tried.

I climb back into the car and glance at Nate in the passenger seat.

"How the hell did you get here?"

He snorts. "I know you're mad but it isn't at me."

I sigh. I hadn't meant to snap at him. "Sorry."

He nods. "I drove, but if you think for a second I'm letting you drive back to campus on your own, you can think again. I'll get Rye to bring me for my car later."

I nod then start the engine, knowing arguing with him will get me nowhere. I drive us back to the campus in silence, my mind reeling with rage and inner turmoil. I don't even know who I'm angry at. The assholes on campus who have spread this vicious rumor? My dad for not being who I need him to be? Professor Cooper for the bullshit he pulled this morning? Or myself for actually fucking believing things would be better here?

I park up in the lot outside my block and, noticing my dad's car, I let my head fall back on the seat, turning it to face Nate. "You might wanna jump out now before me. This isn't going to be pretty."

He sighs softly before taking my shaking hand in his. "Hallie I don't care. I told you, I don't give a shit what they say. Now, put your mean face on and let's do this," he smirks and I snort before pulling away and climbing out the car.

CHAPTER TWENTY-SEVEN

Hallie

The walk of shame has nothing on this. Eyes everywhere watch us as Nate and I walk towards the main entrance of our dorm block. I square my shoulders and force myself forward, one step at a time. Nate reaches for my hand and I link my fingers with his. The only reason The Dean would be in there is because I'm being turfed out of campus. It isn't even worth fighting it. Life here on campus won't be worth living after all of this. The thought causes me to pull away from Nate. I can't hold on to his comfort, when I won't have it much longer.

I take to the stairs two at a time once inside. I just need to get into my dorm, pack my things and I can leave. If I do this right, I can probably get away without saying a single word to Mr You've Gone Too Far.

"Shit, Hallie, you've got to stop running. Like seriously, how do you move so damn so fast?"

I stop outside my door and face Nate behind me. His eyes are desperately searching mine and his breath comes in heavy pants.

"I always move fast. If I stay in one place for too long,

people see the version of me I prefer to keep to myself," I say before turning my back to him. "You've already seen too much of that version."

Silence falls on the room as I walk in. Codie is sat with Ryan on one of the couches, my dad and Dean Vincent on the other. I take a deep silent breath and step further in, prepared for the onslaught.

"Hallie, we have to talk," my dad says, standing and rushing over to me.

I step back defensively as he comes close. A hand wraps around my waist, and from the reaction my body is having, I know its Nate. I welcome the comfort briefly before crushing it and walk around my dad and over to Dean Vincent.

"Hallie we have some very incriminating evidence regarding your relationship with Professor Cooper," he motions to the small coffee table in front of him. I look down and let out a long breath at the images that must have been taken this morning in Cooper's office. Of course. "As you can see, with this, I have no choice but to ask you to leave campus."

I laugh sarcastically, unable to stop it. I hate this, but I've been shit on my whole life. It's time to go home. Nate comes to join me by my side and I flinch from the curses that come from his mouth as he gazes at the images. I look to him, and he brings his gaze level with mine. My heart stops when I see the hurt and anger behind his eyes. But most of all, I see the disgust. *He believes.*

"Nate..." I start but he throws his hands up stopping me and begins to back away.

"Save it, Hallie."

He storms from the dorm and I remain immobile, unable to clear his tortured face from my mind. He believes all of this. He thinks I did this. Ryan rushes after him and I close my eyes, fighting back the tears and letting the emotions leave me. I feel the familiar walls of ice build up around me, guarding me from the sharp ache slicing through my chest. I'll need the cold to get through this without breaking. I'll need the old Hallie to get me home and away from the pain.

I turn to face The Dean, my face hard and unmoving.

"It's not true," I say to him. "I haven't been sleeping with Professor Cooper. Its bullshit but you couldn't possibly believe that. Not when it's your own daughter whispering in your ear. Hell, even my own father believes it so I can't blame you. Whatever, I don't care. I'll be gone by the morning."

With that I leave the room. I walk into my bedroom, shut and lock the door, then finally let the tears fall silently as I slide to the floor. I let it all out. The rage, the frustration, and the pain. I let the ugly fat tears roll down my face as I ignore whoever is tapping desperately on the door behind me. I sit like that for a few minutes before building my walls up stronger than ever before. I mentally stack more bricks up and cover my heart, soul and mind. My guard firmly in place, I stand and look around my room. I pull out the pathetic bag that brought my stuff here and begin packing my clothes into it. I ignore the knocks at the door and the sound of my father shouting me from the other side of it. I can't deal with him. I won't deal with him. He's worse than the kids on campus. He's worse than them all.

I carefully unstick the pictures that Codie stuck all around the mirror of us together, and me with Nate. A dull ache spreads across my chest with just the thought of him.

I drop down on to my bed clutching the photo of the both us laughing together. Codie snapped it without us knowing when we were all hanging out in our dorm. I smile small at the memory of playing my guitar as Ryan sung out the offensive lyrics of Tenacious D. I knew I never should have let them in, especially Nate. I should have kept fighting it because he turned out to be just like everyone else, unable to see past the bullshit. He didn't even give me chance to deny it, just left with eyes full of disappointment. My soul is crushed, my spirits flattened under the weight of his reaction. I'll be seeing that face in my dreams, reminding me of how I failed over and over again, and I hate that I'm letting myself feel that devastation. I hate that I've let him worm his way inside me so much that I care what he thinks. Because I do. I do care. And it hurts like hell.

I don't bother packing that image. Instead, I chose to throw all the ones with him on in the trash and just stuff the ones with Codie in my bag.

After I've emptied my room, I hang my guitar over my shoulder and leave. I stroll into the bathroom and grab my stuff from there. When I'm done I walk back towards the lounge area. Codie runs over to me and hugs me hard as I reach the kitchen, causing me to drop my bag.

"This is horseshit, Hallie, and I'm so pissed this happening to you. I love you and I'll call you every damn day," she says into my hair.

I bring my arms around her and let myself have this last moment with the only real friend I've ever had. God I was going to miss her over-enthusiastic ass.

"I love you too," I whisper then pull away. "Say bye to Ryan for me."

"I will," she lets out a long shaky breath. "I want you to know I'm on your side and *he* will be too, once he's had time to process."

By the way she says 'he' I know she means Nate. I let my head fall as she continues.

"I don't care who I have to bitch at, I *will* find out which asshole photoshopped those pictures and I *will* fucking murder them."

I snap my eyes up to her and I begin to shake my head slowly. Her mouth forms a silent O as she gapes at me.

"No... Hallie?"

"No! I didn't. But the images are true. It happened this morning when I handed my paper in. I didn't kiss him, but he kissed me," I kick at the kitchen counter. "I pushed him off and took off straight away. I drove to see Willow and clear my head. Nate showed up and shit."

I laugh coldly, unable to believe the cliché irony of the situation. "I swear Codie I was just about to tell him when Rye called him."

"Oh my God, Hallie. You have to go talk to him, explain."

"No," I shake my head. "I can't. His face... he won't believe it. Just keep this to yourself, yeah?"

A watery smile graces her face as she nods and I look away before the sight embeds in my brain. I don't need another face keeping me up all night.

I pick my bag back up and walk towards the door. Out of the corner of my eye I notice that not only has The Dean left, but my father too. Pain radiates through me, the same pain I felt when he wasn't at my side the last time a rumor tore my world apart. I push through it and head out the door, ignoring the sniffles from Codie.

Come on Hallie, just get to your car and go home.

It's at the top of the stairs where I see Nate. He's leaning against the wall, his gaze cast downwards. I take a silent breath and force myself to move forward. I feel the exact moment he looks at me, the hairs on the back of my neck standing as goosebumps form along my arms. I still my legs and turn to face him. His eyes are narrow and hard, the usual bright green dark and glazed.

"So you were playing me this whole damn time, huh?"

I stop the gasp from escaping my mouth. It would do no good to defend myself now. What's the point? I saw the look in his eye, he already believes. Nothing I could do or say would make it better. I pack my walls tighter and walk away from him. He doesn't follow me, not that I expected him to. He thinks I've played him, that I've been lying to him this whole time. That cuts me deeper than I ever thought it would.

I ignore the stares and taunts as I haul my things to my car. I pack them in and drive away from the campus after texting Mom to say I'm coming home. I imagine my dad will have already told her what has happened so I don't bother to explain anything in the message.

The drive back to Iowa is grueling and with every mile I put between myself and Michigan I feel the newer, brighter parts of me whimper away. All the progress I've made slips away the closer I get to home, and by the time I'm pulling up in the drive of the simple brick house I called home for 18 years I'm broken.

I drag my stuff from the car and push open the front door. The familiar scent of sweet vanilla candles and my mother's perfume fills me and soothes me with a strange sense of calm. I drop my bag as Mom appears in the doorway. It's early hours of the morning, why is she awake? I study her as she moves towards me, a sad smile on her face.

"Why are you up? It's late."

"Hallie... your dad told me what happened. Of course

I'm awake. Come here," she says and pulls me into a tight hug.

"Mom," I choke and fold into her, emotion pulsing through me. My mom, here and awake for me. Holding me the way I've always wanted and never got. I let the tears fall freely as we stand in the hallway, my guitar clinging from me.

"Oh, Sweet Girl. It's all gonna be okay baby," she coos and I warm inside at the pet name she's always called me. "Come on, let's go get some tea and we can talk."

She pulls off me and I follow her through to the small lounge. I look around, noticing all the pictures she's added around the room. She catches me looking and laughs.

"I missed you whilst you were gone so I pulled all the pictures I could find and shoved them everywhere," she laughs. "It's a bit mental, right?"

I smile as I glance over the pictures of me, some alone and some with her, dotted all over the mismatched furniture in brightly colored frames. My eyes land on the one at the center of the mantle. I walk over, brushing my fingers across the image of me and Mom. It was taken when I was fourteen years old. It was the day she bought me my guitar. I'm sat on the sofa playing it with her beside me, smiling. I wipe away the stray tear falling.

"No, Mom. It's perfect. I missed you," I say.

She smiles kindly before excusing herself and walking through to the kitchen. I pull my guitar off and slump down on the sofa. When she returns I'm softly playing it to try and ease the pain in my chest. She places the cup of tea on the small table and sits beside.

"So, Sweet Girl. Are you ready to talk about it? I've already yelled at your dad so which boy is it that I need to deal with?"

I laugh. My mom is practically a hippie. The idea of her yelling at anyone is hilarious. It's nice though, strange, but nice that she's here for me. I expected her to play ignorant, to let me handle it but here she is being the mother I always needed. The mother she had been when I was just a kid dancing around her bedroom to music that was too old for me.

"I don't want to talk. It won't change anything," I still my hands on the guitar and place it gently on the floor, wincing from the sounds its making. "I need a new guitar."

"Well, that I can fix. We'll go get you one tomorrow."

"I guess I better ask Lenny if I can have my old job back at the record store."

My mom takes my hand gently. "Don't rush things, Hallie. How about we spend the day tomorrow just us. We can go shopping and for lunch. Things might seem better after some time away from thinking about it all, okay?"

I look at her face, hopeful and desperate. I nod my head slowly before settling back on the chair and lifting my knees to my chest. Mom reaches for the remote and puts my favorite Channing Tatum movie on. Together we stay quiet and watch the TV. The ache is there, but I lay it to rest for the night and enjoy my time with my mom. I need this, need her, and she's come through for me.

Tomorrow I'll spend the day with her like she wants, and then I'll attempt to piece my life back together.

CHAPTER TWENTY-EIGHT

Nate

"You're a fucking idiot, Nathan Harris."

I spin to face the pouty blonde behind me. Her eyes are wide with fury racing through them as she stares me down. I barely feel the sting of her anger, my own making it impossible to acknowledge anything else.

"Excuse me?" I question.

She takes a step closer to where I'm standing at my doorway. She barreled up here and banged loudly on the door, forcing me from my comfortable position on the couch. I assumed she was mad at Rye over something but I was wrong. The girl is out for blood, apparently mine.

"It's been an entire week and I'm wondering why the fuck you haven't got your shit together and gone to get our girl back," she growls.

Oh. This is about Hallie. Of course.

My stomach tightens at the thought of her. I've been in a really dark place since I found out about her *relationship* with that asshole professor. I've never felt so damn low in all my life. I was stupid. I should have listened to my dad and stayed away from her. That girl is trouble and I don't need that shit in my life. She played me, damn it, and that is what pisses me off the most. I don't get played. I'm *always* in control and I'd given it to her, knowing she needed it in order to let me in. I ran to her every need, gave her exactly what she wanted. I loved her, I hadn't told her, but I did and she stamped all over that.

"Why the fuck would I go to *her* after everything?" I growl back.

My mind flashes the images through my head. Her, with him. His hands caressing her face as she kissed him. How long has it been going on? *Is she with him now?* I believed her when she had told me it was bullshit. I defended her to everyone on campus and now I look a damn fool. Even Tami knows and hell didn't she enjoy coming over to gloat. If she wasn't a chick I'd have punched her out.

"Because you and I both know that those pictures were horseshit and it's all going to come out soon enough that it was lies. How fucking bad are you going to feel when you realize what you have done?"

I don't get to reply as Ryan come stalking out of his room.

"Babe? What's going on?" He asks, his head clearly half asleep.

"Nothing," she snaps then walks away.

I shake my head and step back into the dorm. Rye is watching me closely as I walk over to the fridge and pull a soda out. I ignore his stare and sulk to my room, slamming the door shut behind me. I don't need to hear his opinion on the whole thing either. I've been listening to it for an entire week. He'd come after me when I left Hallie in that room, pleading with me to go back to her and hear her out. I didn't need to though, I saw the fucking evidence. Still, I couldn't stop myself from waiting by the stairs for her. I knew she'd have to come out at some point. I almost broke when I saw her face. She'd been crying, I could see the puffiness around her eyes, but when she looked at me her eyes were ice. There was no explanation in them, no apology. She hadn't even responded when I asked her if she had been playing me. She just walked away without a word whilst I watched, painfully trying to keep my shit together.

I didn't go back to my dorm that day. I went straight over to the gym and punished my body for three solid hours before getting into my truck and driving around all night. I've almost drove to Iowa at least twice over the past week, something stopping me before I hit the highway every time. I did drive into Dexter though, parking up and walking the streets on several occasions. Willow spotted me on one occasion and dragged me into her music store. I humored her, unable to say no to the crazy bohemian chick. She sat me down with a cup of god knows what and forced me into telling her what was going on. She had received a cryptic message from Hallie to say she wasn't coming back but that was all. I'd almost laughed. It was more than I'd received.

I look down at my cell, as if accusing it for the reason she hasn't called or texted. What am I expecting? This is Hallie Clarke. She doesn't explain herself, doesn't apologize for doing something wrong. We were destined to fail from the start. She'd have never opened to me fully, no matter how hard I tried. I'm better off without her and her mood swings.

I throw my phone onto my bed and slump down after it, lying back and staring at the ceiling. I close my eyes, forcing my mind blank as thoughts of Hallie fly through it. This is ridiculous. She's just a chick, and there are plenty more in the world. I'm only nineteen, I have all the time in the world to find a new girl. A better girl. One I don't have to work so damn hard for. That's it. I'm done with this.

I stand suddenly and pocket my cell. I grab my keys from the bedside cabinet and leave the room. Ryan is still in the kitchen when I walk through.

"I'm going home," I tell him.

He nods slowly. "I think that's a good idea bro," a short laugh escapes his mouth. "You've been pacing around campus like a caged animal all week."

I snort. He isn't wrong. I've been on edge since *she* left and it's finally taking a toll on my sanity. I needed to get away, to go see Dad, and get my head straight.

"Can you give me a ride to the airport? Fuck driving."

"Yeah man sure. You wanna go now?"

I nod, eager to see the back of this dorm for a while. We head out and down to the parking lot and pull my cell out and buy a plane ticket over the phone. When I'm done, I stare out of the window as get further away from UM. It just isn't the same anymore. I see her everywhere. The faces of nameless strangers morph into hers on the street and it seems I'll never get the smell of her out of my room. The sweet honey scent has seeped into everything. I don't know what I'm feeling, but I'm more than ready for it to be over.

Ryan's voice distracts my wallowing.

"So, have you spoke to her?"

"To who?" I ask, even though I know exactly who he's talking about. I can feel the slight annoyance coming from him, but I keep my eyes focused outside and let out a heavy sigh. "No I haven't."

"Don't you think you should call her? Find out what the fuck happened?"

I turn sharply to face him. *Was he fucking insane?*

"I know what the fuck happened. She was fucking her English professor."

He shakes his head, clearly amused by something I said.

"Come on man, this is Hallie. If she was fucking someone else, she'd have told you," he says eventually.

"Obviously not."

The subject is dropped then and we spend the rest of the drive, thankfully, in silence. At the airport I thank him for the ride.

"No problem, bro. Say hi to Clay for me yeah?"

I nod and assure him I will before heading inside to collect my ticket.

The flight is short and I breathe a small sigh of relief when I'm finally in the cab heading home. I'd grown up in a large house in Tribeca. The house is a lot bigger than what Dad and I need, but he bought it back when Mom was still around. They had plans of a big family but she skipped out when I was six years old, never to be heard from again. Dad hasn't remarried and never fathered any more children but he kept the house. The only thing he had done was redecorated. There are no feminine touches to our place. It's a bachelor pad, complete with games room and home cinema. I loved growing up here, me and Rye. Our dads are partners of a highly successful law firm and so we were practically raised together. The Turners live only a block over from us so we spent most of our lives at each other's houses. The memory of the shit we used to get up to causes a small smile to play on my face as the cab driver pulls into my drive. I pay him and climb from the car, breathing in the familiar scent of home.

Damn that feels good.

My dad greets me at the door. I called him from the airport earlier to let him know I was coming home for a few days. We exchange a few words before settling down in the lounge.

"So, Nathan, you going to tell me what all this is about?"

I look to him at his words, slightly amused by the pointed look on his face. We are close, Dad and I. So close, in fact, that I know more about his 'relationships' than I care for. I let out a sarcastic laugh and tell him everything. I let my frustrations pour out of me to the only person I know won't judge me for it.

He is my dad after all.

CHAPTER TWENTY-NINE

Hallie

"Later, Hallie!"

I turn and offer a small wave to Rory as I exit the music store. It has been a long ass day and I can't wait to get home, eat, throw on my running shorts, and re-visit my favorite running track. The thought alone has me picking up my pace to the parking lot.

I've been back in Des Moines for almost two weeks now and it is as though I never left. Nothing ever changes here, the same people with the same problems. No one ever leaves, most staying for the 'up and coming' city life. I don't know what's wrong with people. It's still Iowa, still surrounded by corn, and still in the middle of nowhere. Not a single person here is going anywhere fast and they are likely to settle down with their two-point-five kids and live the same lives as their parents. And to prove my point further, I walked into a few of my old classmates this morning and had to endure the usual bullshit from them, snickering and taunting. I figured they would have heard about Cooper and Michigan. Damn social media. It has been branded all over the stupid Facebook page in my honor, the pictures and everything. *I bet Jason Evans loved that.* Codie had been the one to inform me that it was Tami who had shown them to her dad, The Dean. She apparently showed up at Nate's dorm after to 'console' him and slipped out that she'd been the one to witness the whole thing. I hadn't admitted out loud the small sense of joy I'd gotten when Codie told me how he'd shut the door in her face without saying a word.

After that Tami set her sights on making sure I was ruined everywhere I went by uploading the images where everyone could see them. I may as well have been back in high school. I'm still a social pariah, still work in a music store, and still hate the world. My cell begins to ring from my pocket as I reach my car so I pull it out, reluctantly smiling at the caller ID.

"Hey Codie."

"Hallie! Oh my God I miss you, I'm so fucking bored! How the hell are you?"

I laugh into the receiver as I drop down into the driver's seat of my car. Codie has called me at least once a day since I moved back home. She tries to keep me up to date with everything and gives me all the gossip she knows I don't care about. I know what she's doing though. She's saying everything she can without mentioning Nate. I'm grateful. Just the thought of him causes pain to sear through my chest. I see his tortured face in my sleep every night and feel the stab of betrayal from him all the damn time. I'm mad at him because he didn't let me explain, but mostly I was mad at myself for letting him consume me so much that I felt I had to. I let him in and now I'm learning my lesson. I squash the feelings down and reply to Codie.

"I'm okay, just got off work. You good?"

"No!" She exclaims. "I'm meeting Ryan's parents tonight. What do I do? What do I *wear?*"

I can hear her rifling through clothes on the other end of the cell. The sound makes me smile small to myself, the now familiar sadness on my shoulders getting heavier. I miss her more than I ever thought I could. She's my only friend and I got used to seeing her every day, even if she is a little too 'out there' for my usual liking.

"Wear anything. You look great in everything," I tell her and she huffs before informing me that was exactly the same as what Ryan said and it was not helpful. I laugh in response.

"Are you still getting those goofy messages?" She asks.

A heavy sigh escapes me.

Ever since I came home I've been getting text messages from the familiar 'JC'. It seems now I was no longer on campus, they've found a whole new way to annoy me. I'm never going to get away from it all.

"Yeah, I got one just this morning," I tell her then put on my best aggravating asshole voice to mimic the text. "Hallie, I can't wait to see you again. Things can finally be as they should now." Codie laughs as I gag down the line.

"You know you should probably change your cell number, Hal."

I laugh. "What? So they can turn up at my house? I already moved out of one place, and they found my number. I change that and they'll find my house."

She chuckles down the line. "You're probably right."

We talk for a few minutes longer before she hangs up to go and get ready. I start the engine of my Focus and make the short journey home. After talking to her I'm entering the ditch of depression I've been fighting hard to avoid for the past fortnight. It's going to take a long, hard run to numb the pain, it always does.

The house is empty when I arrive home, but that's to be expected. It's Friday which means Mom will be at her Yoga class with Hazel, her friend. I kick my boots off at the bottom of the stairs and stroll through to the lounge. After clicking the button on the landline, I half-listen to messages and wander over to the fridge. We always have a million messages on the phone. Usually it's men my mother has dated, or someone wanting money from us. Neither is overly welcome. I ignore their voices as I pull out everything I need to make the grilled cheese sandwich I've been fantasizing about all day. I almost drop the cheese when I hear the next voice.

What does he want?

I walk over and stare at the phone accusingly as my father's voice filters out.

"Hallie, I think we need to have a conversation about what happened in Michigan, and I hope for your own sake that you aren't still seeing that professor," I hear him release a long frustrated breath. "Call me back."

Fat chance.

I erase the message, as I have with all the others, and go back to the kitchen. Whilst my grilled cheese is cooking to perfection I flick on the CD player by the window and turn the volume up full. The Byrds fill the room and I can't help but smile. Roger McGuinn is a God.

One good thing about being back home was the music. Both Mom and I are obsessed, and she likes all the older rock anthems like me. It is how we bonded when I was younger, and again now when I'm older. Ever since I came home she's been so different. It's almost as if the last six years hadn't existed and I'm back to being thirteen again, dancing around in her bedroom, and listening to her old records. I smirk to myself. *I still listening to her old records.* She'd been ecstatic when I showed her my collection of Bon Jovi records. The pride in her eyes had floored me. My mother is never proud of me, or she's never showed me she is anyhow. Things are better now though. The last couple of weeks she has helped me to dull the loss I'm feeling from college. She's kept my father away too and one night I sat and listened to her yelling at him down the phone. We are closer than we ever have been before and I'm kinda' loving it. I even played her some of my own songs, causing her to tailspin off about how I should be on a stage. I poured my heart and soul out to her after the first few days of being here, telling her everything that had happened back on campus. Codie, the rumors, Cooper, the attack, the notes/texts, and Nate. She held me as I cried and I let myself take the comfort she was giving, needing it more than I needed my next breath.

At least something good came out of all this drama.

I take my food upstairs with me and eat as I change. Friday evenings to me mean my favorite running trail at Gray's Lake.

The air has cooled by the time I'm pulling up in the parking lot of the lake. It's why I wait until this time to come here. When I was younger, before Michigan, I came here every Friday and every Wednesday at seven pm. I seem to have fallen into that same routine now I'm back. My cell beeps signaling a text. I glance at the screen, noticing its 'JC' again and decide to ignore it. I'm not about to let that crazy fool ruin my run.

I climb out my car and stretch out my muscles as my eyes scan the area. There are a few people dotted about and a couple heading up to the trail but it's fairly empty. I smile at the thought. Not that it matters. I rarely stick to the track anyway. I have my own path, through the trees where the ground is tougher and I can punish my muscles harder.

I push my earphones in, click shuffle, and set off. Billy Joel pounds through and I match my strides with the beat of the music. The world around me fades until I'm left with only myself, the beat in my ears, and the ground beneath me. At the first curve of the path I veer off into the light woodlands. I take the first lap of the lake at ease and then push harder for the second. By the third my breathing is labored and my throat is raw.

As always, my thoughts drift to Nate. No matter how hard I try, I can't get his face out of my head. My body responds as images of what once was begin to flash through my mind. I pound my legs harder on the ground, as if somehow the harsh strides will force him back to my subconscious. It doesn't, it never does, and the pain rips through me. It feels as if something has reached inside me and torn my heart from my chest, thrown it to the ground, stepped all over it, and then put it back in not quite beating the same way. The pain is so deep, so agonizing, and so intense, that my heart is mangled beyond recognition. My mind is numb, racing in circles, unable to make sense of what I'm feeling. I've gone so long without letting anyone past the ice walls I built so high, that I forgot how much it hurts to reconstruct them. Forgetting is impossible and I'm not sure I'll ever heal.

I stop and lean against a tree when my own conflicting emotions almost make me fall. I have to get a damn grip on this. My chest heaves as my lungs fight for clean air. I bring my water bottle to my mouth, the cool liquid soothing the harshness in my throat but doing nothing for the coldness of my heart. My gaze falls over my surroundings. The sun is just starting to set, making the green of the leaves seem brighter under the burnt orange glow. It seems a direct contrast to the stormy darkness that's blooming inside me. I can see the main path through the trees and my body begs me to take the shortcut and head back to the car but I know my mind won't rest until I finished. I switch my music to Guns N Roses – Don't Cry and set off down the trail at a slow pace.

I don't make it ten strides before I'm stopped short by a hooded figure standing in my way. I step back as he steps forward, confusion clouding my already messed up mind. My nerves frazzle, holding me in place as I try to recognize who's blocking me. Only the bottom half of the face is visible, but that mouth. I've seen it, I know I have. I pull my earphones from my ears and let them hang from my neck, the music still faintly hearable in the background.

Who the hell is that?

"Hallie," he breathes, a lazy smile spreading across his face.

He pushes the hood of his jacket from off of his head, allowing me to see him fully as he moves closer.

Oh crap.

"Professor Cooper?" The hairs on the back of my neck stand to attention. "What are you doing here?"

He laughs, almost wickedly, a sound that punches at my eardrums.

"Please, I think it's time you call me James," when I don't respond he continues. "You weren't responding to my messages, what was I supposed to do?"

Messages? What messages? Wait... *No.* JC. James

Cooper. Damn it! I should have figured that out sooner. It's painfully obvious now. He must see the recognition on my face as he smiles knowingly and steps closer again. I will my body to react and move away but it betrays me, the gleam behind his eyes making me immobile. The foul smell of stale alcohol radiates from him in waves, his steps slightly staggered.

"I wanted to keep my distance. I knew you were a little upset about college and everything but don't you see," he takes my hand and clings to it. "This all had to happen, Hallie."

I look up into his eyes, the desperation behind the drunken glaze scaring the shit out of me. The man is crazy, drunk and crazy. A ball of dread begins to crawl up my throat as my heart pounds harder. Why is he doing this? I've never lead him on or given him any reason to think I felt anything but platonic teacher-student feelings for him.

"Mr Cooper," I start but I'm stopped when he grabs at my wrists.

His eyes harden, his voice mean. "Hallie for fuck sake, call me James."

"Sorry," I choke as I pry my hands free from his. "James... this can't happen."

I think carefully about my words and speak slowly. "You are, I mean, *were* my teacher. I don't look at you like that."

His arm swings and connects with my cheek before I can register the movement. I feel the sting of the hit all over my face, the momentum forcing my head to snap back as I crumble to the ground. My hand flies to the sore area and I wince from the pain. Tears burn in the corners of my eyes but I manage to blink them back, my mind already acknowledging that this isn't a situation where crying will help me.

You can't negotiate with crazy.

"Is this about that boyfriend? Where is he now, huh?" He growls, his long frame towering over me.

I flinch from the venom in his voice and he hauls me back to a standing position. My entire body trembles, fear pulsing through me in sharp waves. I keep my eyes trained on the floor, not wanting to look Cooper in the face. He's lost his damn mind completely. My gaze lands on my phone, the music still faintly playing through the headphones. If only I could get to it without him knowing. As if sensing the ideas running through my head he pulls my attention back to him, his voice back to the usual soft southern tones.

He cups my face gently. "I don't want to hurt you," he says. "You need a *real* man baby, one that can look after you properly and give you what you really want."

His hand moves to the back of my neck as he forces his lips against my own. His mouth moves urgently against mine, the bitter taste of cheap alcohol making my stomach turn. I fight myself free of him, pushing him as far back as I can then turn to run. I'm fast, he'll never catch me.

Wrong.

He's on me within seconds, forcing me back against a tree. The rough bark scratches my back through the thin shirt I'm wearing as Cooper presses his body into me.

"Why do you fight this, Hallie? We're meant to be," his damp forehead rests against mine, the sweat dripping from his face to mine. I shudder for a whole new reason as he continues. "Can't you see that?"

I shake my head in response, unable to open my mouth to let any words out. He sighs heavily and lifts back from me. Maybe he's regaining some sense and is about to let me go. He reaches his hand to the back of his neck.

"I didn't want to have to do this, Hallie." His hand moves to behind him.

Do what?

"But I need you."

I catch the small glimmer of silver before I feel the pressure in my stomach. I groan, my eyes watery and wide as I drop once again to the ground. I don't scream, my throat clogged with fear and pain. Cooper crouches down beside me and runs his hand through my hair, the knife hanging loosely in his other hand.

"I can't watch you be happy with someone else."

I press my own hand against my abdomen as if I can somehow stop what has already happened. My shirt is wet to touch and when I pull my hand away, I can see the red stickiness of my own blood. The sight seems to amplify the pain and it burns across my body. I'm numb but I can feel, hot and cold all at the same time. It's too much, a dull ache heating my entire torso. Cooper kisses the top of my head then stands and turns away.

"Please," I say, my voice nothing but a rasp.

He doesn't turn and through my now blurring vision, I watch him walk away. My mind blanks, and despite the agony coursing through me, I welcome it. For the first time in what feels like forever my head isn't spinning, my heart isn't aching and my brain is at peace.

I close my eyes and let the darkness wash over me.

Peace.

NATE

"Here's your ticket, sir."

I mumble a thank you at the overly polite woman behind the counter and stalk away. It's time to go back to Michigan and deal with my shit. Or move on from my shit, at least. I don't know. All I know is that I can't hide out at Dads anymore. I flick a glance at the flight board and groan inside when I see I still have three hours before my plane. I didn't plan this very well, at all. My cell begins to ring from my pocket. I pull it out and check the caller ID before answering.

"Rye, what's up?"

He hesitates. "Hey man, where are you?"

"Airport, why?"

I can hear Codie muttering something in the background, but it's too distant for me to make out the words. I stroll towards the coffee shop in the corner. Might as well sit in there. Ryan's voice comes back through the speaker.

"Look, it's about Hallie."

My muscles tense from her name. I didn't want to hear it, or anything about her. She's torn me apart, and I don't want to know. After everything, all the time we spent together, all the assholes I chewed out for her, she betrayed me anyway. I've been an idiot, believing her when she said she isn't the girl everyone makes her out to be. I believed her when all along she is exactly that girl. I bet her and Cooper had a good fucking laugh about it. Man, I wish I could punch that guy. Really fucking punch him. But he's been MIA since he was 'escorted' off the campus. He looked about as sorry as Charles Manson. Fucker.

"I don't wanna hear it," I snap to Ryan, then disconnect the call.

I'm being a dick, but I can't listen to what he has to say. Hallie Clarke is no longer my problem, and can do whatever, or whoever, the hell she pleases. I order a coffee from the counter and saunter to a table at the back. My eyes drift over the rest of the people in here, landing on a familiar man seated two tables down from me. He's muttering to himself as he taps his fingers on his laptop. He lifts his cup to his mouth, his gaze transfixed on the screen. *No way.* I sip at my own drink, unable to keep from staring at him. I'm searching for the similarities between him and Hallie. They don't exactly look alike, but I can see it. The way he's sat, unaware of the world around him, is all Hallie. She's the same. Ignorant to other people, lost in her own damn bubble. As if sensing my stare, George Clarke looks up and locks eyes with mine. I offer him a slight nod when I see the recognition cross over his face. He stands, reluctantly, and walks over to me. I lean back in my chair, amused that he feels he needs to acknowledge me. Suit stiffs are always the same. Their manners mean they have to have a conversation with everyone they know. He sits opposite me, his mouth pressed in a hard line.

"Nathan, hello."

"Mr Clarke," I respond, then take a large gulp of my drink.

"How are you?"

"Fine. Yourself?"

He nods his answer and I inwardly groan. I hate these conversations, but I'm luckily well versed in them. It's like some standard script for those who have money. I hate the whole damn thing. It's all unspoken words, and assholes being nice to your face, even though they hate your damn guts. This is a prime example. I have nothing in common with this man, and I know from the look in his eye that he doesn't approve of me. It's there, hidden behind the professional courtesy.

"And how is my daughter? It seems she doesn't want to talk to me," he says.

Something flashes across his face, but it's too quick for me to really decipher it. Again I can't help but think of Hallie.

"I wouldn't know," I mutter back at him, wanting to end this conversation as quickly as possible.

"What do you mean? You're her boyfriend, correct?"

No, dude. I'm just another sucker, left in the wake of Hurricane Hallie.

"We're not dating anymore."

He has the decency to look at least a little shocked, before nodding slowly. I mean, he was there. He saw the photos too. Why is he asking me this? Like I'd stay with her after that.

"I see," he says. "I'm sorry you have been caught up in the destruction that my daughter leaves behind."

He releases a long breath. "I'd like to be able to tell you that this is news, but she has a habit of making poor decisions. You're not the first to be tangled up in it."

My gut clenches at his words. I may be mad at her, but I don't need to hear her being bad-mouthed. This is her dad! He should be sticking up for her. A memory pulls at me, a conversation between myself and Hallie. She finally started opening up, and told me a little about her relationship with the man in front of me. We were in Dexter, her favorite place to go, sat on the small park as she tried, and failed, to teach me to play guitar. I try to recall the words she said, as he begins to rattle off all the problems he has with his daughter.

"So come on, what's the deal with your dad?"

Her mouth presses into a flat line. The laughter from thirty seconds ago, completely gone. I know this is a hard subject for her, but I want to know why. She's such a vault, always keeping her thoughts to herself. I want to know everything about her, know what's hidden behind the dead look in her eyes.

"There is no deal. We're just not close," she says.

"You're being vague."

Her eyebrow arches. "You're being nosy."

I laugh. Getting things out of Hallie is always a challenge, but the stuff she does reveal blows me away. There are so many sides to this girl.

"Come on, babe."

She lets out a long breath then begins to softly strum the strings of her guitar. I smile inside. This is something she always does when she's about to reveal. It's like the music helps her to get it out. Music helps her to do a lot of things, I just wish I understood it better. I wish I understood her better.

"We've never really been close. He wasn't exactly a hands on parent," she laughs, but it's humorlessly. "When I started high school, he wanted me to be the perfect daughter. He

forced certain friends on me, the kids of his colleagues, and made me go to fancy dinners. I hated those girls."

Her hands still. "When everything happened with Jason, it got worse."

My fists clench automatically. Hallie had already told me the story about the guy she lost her V-Card to. If I ever meet him, I'll enjoy putting my fist through his face. Hell, I wanted to fly down there the day she told me and show him exactly what happens to people who trash talk my girl, but she wouldn't let me and so I reluctantly let it go. I train my face straight, not wanting to interrupt her whilst she's finally sharing.

"He was really pissed about it. Told me I was an idiot for letting it happen. Then when the rumors started, he pretty much disowned me completely. Unless he needed someone to bitch at," she sighs. "Basically, I'm a constant disappointment to him because I'm not the preppy little princess he wanted."

She shrugs, but I can tell she's more cut up about it than she's letting on. "Now, I just avoid speaking to him as often as possible."

I bring my focus back to Hallie's dad in front of me. I have no respect for this man. If it was my daughter that had been treated that way, I'd have torn up the school looking for the asshole that put those tears in her eyes. No wonder she's the way she is. And shit... I've done exactly the same fucking thing to her. I turned my back on her, without letting her explain, just like him. I'm just as bad. The regret fills my stomach, and clings to my organs. I take a large drink of the coffee in front of me, trying to null the bitter taste in my mouth.

"Hallie has never really been a normal girl," George says, his head shaking slightly. "She likes the attention she gets from acting out."

I can see it. The disappointment, the shame, etched all over his face. He has no idea who she is, or what kind of person she is. He doesn't know anything about her. Likes the attention? Shit... he really doesn't know her. Hallie does nothing but avoid people and attention.

"Do you know what she does with her spare time?" I ask.

My question throws him off. I can't blame him, it's pretty fucking random. And I've been mute for the past fifteen minutes. But it's about time he had an actual insight into who his daughter was.

"Excuse me?"

"When she isn't working her ass off with school work, she's at homeless shelters. Feeding them, playing music for them, generally just spending time there. She volunteers at the centers, and has spent the past three months teaching one of the older regulars how to read," I smile small at the memory of Howard. I've met him a few times, and he is one of the best people I've ever known. His stories from his youth are hilarious. "She spends her weekends helping a woman run a music store, and refuses to take payment for it. You know, she got accepted to Yale and Harvard, but refused them. They wouldn't accept her scholarship because you earn too much money. She wanted to do it all on her own. So please, don't sit there and tell me all the things you think you know about her, when in reality, you have no idea who, or what, she is."

His mouth is agape as he stares at me and I fight the urge to lean forward and close it for him. Just before he replies, his cell begins to ring. He glances at the caller ID and lets out a frustrated huff before answering. I should leave, I know I should, but, I want to hear his response to my rant so instead I listen in on his call, and wait.

"Hello? No, I haven't gotten your messages yet, I've just

arrived in New York. Levi, calm down. What's happened?" His face is paling. *Levi?* Isn't Hallie's mom called Levi? "What do you mean hospital? How bad is it? Have the police been called? I'll get the first flight out. Tell her I'll be there soon. And Levi? I'm sorry."

He places his phone down with a hand that's trembling slightly. My own are shaking too. Hallie's mom. Hospital. Police. Hallie. George looks at me, his eyes wide in something closely relating to horror. Scenarios are flashing through my mind. Was this why Ryan was calling me? Shit. I'm a fucking idiot.

"I..." He stutters. "I have to go."

He stands, rushing back to his own table and collecting up his things. I can't move, panic immobilizing me to the chair. All I can do is watch him as he clumsily pulls at his belongings, stuffing them into his briefcase. Gone is the stiff, uptight man from before. Now, I'm looking at an out of control, worried father. Something is definitely not right. He hurries away from the table, then stops dead barely two feet from my own. He turns back, squaring his eyes with mine. I sit up, preparing myself for what I'm already guessing.

"Hallie is in the hospital. She's been hurt, badly."

CHAPTER THIRTY-ONE

Hallie

My entire body aches as I try, but fail, to reach the water on the side of the bed. Hell, even my eyebrows were aching. How is that normal? I woke up in the hospital yesterday, and I'm already desperate to get out. I attempted to leave earlier this morning, only to be stopped before I even made it off the bed by a pushy nurse. I don't want to be here. I want to be home, in my room, hiding from all of this. It's crazy, and I don't like crazy. With crazy comes drama, and drama is a huge no.

I was found on the trail by another runner. She called an ambulance straight away, and they found my cell phone and called my mom. I'm lucky, apparently. If I'd been left any longer I would have bled out. The knife punctured the left of my stomach, leaving damage to my spleen. It's mild, thanks to Cooper's bad aim, but it still hurts like hell. Hopefully though, I can get out of here soon. I'm desperate for solitude, and a bed that doesn't make my ass itch. I shudder, just the thought of all the people that might have lay here before me is sickening.

The door to my hospital room flies open and I almost

laugh at the sight of my mother. She's got my guitar hanging from her body and holding a bag in one hand, whilst balancing a box in the other. Her long hair is sticking to her face, messy, and still damp from her standard morning shower. I look down at her outfit: long wavy skirt with Aztec patterns covering it, white tank, and a soft cream cardigan. Most people would be embarrassed by her, personally I love her individuality. My mother doesn't give a damn what she looks like, or what people think of her. It's refreshing to see.

Her flip flops slap against the floor as she walks further into the room, cursing when she hits the visitor's chair with her hip.

"Hey, sweet girl," she says, dropping the bag and box onto the chair. "I brought you some things to help keep you sane until we can spring you outta here."

She dives into the box and begins pulling out candles and incense sticks. I watch her in amusement as she begins to put them around the room. She's such a hippie.

"Mom, I don't think the hospital are going to let you burn incense in here."

She turns to me and smirks. "Who says I was going to ask permission?"

I let out a short laugh and settle back on the bed. Once she's finished decorating, she comes to join me, finally handing me the drink I'd been desperate before. I shift uncomfortably to a complete sitting position so she can cross her legs opposite me. Her eyes are kind as she studies my face, lingering on the nasty bruise I know I have across my cheek. I remember the sharp bite of Cooper's hand connecting with my skin and stifle a shudder.

"How are you feeling today?"

I sip the water, frowning at the warm taste. "I'm okay. The cops are coming back later."

Mom frowns, her eyes darkening a little. "They better damn well find that guy before I do."

My fingers tremble around my drink without my permission. I hate this, hate how jittery I've become. It has been two days and they still haven't found Professor Cooper. I see him all the time though, his drunken face etched permanently into my brain. Every time I close my eyes, I see that dark gleam in his. I feel that harsh tear into my stomach as though it's happening all over again. My free hand moves to my stomach, pressing over it as if to somehow protect me from the wound that is already there. I fight back the flashbacks and memories, and force all my attention back on Mom as she continues.

"I brought your guitar. Not the new one, the old one. Figured you couldn't go running but at least you could play."

I smile, grateful for the gesture. My new guitar makes better music, but my old, beat up one brings me comfort like no other. The scratchy, out of tune sounds give me a sense of peace that I can't describe. It's familiar, mine.

"Thanks, Mom."

Her hand drops onto the thin sheet covering my legs. "Of course, honey," she lets out a long breath. "I finally got a hold of your dad."

I feel every muscle in my face harden. Mom has been leaving him messages since I was found yesterday. Over twenty-four hours it has taken him to get in touch. I shouldn't be surprised. This is George Clarke. He doesn't give a damn about me. Still, it hurts more than I care to admit. I thought I'd at least warrant a phone call.

"Great," I say dryly.

Her face showcases her distaste. "He's flying out, had just arrived in New York for a business trip apparently."

"How very decent of him," I reply, my voice laced in sarcasm.

Mom scoffs. She's been arguing with him constantly ever since I came home. She's furious with the way he handled everything in Michigan, and the rest of my life. We've become so close lately, Mom and me, it was almost as though we are friends. I've told her the full story about Jason Evans, and high school, and she coached me, giving me the advice I needed then. That was after she apologized eighteen thousand times. I told her it isn't necessary. It's not like she knew about it all. Mom isn't into social media, so she never would have known about the rumors, and I wasn't exactly forthcoming with information. Still, her guilt is obvious and she's been doing everything she can to make it up to me. Her anger at my father is also obvious, now more than ever. I heard her chewing him out on the phone a few times, livid that he believes the gossip on a social media website instead of seeing it for what it was – a bunch of kids being assholes. Her messages to him over the past day have gotten more and more neurotic as time has passed. I almost feel bad for him, as she is sure to hurl some abuse his way the second she sees him. However, he probably has it coming. I'm not about to save his ass. Not. A. Chance.

"Well maybe this time he'll decide to actually be a father to you."

I offer her a skeptical look at her words. *Yeah, right.*

Mom stays with me for most of the day, talking and distracting me with stories from her day job at the coffee shop. I love hearing about the customers, they do the funniest things. She listens intensely when the cops stop by to ask me more questions, and I have to fight my mouth into a flat line when she starts berating them for having not 'done their job'. It's hilarious. My mother doesn't get mad often, but when she does, she becomes uncontrollable. Her arms were flying around her, and the cops looked a mixture of amused and terrified. It made for great entertainment.

When I'm fighting to keep my eyelids from closing, she kisses my cheek and leaves the room. The little girl in me misses her instantly, but the socially closed off parts of me breathe a sigh of relief for finally being alone. My eyes find my guitar, pulling a reluctant smile from me when I notice Mom has left it completely within my reach. I lie back. I'll just have a little nap, and then let out some frustration on the strings.

My little nap turns into a full blown sleep, leaving me confused when I wake up and see that it's dark outside. I fix my gaze on the small window, the stars twinkling back at me. It's beautiful. The view pulls at a suppressed memory, and lacking my better judgement, I let myself relive it.

"Babe, where are you going?"

I turn back and look at Nate, smiling at his obvious confusion.

"Stop complaining," I say, then walk further into the park.

Nate follows me, jogging to catch up, and then twisting his fingers with mine. I revel in the contact. It had taken a while, but I'm used to it now. I'm used to him. I lead him along the familiar path and up the hill. At the top, I stop and lift my head to the sky. The stars shine above, drawing my attention. The view is spectacular. I glance around me, checking the area. Quiet, solitary, perfect. I drop to the floor and stretch out, turning my head in Nate's direction. He raises an eyebrow at me, so I pat the grass beside me in a silent explanation.

"Seriously?"

"Yes, seriously. Trust me?"

"Always."

He joins me on the floor, his head next to mine. I pull my phone and earphones from my pocket and plug them in. I press one of the speakers into my ear, and hand the other to Nate. I've made it my mission to introduce music into his life. It's not that he hates it, but he rarely listens to it. I can't accept this. He copies my action, and I press shuffle on my playlist. The Killers - Smile Like You Mean It filters through. I smile. I love this song.

"What now?" He asks.

I link my fingers with his and sigh. "Now, we make pictures with the stars."

I push the silly memory back down, and wipe the stray tear that had leaked through. It will do me no good to cry now. After forcing myself into a sitting position, I reach for my guitar. I got lucky in the hospital room department. I don't have any 'neighbors' so I don't have to worry about noise. If the doctors and nurses want to complain, they can bite me.

I find my favorite pick and tease the strings, the out of tune sounds causing me to laugh to myself. I finally get a new guitar and I still prefer this one. I clear my throat and begin to play properly, quietly singing the words that have been on my mind for weeks. I get lost in the music, deep in my own head for what seems like hours. In reality it's barely five minutes, a knock on the hospital door interrupting me, and pulling my attention away. They don't wait for me to respond, and I watch as the door pushes open.

I frown at the sight and loosen my grip on the guitar.

"Hallie," my dad says, his voice wary and quiet. "Can I come in?"

I nod, not really able to form words. The almost apologetic look on his face has rendered me speechless. This is definitely not a typical George Clarke look, and truth be told, I'm a little bit scared. My eyes follow him as he walks further into the room, stopping beside the bed.

"I heard you playing," he starts, his eyes on where my fingers are pressed lightly against the strings. "I had no idea you were that good. Your voice is beautiful."

Holy shit. Now he's going to compliment me, too? Is he trying to make my head explode? I shift uncomfortably, lifting the strap from my guitar over my head and placing it back down on the floor, letting it lean against the cabinet. I miss it immediately.

"Thank you," I reply, finally.

He smiles, a genuine fucking smile. At me! I pull nervously at the loose cotton on the sheets. I'm not used to this person. The disappointment and the shame that normally clouded his face when I'm near is what I'm used to. I have hardened myself to it, can handle it. But now, now he's looking at me like he actually cares a little for me and I don't know what to do. He drags the visitors chair front he corner of the room over to my bed and sits on it. My hand freezes when he places his over it and squeezes gently. I look up at his face, pain and regret flashing all over it. Oh this is too much. Maybe I should call the doctor? He's obviously experiencing an aneurism or something. Maybe he's sick.

"I was so scared when I got that message, Hallie. I swear, my heart literally stopped," he inhales loudly. "I'm sorry I wasn't here sooner."

"It's okay."

What else can I say? It is okay. I'm used to him not being here.

"No, it's not. And it hasn't been for a long time."

My face portrays my confusion, and so he continues.

"I haven't been a father to you, not really. And maybe if I had, you wouldn't be lying in this hospital bed right now."

I stay silent. Not sure if I can trust myself to reign in my own thoughts. His hand on mine, his apology, the way he's looking at me, it's all too much. I don't know how to respond, what I'm supposed to do. I've waited most of my life to have a father that cares, and now... I don't know. I can't trust him. Is this just because I'm in the hospital?

"Cooper would still be a psychopathic maniac whether you were here or not."

His face transforms, the guilt replaced with anger.

"Cooper? Professor Cooper did this? The teacher from Michigan?"

I guess no one told him, huh? Then again, he still thinks I was fucking him. Maybe it's about time I give him the reality check of exactly what happened. It will all come out at the trial anyway.

"Yeah. He's been sending me notes and messages for months," I start, sitting up in the bed fully and pulling my hand away from his. "I didn't know it was him though. He was just my English tutor, you know?"

I force back memories, missed signals, and annoyance at myself for not seeing it sooner. "That picture, the one that looks like us kissing, it's misunderstood," I cross my arms over my chest, a futile attempt at stopping the shiver that's running through my spine. "He... he came onto me. And I pushed him back. But Tami."

I shake my head. *That fucking girl.* "Tami is the dean's daughter, and she had, or probably still has, this thing for

Nate," just saying his name hurts my insides. It more painful than getting stabbed. "She took the picture, showed her dad. She also leads the Hallie Is A Whore Crusade on Facebook."

I ignore the guilt I see wash over him. I don't need to process that. I'm not going there. I push on. "After I left campus, I came home. Cooper got me on the trail whilst I was running. He'd been waiting for me."

I feel a tear fall from my eye as my mind begins to recall the events. The harshness of his voice, the slap of his hand against my skin, the blade slicing through me. "It's my own stupid fault," I spit out. "I should have seen him for what he is."

Dad grabs my hand again, clutching it in both of his. I barely feel it, my mind still lost in the haze of my own self-punishing. I'm exhausted. I'm so fucking tired of trying to keep my shit together. I just want peace, to be left alone, to live normally. The tears fall quicker, big ugly sobs dropping onto the sheets as I bow my head. I can't stop them. It's like a dam has broken, the pent up emotion pouring out of me. I can't do it anymore, I can't keep fighting it, fighting everyone. My dad lifts from the chair leans onto the bed, pulling me close to him. I cry onto his shoulder, his hand rubbing my back gently.

"Let it all out, Hallie," he soothes. "I'm so sorry."

We stay like that for what feels like hours, but in reality is probably only a few minutes. My tears diminish to nothing, my throat hoarse. I pull back, and reach for the drink on the unit beside the bed. Now I've calmed down, I feel awkward. My dad has just held me whilst I cried. Me. He held me. He's never held me, not even when I was a kid. As if sensing my unease, he sits back onto his chair and looks around the room. A small laugh escapes him.

"I see your mom has been decorating."

I flash him a watery smile. "You know how she is. She argued for a full twenty minutes with the doctor about the incense."

"In the hospital, when you were born, she did the same thing," he laughs, really laughs. "The midwife was telling her to push, and she was complaining at me for lighting the blue oil burner instead of the red one."

I join in with his laughing. Mom really is a complete nut.

We spend the next hour or so talking, nothing serious, just actually talking. I talk about Codie and my music, and he tells me about work and some of his more amusing clients. We swap stories about my mom some more, and I get a little insight into George Clarke - before the briefcase. I tell him about Willow and the music store, and the shelters I volunteered at, and he listens, actually listens to me. It's weird, and amazing, and totally surreal all at the same time.

After the second time the nurse comes in to warn him about visiting times, he kisses my head and leaves with the promise of being back tomorrow. I lie back on the bed, and for the first time in too long, I drift off easily.

CHAPTER THIRTY-TWO

HALLIE

My eyes open to the sound of a familiar voice. No... It can't be. Am I dreaming? Shit. I'm hearing things now. For a second there I could have sworn I just heard...

"Hallie! Shit, you're awake."

I turn over. There was no mistaking that one. My eyes land on Codie as she practically jumps up and down beside the bed. Holy crap. It's too early for this. What is she doing here? I groan and lift my hand to my face, rubbing the ruminants of sleep from my eyes. Codie rushes to the door of the room.

"Ryan! Babe she's awake. Get in here."

Great. The other half is here too. Resigning myself to the inevitable, I sit up in the bed, wincing from the pain stretching across my abdomen. The nurses have been trying to force painkillers down my throat since I got here, but it's not happening. I don't need them, and I don't believe in medication being used when it's not completely essential. There are too many people out there that are suffering. Besides, the medical bill is already going to be through the fucking roof. Shit, something else to worry about. I gotta get out of this hospital. Mom and I can't afford this. Codie climbs onto the bed opposite me, pulling me from my thoughts.

"You have no idea how good it is to see you awake right now," she says.

I watch her carefully, the tear stains on her face glistening under the artificial light. The usual sparkle in her eyes has dulled, and now she is staring at me as though I'm some rare artefact at the museum. Her preppy pony tail is nowhere to be seen. Instead, she has her long blonde hair piled up on top of her head as though she's just got out of bed. I've never seen her look this... rough? Is that the right word? Codie never leaves without her make up perfect and hair immaculate. This is so weird. Also, why has she been crying? What's happened? I ask her as much as she deadpans, looking at me as though I've just told her the sky is green with purple spots. Why is everyone always looking at me like that?

"Why have you been crying? Really? You're asking me that?" Her head shakes in disbelief. "Because of you! I've been a mess since your mom called yesterday. I was so worried and scared. I didn't know what had happened or if you were okay."

I frown. I'm not used to all of this. She's worried about me? That's... different. I'm used to people just leaving me be, not really caring. I've been on my own so long, I don't know how to deal with people actually giving a crap about me.

"My mom called you?" I ask, barely believing this little bit of information.

"Yeah. She called me, and I told him," she inclines her

head to where Ryan is just walking through the door, a bleak expression on his face. I ignore the tiny pang of disappointment I feel when I notice that Nate isn't with them. I don't know why I expected him to be, he hates me. I shake off the thoughts, it will do no good to go there now, and tune back in to Codie. "We flew out as soon as we could, and then your dad arranged a car for us."

She smiles sweetly. "He seems different."

"You have no idea," I mutter.

Ryan slumps down on the visitors chair by the bed. His eyes are hooded over as he studies my face. I can see the lack of sleep evident all over him, but then if Codie has been hysterical, I can see why he would have had no sleep. When Codie gets upset, she makes sure everyone suffers with her. I can only imagine what he's had to deal with.

"How you feeling, Hal?" He asks.

His voice is low, too low. His face is pinched as fixes his gaze just below my eye, burning holes through the already bruising skin. His brows furrow, eyes narrowing as a tight scowl flattens on his face. I can't keep staring at that expression. Ryan is a joker, always smiling and annoying me with his 'I want to be a playboy' attitude. I can't deal with him any other way. Too much is changing right now; my mom, my dad, everyone. They've all gone bat shit crazy. It's got to end.

"What have I told you about calling me Hal?" I arch my brow. "It's Hallie, asshole."

He lets out a short laugh, my words having the desired effect.

"Hallie, I really want to hug you right now," Codie says. "I mean, I really need to."

I roll my eyes for form, but I'm secretly grateful that

they came. No one has ever cared enough before. I've never had friends that actually give a shit. I shuffle over to the left of the bed, and pat the right. Codie smiles wide before crawling into the space. She kick off her shoes and tucks her legs under the sheets. Her arms wrap around my neck as she pulls me close. I let her, chuckling when she kisses the side of my head.

"I'm so glad you're okay," she whispers into my ear.

"I'm glad I'm okay, too."

"Can I get in on this?" Ryan asks, and when we look over he has the biggest smile I've ever seen. That's better.

"No," we say, in unison, then laugh at his wounded look.

He sits with us for a short while, before excusing himself to go and check into a hotel. Apparently, they aren't leaving until they're happy I'm not going to die. Codie stays with me, cheering loudly when the doctor tells me I can go later today. She stays in the bed beside me, and we spend the time talking and laughing. She tells me her plans for the summer, and I tell her about the record store and the shelters. She laughs as I tell her about seeing the girls I used to go to school with, saying how she wishes she could meet them. I almost want to introduce her for the comedy value. Codie isn't subtle, at all. The girls from high school wouldn't know what to do with her.

Mom stops by between her shifts and I watch in awe as Codie and her hit it off. Trying to decide which one of them is more enthusiastic is difficult. Their chatter is loud, animated, and too fast for me to keep up. So instead, I just sit and stare. I'd forgotten how awesome my mom is. It's so good to have her back. Watching her like this brings all of my good childhood memories flooding back. The times where we would spend time, just her and me. Picnics on the park, dancing around the house, playing music together. We used to have so much fun, and I'd forgotten just how much. We both got lost in our own lives and drifted from each other. I can't put all the blame on her, I had pulled away just as much, but we're fixing it. We're gonna be okay.

It's my dad who arrives to pick me up and take me home. He smiles as he walks into the room, wearing jeans and a plain shirt. The sight of him almost knocks me on my ass as I stand and stare. I mean, I don't remember ever seeing him in anything but a suit. After a brief argument, he lets me walk out the hospital, instead of being wheeled out in a wheelchair. His arm stays firmly around my waist though, demanding I put all my weight on him. Any other girl would love her daddy taking care of her. Me? I just put my head down and pray that I don't see anyone I know. Codie leaves at the same time as we do, Ryan picking her up and helping to carry my things to the car.

At my house, I let Dad help me onto the sofa, then watch him in mild amusement as he attempts to work the ancient coffee maker in the kitchen. *Good luck, pal.* That thing gives out more electric shocks than it does coffee.

It's so strange to see him moving around mine and Mom's house. He doesn't really fit in here, the craziness of it doesn't suit his put together lifestyle and demeanor. I've only ever been to his place once, a townhouse right in the middle of the city. The furniture is all matching and modern, the walls bare, and everything immaculately tidy. You can see that he doesn't spend a lot of time there, it isn't very welcoming. There are no pictures on the walls, no personal things around the place. It's an outer shell, somewhere to sleep and nothing more. I only stayed for the one night, after being forced to attend a company function with him. I didn't want to, but it was easier than going home. I felt like a spare part there, sleeping in a spare room that had no identity. My room here is filled with posters and piles and piles of records. I like things tidy, but there isn't a lot of room to hold my stuff. Our house is small, only just enough for Mom and me, and we both have a ton of stuff.

Dad joins me back in the lounge, handing me the steaming cup. I place it on the coffee table and cross my legs on the couch. He perches on the chair opposite and regards me carefully. I offer him a small smile which he returns. That is still hard to get used to, George Clarke smiling. It's definitely going to take a while. His eyes are scanning the room, a nostalgic look about his face as he lingers on the pictures mom had recently put up.

"She went a bit crazy with the photos," I say, not enjoying the silence.

"It's nice to see," he brings his focus back to me. "How are you feeling?"

"Better, thank you."

His cell rings from its position on the coffee table. There is an apology in his eyes, but I still frown slightly as he answers it. His job and work have always been the problem. I've never been able to compete with it, never been important enough to even come close.

"George Clarke," he barks down the phone. "No, I can't right now. I'm with my daughter, and will be with her for the next few days at least."

He releases a frustrated breath whilst I sit gaping at him. "Well, you'll have to get Charlie to handle it as I'm spending time with Hallie. This is why I hired him. I see. And have we heard back from Michigan?" What business does he have in Michigan? What is he doing? "Okay, that's good news. I will let you know when I've spoken to her.

Has Karl been briefed on her case? Good. Okay. Bye, Sylvia."

He places the phone back on the table and picks up his own drink, sipping it carefully. He winces from the taste.

"This is really bad coffee."

I snort a laugh. I can absolutely agree with him on that.

"I think the coffee maker is older than me."

"That explains it."

He places the cup down, and squares his gaze on me.

"Do you want to go back to college, Hallie?"

Huh? Do I want to go back to college? After everything, could I face it? Tami, Jace, Nate, all of them. I don't know if I could go back to seeing them every day, to dealing with the crap. Everyone would know about Cooper, and I don't want to re-live it. I don't want to talk about it or deal with it at all. But then, I really want my degree. My walls crumbled yesterday. The bricks melted into tears when I finally give in my fight with my dad, with the world. I need time. I need to figure all the things in my head out. I need to silence the noise of other people.

"I want to," I start. "But I don't think I can. Not yet."

I exhale, defeated. "I can't anyway. I lost my scholarship and I have to pay the medical bills and-"

He cuts me off.

"Hallie, don't worry about medical bills and college tuition. I have enlightened Dean Vincent to the actual events, and he's more than happy for you to go back. I can pay for college, Hallie, I want to."

"I'm not ready."

A look of understanding clouds his features, as he nods his head slowly. He picks up his cell and begins to tap away at the screen. I leave him to it, assuming he's organizing some work, and pick up my coffee. I sip at the harsh liquid.

It really is bad coffee. Buying a new maker may have to become a priority. Dad mutters to himself as he stares into the screen. I almost laugh. I know I do this too when I'm concentrating. Who'd have thought we actually have something in common? I sure as shit wouldn't. After a few minutes, he looks up and at me. There's a smile behind his eyes.

"I have a proposition for you."

"Okay..." I say, uncertainty lacing my voice.

"I know I haven't been great father to you, but I want to change that. I really want to get to know you, Hallie. Despite what you must think, I do love you," my breath catches in my throat as I grip onto my coffee cup. It burns my hand but it's the only thing keeping me anchored to the moment. *Did he just say he loves me?* He continues. "I was thinking, maybe you could take your classes online for a year and come with me? Then go back to Michigan when you're ready. I have some travelling to do, New York, San Francisco, lots of places. We could travel together, and you could see some of the country."

His face drops a little. "It's just an idea."

My mind reels with his words. Could I just take off for a year? Could I spend it with him, getting to know my dad, getting to know myself? If I went to New York, I could try and catch up with Bobby. That's where he is. I have his address somewhere, he's always sending me demos of his new band. And San Francisco is on my places to visit list. But no... I couldn't. *Could I?*

"Is that possible? Like, could I really do that? Take my classes online and travel with you? Won't you be really busy?" I ask.

He laughs. "I can do whatever the hell I like, Hallie. It's a perk of being the boss," his eyes are all but twinkling as he smiles at me. "I'd love to show you around the country. If this is something you want Hallie, then I will make it happen."

I take a deep breath. I'm going to do this. I need to do this.

"Okay," I say. "I want this."

An entire week after the attack, Cooper is finally caught and arrested. They found him holed up in some shit pile motel, just outside of town. His room walls were covered in my pictures, pictures he had taken himself. Creep. The news gave me shudders, but a weight is lifted now that I know he's no longer out there. My dad has hired a lawyer to represent me for the case, but as Cooper is pleading guilty there will be no trial, only a sentencing, and I sure as hell won't be present for that. I don't want to look at his face again. I just want the entire thing behind me.

Dad has also arranged everything for our trip, including informing my mother. She's over the moon with the idea, happy that we were finally going to get some father-daughter time. I'm a little more apprehensive on that, but I'm trying out my new optimistic disposition. We're leaving tomorrow, starting our trip in San Francisco. I'm actually kind of excited. Or I would be if I could get this packing finished. I've been in my room for the past three hours, with Codie, trying to decide what I need to take with me. By that, I mean, she's throwing clothes at me and I'm stuffing them into a bag. Except for the pink stuff she's managed to find. That does not make it into the bags, hell no. I eye her skeptically as she thrusts a denim skirt in my direction. I don't remember buying this. Hell, I know I never bought this.

"No," I warn. "Where did you even find that?"

She sucks her lips into her mouth, her eyes touching the ceiling.

"It may have been in my suitcase at the hotel."

I let out a laugh, shaking my head at her. I add the skirt to my things, just to please her. I'll never wear it, but the smile on her face is worth the charade. I'm really going to miss her whilst I'm away, but she has already told me that she will be visiting me, wherever I am. I hope she can make it to New York, I'd love for her to meet Bobby. I'm also going to send her postcards of all the places we visit. She's told me she'll decorate her walls with them. I'll have to keep that in mind when I'm picking them out. I'll find the most inappropriate ones possible, she'll love that.

It takes us another two hours, but I finally have everything packed up and ready to go. We lie, side by side, on my bed and stare up at the ceiling. Our feet are splayed on the wall whilst we wait for the nail polish we just applied to dry. Smash Mouth - You're a Rockstar is playing low in the background.

"I kissed the kid next door when I was eight, then ran away," Codie whispers. "He smelt like Cheetos."

I laugh, unable to stop it before it bubbles out of me. Damn it feels good. We've been sharing silly secrets for the past twenty minutes. It was her idea, obviously, but I'm enjoying it.

"When I was fifteen, I stole my mom's old truck with a high school senior. He taught me to drive the stick, and I let him fondle my chest."

It's Codie's turn to laugh now. And she does, loudly, rolling over to her side and into me. I chuckle with her. It's times like this that I feel really grateful I found her. Her eyes grow serious after a few seconds, her hand touching mine softly.

"He misses you too," she says. "He's just being an idiot."

I offer her a tight smile. I wasn't about to have that conversation, not now, not ever. Nathan Harris is a no go area.

It's late when I walk her down stairs and to the door. Ryan is waiting in the driveway, talking on his cell. He offers me a one finger salute before walking a few steps away from us. I know this action means it's Nate on the phone. It has happened a few times over the past couple of days. They both avoid mentioning him, and I avoid thinking about how much it hurts that he isn't with them. He still believes I was cheating on him, and I'm not about to correct him. If he thinks that I could do something like that to him, then he obviously doesn't know me as well as I thought he did. Besides, it's time to think about me. I need to get my own head straight, before I think about other people. I needed to find my own sound, instead of everybody else's, instead of his. Codie hugs me at the door, careful not to squeeze me too tight. I am still recovering after all.

"Promise me that you're definitely going to come back," she says, the tears beginning to build at the corner of her eyes.

"I promise. I'll be back for junior year."

"You better had be, or I'm coming to get you," she sniffs, leaning into Ryan as he comes back to join us. "I'll have a room ready for you when you come back because like hell I'm gonna let you live with anyone else."

"You only want me for my cooking," I laugh.

"And your bad taste in music."

We exchange a few more words before she climbs into

the car with Ryan and drives off. I watch as they get smaller in the distance. I never thought I'd have actual friends, and now I do, I can't imagine my life without them. Mom comes out and wrap her arm over my shoulders.

"She's a nice girl."

I smile to myself.

"She's my best friend."

CHAPTER THIRTY-THREE

HALLIE

"Maybe you'll get noticed and become super famous."

"Mom."

"What?" She laughs. "It could totally happen. My girl has got talent, hasn't she George?"

I look over to my dad who's flicking his gaze between us. He shakes his head, apparently deciding to stay out of this one. *Smart man.* Mom has been badgering me about sending some of my music off to record labels and creating demos. She's in a dream world, lost on the idea of me being some Taylor Swift wannabe. She spent a whole twenty minutes discussing how much fun it would be if she came on tour with me. The thought is both terrifying and hilarious.

"Not happening," I turn to Dad. "What time are we leaving?"

Mom has dragged him over here, saying she wants to know every last thing we'll be doing and where we will be going on our trip. They're apparently all about parental conversations now. They've even been discussing whose house I'm going to for the holidays when I'm back in college.

This year doesn't matter as I'll be traveling, and Dad is going to fly Mom out to wherever we are. Christmas with both my folks. Together. Great.

"An hour or so," he replies.

I nod and excuse myself. I grab my guitar from near the front door and head out, taking a seat on the brick wall surrounding the front porch. I lean back against the main house and bring my guitar onto my knees. Our house is set back, away from the rest in the street. It means we get privacy, and don't have to worry about people just stopping by. And by people, I mean the neighbors. We aren't the friendly neighbor type.

I used to spend a lot of time in this spot as I was learning guitar. I'd play for hours, staring out at the rest of the world from the safety of my bubble. I pull my pick from the pocket of my jean shorts and being to strum. The music comes naturally, flowing through me and soothing every part of my soul. An entire year is ahead of me, just me and my music. Dad will be there, but let's face it, he'll be working. I'll have the freedom to go out and explore different places by myself. I can be myself and not have to worry about rumors circulating, because I have no one to please. I have no one to shelter from them. Dad is already working on having the Facebook page torn down, and after his conversation with Dean Vincent, Tami has been transferred to another college. It will make going back easier, I suppose. Sensing the change in my demeanor, my fingers pluck quicker, the tune transforming from a slow, lazy melody to something more upbeat, and dare I say it, happy. I almost laugh out loud at myself. I'm becoming ridiculous.

I close my eyes, the sun beating down on me, as I begin to play Hotel California - The Eagles. This is one of the first songs Bobby taught me to play. The words escape my mouth, soft and quiet, and I'm lost. In the music, in the moment, in myself.

"Hallie."

My hand stills, my mouth clamping shut. Great. He's now seeping into my subconscious. I keep my eyes closed and breathe in as a soft breeze moves through the air. Sandalwood, aftershave, *him*. He's everywhere, and nowhere, all at the same time. I can smell him, feel him close to me, but logic tells me he isn't here. Still, I refuse to open my eyes. Refuse to feel that rejection again. I have to let it go, let him go.

"Hallie, please."

Wait. I risk it. I open my eyes and turn towards the noise. He stands there, shoulders hunched, staring at me. My eyes roam over him, appreciating every square inch of his frame. He kicks at a stray stone, and I drag my gaze away to meet his. He takes a step further to me, and I let my guitar slide down until it's on the floor, leaning against the wall. He keeps moving until he's right beside me. My heart rate exceeds normality, beating so hard that I'm certain the whole damn town can hear it. I take silent breaths, willing for it to calm down. I'm not ready for this.

"Nathan," I say, my voice barely audible. "What are you doing here?"

"You were hurt."

He says it so simply, as though those three little words are all the explanation he needs. I pull my knees to my chest, wincing from the pain, and wrap my arms around my legs. Nate climbs onto to wall opposite me, leaning his back against the brick column behind.

"That happened a week ago," I answer, finally.

"I know."

His hand rubs at the back of his neck, whilst I pray for

the ground to swallow me whole. I don't want to be here with him. I don't want to have him so close, yet be unable to touch him. I don't want to be fighting the urge to reach out and pull him to me. I don't want to be in love with him, but I am, and it hurts like hell.

"You were never with Cooper, were you?"

A shiver runs cold up my spine at the mention of that name. I force it back down, blocking the memory before it can surface. *Don't go there, Hallie.* Nate is looking at me, expectant and waiting.

"No," I answer, then jump down from the wall.

I pick up my guitar and throw the strap over my shoulder. I take two steps away from him, before I feel his hand wrap around my arm. He tugs it softly, but with enough force to pull me back. I land, my two hands pressed against his abdomen, his arm wrapped around my waist. My pulse accelerates, my eyes transfixed on the rapid rise and fall of his chest. His grip tightens, pulling me closer than I already was. I feel his hand move from my hip and up my back. It stops at my head, his finger running through my hair. Flashbacks of him doing just that begin to run through my mind, one after the other, in a torturous slideshow of what never really was. We were never a couple, not really. He didn't know me, and I didn't know him. He was something I could lose myself in, and I was something he could try and fix. We never could have worked. Eventually he'd have gotten sick of my shit, or I'd have bailed and ran. It's an inevitable truth.

His head dips, his lips pressing against my forehead.

"I should have trusted you," he mutters against my skin. "I never should have let you go."

With all the mental strength I can muster, I push him back.

"But you did let me go," I say. "And now I have to let you go."

Before he can reply, Dad appears on the porch. He's eyes Nathan suspiciously before turning his attention to me.

"Hallie, are you ready?"

I walk towards him, looking back at Nate briefly. The pain on his face mirrors the pain I feel inside. This hurts, this hurts so fucking bad, but I have to do it. I have to walk away.

"Yeah, I'm ready."

The End

The Sound of Us
Sound #2
Coming Soon

ABOUT THE AUTHOR

Thank you for reading. I really hope you enjoyed it. As an indie author, I'd be extremely grateful if you could leave a review on Amazon, or even Goodreads if you're on there.

Also, I'd love to hear your views for myself so please feel free to find me on Facebook and Twitter at the below links.

Or you can email me at anniehughesauthor@gmail.com

I look forward to hearing from you all.

Printed in Poland
by Amazon Fulfillment
Poland Sp. z o.o., Wrocław